The Dating Dilemma

The Dating Dilemma

MARIAH ANKENMAN

Entangled Publishing, LLC
10940 S Parker Rd
Suite 327
Parker, CO 80134
rights@entangledpublishing.com

Amara is an imprint of Entangled Publishing, LLC.

Edited by Stacy Abrams
Cover design by Bree Archer
Cover photography by The Killion Group Images

Manufactured in the United States of America

First Edition January 2022

To E.L. aka Elmojedi10

Some dreams we work hard toward, some we don't even realize we have until someone else fulfills them. Thank you for fulfilling mine.

Chapter One

"Hey, Lexi, there's a super-hot firefighter out in the hallway who says he needs to see you."

Lexi Martin looked up from her mountainous to-do pile. The paperwork never ended for the assistant director of the Denver Youth Center—or DYC for short, as all the kids called it…pronouncing it so it sounded like a part of the male anatomy because, well, teenagers.

But in addition to the red tape, grant applications, and a host of other annoying bureaucratic headaches she had to deal with, Lexi also got to work with kids, offer them a safe space for a few hours of the day, provide homework assistance, recreation fun, and overall, show them that somebody out there cared about them.

It was the very best part of her job.

"A hot firefighter?" she asked Zoe as the woman closed her office door.

The twenty-two-year-old college intern lifted one hand to fan herself. "Five-alarm-fire hot! I would risk arson charges and set a blaze in my bedroom to have this man come put it out, hot!"

She laughed. "No you wouldn't."

Zoe was a stickler for the rules and a certified angel. Lexi would be lost without her. She dreaded the day when Zoe's internship was over and the younger woman left for better opportunities.

"You're right, I wouldn't, but I might stick your cat up in a tree and give him a call."

"Lucifer would scratch your eyes out and you know it."

"True." Zoe shuddered. "Your cat is adorable, but a bit of a prick."

He was just living up to his name. Not that she had given it to him—it came with him when she picked him up from the shelter three years ago. One look at those sweet little green and blue eyes and she'd been hooked. The shelter tried to warn her the cat had what they called "behavior issues," but Lucifer just needed someone to show him love. Something Lexi excelled at. She didn't believe animals *or* kids were bad. That was nonsense spewed by people who didn't want to take the time to understand the pain underneath the lashing out.

Lexi believed everyone had a chance to be saved, a chance to change. All they needed was someone who cared.

"Anyway," Zoe continued, "I don't think this guy would rescue a cat. He's too hot to be a real firefighter. Looks too polished, ya know?"

No, she didn't. Were real firefighters supposed to be grubby looking?

Zoe took a few steps closer to Lexi's desk and spoke in a hushed tone. "I think someone sent you a strip-o-gram."

A strip-o-gram? Wasn't that used only for bachelorette parties?

"Your birthday is tomorrow, right?"

She groaned. "Don't remind me."

No one wanted to be reminded that in less than a day

they would be turning twenty-eight and all they had to show for it was a massive pile of student loan debt, a crappy two-bedroom apartment they shared with a roommate, a nonexistent social life, and a cat as the closest thing to a life partner.

At least Lucifer gave her the occasional snuggle and didn't run up a buttload of credit card debt in her name, then ghost her like her last disaster of a boyfriend. Men sucked, full stop—give her a cat companion any day.

"Who would have sent me a strip-o-gram?"

Zoe shrugged. "Jordan?"

Probably. Sounded like something her outrageous roomie would do. He was always pushing her out of her comfort zone, but in a good way. Making her try new things, opening her eyes to new experiences, but he did usually keep the adventures to after work hours. Still…he *had* said this morning that he and his boyfriend, Angel, sent her a special birthday surprise to start her workday. She had figured it was probably going to be one of those fruit bouquets she loved so much but could never afford to indulge in.

Could they really have sent her a strip-o-gram?

She glanced at the clock. Technically the center didn't open for the kids for another twenty minutes. Maybe Jordan had sent her a little start-her-Friday-off-right fun. She didn't know if she should be horrified or grateful.

"Well?" Zoe asked, dark eyebrows lifting high on her forehead.

She couldn't very well send the man away, not when he might have been paid for a job. And none of the kids were here yet, her office had blinds, so…

"Send him in, I guess."

Zoe gave a little hop and an excited squeal. "On it! I'm so going to peek from the window."

"Don't get too excited—he might not be a stripper."

But the second Zoe returned to deliver Hottie McFirefighter, Lexi changed her tune. This man *had* to be a stripper, or model, or Greek god in disguise. Holy cow! Five-alarm fire didn't do the guy justice. He was more of an explosive volcano of sexiness.

"Ma'am, I'm here to check you for fire issues," Hottie said.

Yup. Definitely a stripper.

Kudos to Jordan for the best birthday surprise ever.

Lexi's gaze greedily took him in, from the top of his closely cropped sandy blond hair, to his gorgeous hazel eyes, down to the sharp, square jaw softened by a pair of full lips that should be illegal on any man. He was tall, though not overly so. But he definitely had the muscular build of a man who did a lot of hard labor—or took off his clothes for a living.

He wasn't dressed in typical firefighter gear, which was a bit disappointing, but she supposed that kind of stuff was hard to strip off. Instead, he was wearing a tight-fitting dark blue polo shirt that had the words *Denver FD* stitched on the high chest pocket and a pair of pressed khakis. In his hand he held some kind of clipboard. A prop maybe? All in all, the man looked scrumptious.

"I'm going to owe Jordan an entire month's rent for this present."

The man's right eyebrow quirked. "Excuse me?"

"Nothing." Lexi shook her head. "Go ahead and do your thing. Do you have music you need to play or something?"

The man looked even more confused as the words poured from her lips. "Why would I need to play music?"

"For...you know, for the *stripping*?" She practically whispered the last word, feeling her cheeks heat. Did he do it silently? That sounded weird and a little creepy. The music was half the fun.

Now both eyebrows climbed high. *"Stripping?"*

"I'm sorry." She winced. "Do you have a script you're supposed to follow or something? I've never gotten one of these before. Am I supposed to pretend you're a real firefighter, get all concerned I might have a *fire code violation*?" She winked.

He stared at her like she'd grown another head. "Ma'am. I'm here to check you for *fire issues*," he repeated.

"Oh, there's gonna be a fire issue, all right," she said, getting into it, "as soon as you strip off those pants and get to the show, my panties might just burst into flames." A giggle left her. She felt so naughty, so unlike herself, flirting with the man in front of her.

She had to hand it to her roomie, he sure knew how to break her out of her shell. Jordan would be so proud if he could see her now.

The man's jaw dropped wide. He held up a hand. "I think there's been a terrible mistake here. Who do you think I am?"

"A-Aren't you a strip-o-gram? It's my birthday tomorrow, and my roommate…" Lexi trailed off as the man's expression remained confused and slightly horrified. Heat burned her cheeks, flaming down her body. "You're…um, you're not a strip-o-gram, are you?"

Mr. 100-Percent-Not-A-Strip-O-Gram dipped his head, but not before she caught the smile curling his lips. Well, at least someone thought it was funny.

She was currently wishing the ground would open up and swallow her whole.

"Not a lot of sinkhole activity in this area, so that's not a high probability," he said with a small chuckle, letting her know she had spoken out loud.

Perfect. Just perfect.

With a loud groan, she plunked her head down on her desk, cheeks still fully aflame. Would the embarrassment ever die down? Probably not until her next birthday. Whatever this man was here for, she had to deal with it, and apologize.

With a deep, fortifying breath, Lexi lifted her head. Somehow, she managed to put her embarrassment away and find a professional smile. "I apologize for my assumption, sir. I'm Lexi Martin, assistant director of the Denver Youth Center. How can I help you?"

"Dyson O'Neil." He dipped his chin in greeting. "And I'm here to help you. I'm here for the center's annual fire safety inspection."

Inspection? But that was... She swiveled in her chair to glance at the large wall calendar where she kept track of all the center's important events and meetings.

"Sorry, I'm a bit early," Dyson apologized. "I had a teacher once who told me if you weren't ten minutes early, you were ten minutes late."

She'd had one of those, too, but according to the calendar, and her watch, Dyson wasn't ten minutes early; he was half an hour early. And how the hell had she forgotten he was coming today? It would have saved her a boatload of embarrassment if she just would have remembered about the inspection when Zoe mentioned the hot firefighter. Now she'd gone and made an ass of herself.

"Of course, not a problem. It'll be easier to work without the kids here anyway. Come with me and I'll show you around." Great, and now she was babbling.

Pushing out from her desk, she stood and came around to stand in front of Dyson.

Mistake.

The man was even sexier up close. She could see the small freckle on his upper left cheek, just below those gorgeous eyes. Not a hint of stubble indicating he'd either shaved very recently or was one of those people who didn't have his hair grow back two seconds after the blade left his skin. He really did look like he'd just stepped out of the pages of a magazine.

Could she really blame herself for thinking he was a strip-o-gram with those sensual looks?

"I assure you, ma'am, I'm not a stripper, just here for the inspection."

Crap! She'd used her internal voice externally again. It happened when she got nervous, and Dyson made her very nervous. Mostly because she kept thinking about all the completely inappropriate things she wanted to do to him... and with him.

"I'm sorry, Mr. O'Neil—"

"Dyson," he said with a small smile. "You can call me Dyson."

"Thank you, Dyson." Grateful he seemed to be taking her missteps in stride, she smiled back. "And you can call me Lexi."

"Okay, Lexi, shall we get to the inspection?"

Please, before she said anything to dig herself deeper into the hole of humiliation.

Opening her office door, she motioned to Dyson, enjoying the view as he moved past her into the hallway. The man had a delicious ass. Oops! Hopefully she hadn't said that out loud. A quick glance up revealed Dyson focused intently on the clipboard in his hand. Oh good, either she hadn't, or he was being polite and not saying anything.

She led Dyson around the entire facility, ending back in the hallway right outside her office door, her nerves rising with each "hmmmm" and scribble he made. He was writing down a lot. Was that good or bad? She couldn't tell.

He let out a heavy sigh. Oh no. Sighs like that were never good.

"Bad news?" She crossed her fingers and toes inside her five-year-old outlet mall sneakers, for extra good luck.

"I'm afraid so." He nodded, bringing up the clipboard he'd been writing on for the past half hour. "Unfortunately, you have some serious violations here that need to be addressed."

Dammit, dammit, dammit!

"What kind of issues?" *Please don't be expensive ones.* The center was running on fumes as it was. They couldn't afford any big repairs.

"You have fire detectors with failing batteries, and two don't even have any batteries in them."

Shoot! One of the kids must have borrowed them and forgotten to replace them again. It happened. She told them all if they needed batteries to come to her and she'd do her best to help. Unfortunately, a lot of her kids didn't have the means or access to things like that. She didn't mind helping them out, but it put her in a real pickle when they were too embarrassed to ask and just borrowed from the fire alarms.

He continued down his list. "You have exposed wire in a back room—"

"The kids aren't allowed in there," she explained. "We use it only for overflow storage."

"Be that as it may, it's still a fire hazard. You have no lighted exit signs, and your fire extinguishers are way past their expiration date."

The news kept getting worse and worse. Those things weren't super expensive, but again, shoestring budget stretched thin enough as it was.

"You have at least three major violations and half a dozen minor ones." He tore off the top sheet of paper and handed it to her. "You'll need to get these all fixed within the month."

"A month!" Her jaw fell open. A month to fix... She glanced down at the paper, little boxes checked where the center had failed to pass inspection with notes on how to fix the problems. Okay, some of these were easy fixes like the batteries in the fire detectors, but others... "How am I supposed to get all this done within a month?"

"Do you need the number of a contractor? I have a few great references."

"Only if they work for free," she grumbled, because that's all the center could afford.

"I'm not sure any of them do pro bono work," Dyson said with a slight grimace.

"I know, I wouldn't expect them to," she said, a heavy sigh leaving her lips. Just wishful thinking on her part.

First, she mistook the safety inspector for a stripper, and now the center was in code violations she knew they couldn't afford to fix. Could today get any worse? She was two seconds away from drowning this horrible day in a pint of cherry-berry-tastic ice cream.

"I'm sure I can get these repairs done myself," she said hopefully. Duct tape fixed everything, right?

Dyson frowned. "I wouldn't recommend that, ma'am."

Ma'am? She blinked at his stern tone. What happened to *Lexi*?

"Some of this work requires the skills of a professional."

Yeah, but they didn't have the money for a professional. What did he expect her to do? Pull a free contractor out of thin air?

"I understand that, but the center can't afford these repairs right now."

"Then I'm afraid I'll have to fail the inspection."

"But the center could close!" How could he do that to them? Didn't he realize the kids needed this place? How could he be so heartless?

"I understand, but rules are rules. They're there for a reason. For safety's sake and—"

"Ms. Martin, the basketballs are deflated again."

Lexi glanced down the hall to see Mateo standing a few feet away. The tall, lanky sixteen-year-old had been coming to the center almost every day for about six months now. He was a good kid, smart, kind, but closed off, as most of these kids were, due to crappy circumstances and society's failure to protect them.

Shoving down the absolute heartbreak of the possibility of the DYC closing, she pasted a smile on her face and addressed the young teen. "The pump is in the equipment closet, Mateo. Zoe has the keys."

Zoe also must have let the kids in. Lexi glanced at the clock on the wall to see it was indeed fifteen minutes past doors open. Huh, time flew when you were receiving terrible news.

"Okay…" The young teen's eyes narrowed on Dyson. "Is, um, everything okay?"

Poor sweet boy, so suspicious of everything and everyone. Took her weeks to crack his tough shell enough to get Mateo to trust her even the smallest amount. Not that she blamed the kid. He had his reasons.

"Everything is fine, Dyson here is just performing our annual fire code inspection. Need to make sure we're keeping all you kids safe and the center is up to code."

"Will they shut it down if it's not?"

Oh dear. Her heart clenched, the slight tremble in his voice killing her. She knew how much this place meant to Mateo, to all the kids who needed a safe haven. It couldn't get shut down. Didn't Dyson see that? Or was a "dependable space for kids to go" not on the fancy checklist on his clipboard? She knew rules were in place for a reason, but sometimes they needed to be bent a little.

"Don't you worry about that." She gave him a soft smile. "Now, go find Zoe and pump up those basketballs for me, please, would you?"

"Yeah, sure." His eyes shifted back and forth between Lexi and Dyson, the doubt in them evident. "No problem, Ms. Martin."

Once Mateo was gone, she turned back to face Dyson. He was staring after the teen with a look of…familiarity in his eyes. Like he knew what the kid was going through. Maybe he did, how would she know? Aside from calling the man a stripper and now knowing he was an actual firefighter—with a bit of a stick up his butt when it came to the rules—she knew nothing about the guy.

"Seems like a good kid," Dyson muttered.

"He is. In fact, they all are." She believed that with every fiber of her being. "That's why this center needs to stay open. These kids depend on it. I know we have to get these violations fixed, but the budget is kind of in the red at the moment and—"

"I'll do it."

"What?" She blinked, his declaration not computing in her harried brain.

"I can help fix up all the code issues." That soft hazel gaze came back to her. "My dad was an electrician. I used to help him out on jobs before… Anyway, I know what needs to be done to get this place up to code."

That was very kind of him, especially after he'd just informed her he would need to fail them but… "As I said, we don't really have the money to hire—"

"The department gives us Kelley days."

"What's a Kelley day?"

"It's a mandatory paid day off. A lot of us use it for volunteer work in the community."

Wow, that was pretty amazing. Of course, she supposed, to be a firefighter, running into burning buildings to save perfect strangers, it took a special kind of person. A giving and caring one. And Dyson wanted to use his volunteer time to help out the center. Shame burned her gut, and she was really glad she hadn't said any of the unkind thoughts she'd just had about the man out loud.

"I suppose I should try and go with the polite 'oh no I couldn't possibly ask you to do that' refusal, but I'm not going to." She winced, pained to admit it. "The center could really use any help it's offered."

Nonprofits ran on a wish and the kindness of others. She would never turn down free help when generously given.

"Happy to offer." His attention wandered to where Mateo had disappeared before turning back to her. "I can drop by Wednesday if that works."

"Yes, um, I'm here starting at nine and we open for the kids at two." Weekends they were open all day, but weekdays they didn't open until school let out.

"I'll drop by around nine thirty?"

"Perfect. And thank you so much, Dyson."

He nodded and turned to leave. She should have let it end there. Should have kept her mouth shut, but instead she found herself opening up and shouting after him, "And I'm sorry again about the whole stripper thing."

He glanced over his shoulder with a small smile. "No worries. I take it as a compliment. My buddy in college was a stripper—guy had more talent and skill than I could ever imagine. He tried to get me a job once, but I have two left feet and ended up tripping over my tearaway pants and falling onto the table of drinks. Spilled jungle punch everywhere. The maid of honor was pissed because her parents had just redone the carpet in the pool house."

Sexy, sweet, generous, and told his own embarrassing story to help her save face. Dyson was too good to be true. He had to be a secret serial killer or something.

Either that or he was a dog person. That would be just her luck. Lucifer hated dogs more than he hated baths and her cat really, really hated baths.

"See you Wednesday, Lexi." Dyson turned, waving over his head as he went down the hallway and left the building.

"Guess he wasn't a strip-o-gram." Zoe's voice sounded from behind Lexi. "Too bad."

Yes and no. She hadn't gotten a special birthday surprise, but they *had* gotten free labor to fix some desperately needed issues at the center. She might not have gotten a glimpse of that scrumptious-looking body, but she had seen a glimpse of his generous heart, and damned if they *both* didn't seem deliciously tempting.

"You got a delivery," Zoe said. "Put it on your desk."

As Zoe headed off to check on the kids, Lexi opened the door to her office where she saw, sitting directly in the middle of her desk, a caramel-dipped fruit bouquet complete with a card that read: *Happy Birthday Lex! Love Jordan and Angel.*

She choked on a laugh, wishing her BFF's gift had come just a few minutes earlier. It certainly would have saved her from the most embarrassing situation of her life.

• • •

She was still chuckling when she arrived back at her apartment after work. The moment she opened the door, Lucifer headbutted her leg. She bent down to scoop her cat into her arms, nuzzling the soft black fur on his head.

"Hello, baby. Did you have a good day?"

She got a small yowl and a tiny nip for her affection before he leaped from her arms and sauntered away to his cat bed in the corner of the living room. Ornery cat. She loved him though.

"What's got you shining like a sunbeam in July? Did you get the present?"

"Yes, thank you! It was delicious."

Lexi's grin widened as she spied her roommate, Jordan, and Angel cooking away in the kitchen. "A sexy new helper at the center *and* I don't have to make dinner. Win-win for me today."

"What sexy new helper at the center?" Jordan asked. "Did you get a new intern?"

"No, Dyson is definitely not a college intern." She sighed, remembering how tightly his polo had clung to his muscled arms. Dyson was all grown up in the most delicious way.

Jordan wiped his hands on a kitchen towel and moved from the small space to stand in front of her. A frown marred his dark brown forehead, and he ran a hand over his shaved head.

"Lex. You remember our bet?"

For cripes sake, she hadn't even put her purse down yet.

Tossing the small bag on the floor and slipping her shoes off, she moved around her best friend. Heading into the kitchen, she leaned over Angel's shoulder to see what he was cooking. She had no idea what the contents of the pot were, but heavenly spicy smells surrounded her as she took a deep breath.

"Angel, I love you. What is that amazing dish you're making?"

The dark-haired man gave a small laugh. "Green chili veggie stew, and don't think you're getting out of answering Jordan's question."

Damn, they were both against her tonight.

"Leeeeeexi."

Jordan dragged out her name as if it had seven syllables instead of two. With a heavy sigh, she turned, cocking her hip and crossing her arms over her chest.

"Yes, I remember the bet." An utterly ridiculous bet made a month ago after a painful breakup and way too much wine. "No dating for six months."

Jordan nodded, but his smug smile burrowed under her skin a bit. Lifting a hand, she pointed at him.

"You said no dating—we never agreed I couldn't look."

Especially at a man as fine as Dyson. A man so sexy, she'd confused him with a strip-o-gram.

"You did what?" both Jordan and Angel asked at the same time.

Welp, her big mouth had done it. Might as well lay it all out.

She explained to the men about mistaking Dyson for a birthday present from Jordan, the following embarrassment when she realized who he really was, and his generous offer to help the center. By the end of her story, both of them were holding back laughter.

Angel more politely than Jordan.

"Lex, you know I love messing with you, but I would never send a strip-o-gram to your place of work." Jordan's laughter dimmed. "So, there's nothing going on with this guy, right?"

Nothing but him helping her fix the center.

She shook her head. "Nothing. Don't get your hopes up. I am not losing the bet."

Crossing her arms, she grumbled under her breath. "I don't even know why we made it in the first place."

"Yes you do," Jordan insisted. He stepped closer, placing a gentle hand on her shoulder. "We talked about this. You give too much of yourself. To everyone. You need some time to focus on you and what you deserve."

A common refrain her friends had been telling her for years. She compromised too much in her relationships, which was why they never worked out. After her last heartbreak, her bestie made her promise she'd take six months to focus on her or face the penalty of cleaning the entire apartment while dressed as her greatest fear...a clown.

She shuddered at the thought. Not only did she hate cleaning—and clowns—but she knew Jordan would film the winnings and post it to social media. She worked with teens:

their entire life was social media. If she lost the bet and a video of it got posted, she'd be hearing about it for months from her kids. She'd never live it down.

No. She could *not* afford to lose this bet.

And truthfully, she *was* tired of being walked all over by the guys she dated. Not every one of them meant to do it, but it happened regardless, and she had to admit the truth that she often allowed it to. She wanted to win the bet for herself, too. And so far, not dating had been fairly easy.

Until today.

Dyson was temptation personified.

"I'm not going to date the man who's helping at the center," she assured her best friend. "He's not even my type. So don't go shopping for a clown costume just yet."

Jordan gave her a hard look, but nodded.

"Well, now that that's settled, let's eat," Angel said. "Babe, get the bowls please."

"On it." Jordan gave his boyfriend a kiss, opening the cupboard and grabbing some bowls.

Dinner did smell delicious, but all Lexi wanted to take a bite of was a certain sexy firefighter. But her friend was right. She needed to focus on herself and what she needed. As horrifying as the bet was, it was made with good intentions and she planned to follow it through. Besides, if—*when*— she won, Jordan would have to fulfill his end of the bargain. Finally agreeing to Angel's plan to move in together. His boyfriend had been asking for months and Jordan had come up with one reason to delay after another. She might have doormat written on her forehead, but her bestie had commitment-phobe written on his.

Jordan was right. She was so used to giving to everyone: the center, her friends, her boyfriends. It was time for Lexi to put herself first and get what *she* wanted.

If only she knew what that was.

Chapter Two

Dyson stepped into Station 42 firehouse, letting out a deep sigh. This place felt like home. No, not just felt—it *had* been his home for the past six years, since he finished his fire science degree at age twenty-six. It'd taken him longer than his classmates to graduate, since he'd been able to take only a few classes at a time. The result of working two jobs while trying to care for his two younger sisters. But his sisters were both healthy and thriving with their own jobs and lives now, so he supposed he did all right.

He moved past the brick-lined hallway into the main space. The kitchen was off to the left, the large wooden dining table housing a couple of his crewmates as they played a game of cards. To the right was the common room where most of the crew liked to relax and watch TV or read. The furniture was a mismatch of donated items from the community, but it was comfortable and suited their needs, so no one cared much if the blue couch didn't match the brown recliners.

"Hey, O'Neil." Eli Ward glanced up from the bunk gear he was checking as Dyson came into the common room.

"How'd the inspections go?"

"Most passed. Except for the Denver Youth Center." He held up the clipboard, sinking into the comfy recliner chair across from where Ward sat on the couch. "They have a bunch of violations."

"Shit, anything major?"

"A few things need an electrician's skills, but most of the stuff is minor. Problem is they don't have the funds to hire anybody for the fixes."

"Double shit." Ward grimaced, putting down the helmet he'd been checking for damage onto the wooden coffee table between them. "What are they gonna do?"

Dyson glanced at the copy of the report held on his clipboard. "I offered to help. Got some Kelley days and I know enough from my dad to bring it up to code."

"Oh yeah, he was an electrician right?"

Dyson nodded. For twenty-five years, until a house fire took his and Dyson's mother's lives. Some people might say Dyson became a firefighter to make up for not being able to save his parents, but he didn't give a shit what people said. He did what he did because he was good at it and yeah, okay, maybe because it gave him a small sense of redemption every time he pulled someone from a burning building. Which was a lot less often than people and the media made it out to be.

Honestly, most of the time they were responding to false alarms, medical calls, and educating the public on fire safety. And despite what every children's book ever said, not once had he rescued a cat from a tree.

"You need any help with the repairs?"

"Ha!" The loud laugh cracked through the air as Stephanie Díaz came into the room, holding a plate of food and a glass of water in her hands. "Only if he wants the place to blow sky-high."

"Hey!" Ward glared at her. "I can fix stuff."

Dyson shared a look with Díaz and they both burst out laughing.

"What? I can," Ward insisted.

No, he really couldn't. The man was a fantastic firefighter, shit cook, and had two left thumbs when it came to fixing any type of electrical equipment.

Díaz grinned as she spoke. "Remember when you tried to fix Turner's VCR and it ended up shooting the tape halfway across the room?"

"In my defense, he said the thing was crap and I could have a whack at fixing it." Ward slouched back into the couch, crossing his arms over his chest. "And who still owns a VCR anyway? The last time I used one of those I was like…wait, I don't think I've ever had a VCR."

"It's all right, man." Dyson tapped the clipboard. "I got this, but thanks for the offer."

Ward was a nice guy, always willing to lend a hand, but his help sometimes just made things twice as hard. Still, he was crew, which meant he was family, and Dyson loved the guy. He loved all his crewmates and he wasn't afraid to say so. You had to trust the people protecting you in a fire because flames don't care about anything but devouring.

Ward shrugged, glancing at the plate and cup in Díaz's hands. "What's that?"

"Sustenance." She shoved them toward him. "You haven't eaten since you got back from the elementary safety demo."

"I'm doing gear check, Díaz."

"Yeah, and you can do that while eating." She pushed the offerings at him until he took them. "Don't need your stubborn ass fainting from lack of food while on a call."

"Thanks, *Mom*."

"Shut up and eat."

Dyson grinned at their antics. See, family. Always taking care of one another while simultaneously harassing one another. Though with Ward and Díaz, everyone could see the spark except for the two of them. Dyson stared as Ward watched Díaz turn and head back out of the room, a hungry look of longing etched on his features. Okay, maybe one of them did see it, but they were just ignoring it.

Couldn't fault them for that. Getting involved with someone you worked with was a monumentally bad idea. Nothing he had to worry about. Dating was not on Dyson's radar. Period. He didn't need that kind of heartbreak again.

Suddenly the memory of Lexi's dark brown eyes, her soft round face, her flushed pink cheeks hot with embarrassment, filled his mind. She was beautiful, no arguing there. But also...approachable. He found the way she spoke without even realizing she was talking out loud endearing. And the fact that she'd confused him with a stripper? As hilarious as it was flattering. He hadn't been lying when he told her the story of the one ill-fated night of his stripping experience. He could have used the kind of money his buddy had made, but sadly he did not have the skills the job demanded.

No, he wouldn't be stripping for Lexi, but he would be helping her repair some much-needed code violations. Which meant he'd get to see her more than once. A fact he shouldn't be excited about, but the tiny uptick in his heart rate when he'd seen her smile back at the center revealed he was. Still, he knew he wasn't cut out for long-term. Life had slapped him upside the head with that fact nonstop. The final straw being the moment he found his fiancée in bed with his best friend.

Their apologies still echoed in his head from time to time, but the betrayal...a thing like that was hard to forget. He'd lost the woman he loved and his best friend all in one night. An incident like that tended to sour a person on trust, love, and happily ever after.

After finishing his shift, Dyson went back to his apartment

for a quick shower before heading over to his sisters' house. They had a weekly family dinner, which he both loved and dreaded. His sisters were great, but they tended to...get into his business a little too much. He knew they just cared and worried, but that was *his* job. He was the big brother. The one who took over the role of guardian when their parents died.

He knew they cared, but sometimes the caring felt crushing.

The two of them rented a bungalow near Wash Park. Dinner nights shifted depending on their schedules, Dyson having the most hectic one.

He pulled up to the house, thanking the parking gods he managed to snag a spot only one block away from their house instead of five. Grabbing the chocolate fudge cake—because there was no way he would ever show up to his sisters' house without chocolate—he made his way to the front door and knocked.

"Dyson!" Gemma, his younger sister by two years, smiled. "You made it, and you brought cake!"

"Always." He grinned, passing the dessert off.

Gemma kissed his cheek, turned, and hurried off into the house with the treat, her brown curls bouncing as she walked. He followed her into the kitchen where Macy was standing at the counter, dishing out food onto plates.

"Dyson's here and he brought cake!" Gemma announced.

"Hey, Dy," Macy nodded, not looking up from her task. "You want to set the table?"

He nodded, grabbing the plates and silverware Macy had set on the counter and bringing them into the small dining area just off the kitchen, where a square oak table and four chairs stood.

"What are we having?" Whatever it was, it smelled delicious. His stomach had been growling ever since he watched Ward eat the sandwich Díaz made for him.

"Stuffed bell peppers." Macy answered.

"Smells amazing."

Macy brought the ceramic dish of steaming food into the dining area, setting it in the middle of the table while Gemma got everyone drinks. The three dug into their meals that were, as he expected, delectable. The peppers were stuffed with spicy meat, deliciously sautéed onions, and topped off with an unhealthy amount of cheese. He didn't care, it was so damn good he'd clog every artery in his heart for another bite.

"This is so good," Gemma moaned.

"Thanks," Macy smiled. "I got the recipe from a new teacher at school."

Dyson swallowed the heavenly bite he just took and sent a thanks to the universe for new teachers with awesome dinner recipes. "How is work going, Macy?"

And so the tradition of family dinner began. Starting with the youngest they all went around and talked about their week. Macy shared hilarious stories from her seventh graders, one of whom took a dare from his best friend and ate a slice of the flatworm they'd been dissecting in science class leading to the kid puking and a very stern talk about how immature dares are.

Gemma, who worked at a branch of the Denver Public Library system, talked about the nightmare the staff was enduring as the cataloguing system was updated. When it came time for his turn, Dyson shared his stop at the youth center and his promise to help with the repairs.

"Don't they have someone in, like, maintenance to do that for them?" Gemma asked with a frown.

He shook his head. "I don't think they even have a maintenance department. The center seems to be running low on funds."

"I'd believe it." Macy nodded, taking a sip of her drink. "I think a few of my kids head there after school. It's a lifesaver, but not exactly a moneymaker. I bet everyone there wears seven hats."

Sure seemed that way to him. He'd seen the calendar on the wall behind Lexi, scribbled with endless notes, appointments, and tasks. He hoped she didn't have to fulfill them all herself. Poor woman seemed stretched thin, but the second that kid came up and asked if anything was wrong, she put on the most convincing smile he'd ever seen. She might be holding the center together with string and hope, but she didn't let those kids know. He respected that.

"I'd say so. Which is why I agreed to help Lexi out." That and he knew what it was like to lose the only safe space you had in the world.

"Who's Lexi?" Gemma asked.

"How old is she?" Macy leaned forward in her seat. "Is she single?'

His sisters' questions hit his ears all at once. Took him a second to process each one, and he knew exactly what they were after. The same thing they'd been trying to get him to do for the past year.

"She's the Assistant Director of the DYC. An adult, but I'm not about to guess a woman's age. I have no idea. And both of you can stop it right now."

"Stop what?"

Dual voices chimed in perfect harmony. Yeah right. He wasn't buying it. They knew exactly what he was talking about. Pointing at each of them in turn, he spoke. "I'm just helping out the center. I am not dating Lexi."

Maybe if they had met at a different point and time in his life, a time before the betrayal he suffered from his ex. Lexi was beautiful and had a generous heart, from what he'd seen. Had to, for the kind of work she did. But unfortunately, he hadn't met her before. He met her today. And today he was still sworn off relationships.

"Dyson," Gemma said softly. "It's been three years."

He knew how long it had been.

"Don't you think it's time to move on?" Macy pointed out for the millionth time. "You shouldn't cut yourself off from love just because of what happened."

Couldn't get hurt if you didn't make yourself vulnerable. Rule number one: no girlfriends. One romantic heartbreak in a lifetime was enough for him. How much loss could a heart take before it stopped beating? He didn't know, but why risk it?

"I'm not cutting myself off from anything."

"We're not talking sex, Dy." Macy said.

The word "sex" spewing from his little sister's lips made him shudder. Yes, he knew they were both adults with their own lives and he didn't kid himself that his sisters had experienced…things. But that didn't mean he wanted to talk to them about it…

"There's no way in hell I'm discussing m-my"—he stumbled over the next word—"sex life with you two."

"Whatever you say, *One-Night O'Neil*," Gemma snickered.

Dammit. He hated the nickname the crew at the station had given him. Hated even more that his sisters knew it. So he indulged in the occasional one-night stand. No big deal. He was an adult with a healthy sex drive, he always used protection, and the women he hooked up with knew the score. He never promised them more than he could give. Which was one night.

"You have been a bit of a man-whore these past few years," Macy agreed.

"Okay, one, that's really offensive. And two, I don't need to start dating or get in any kind of relationship. I'm fine with things the way they are."

"You're hiding." Macy insisted.

"I'm healing," he insisted.

"Grace and Adam were totally asses." Gemma said, a tiny hitch in her voice. "You shouldn't let their actions dictate your life."

He squeezed his sister's hand. Sometimes he forgot how integral his best friend had been in his sisters' lives. Adam had been there after their parents died, helping out, lending a hand whenever they needed it. He'd practically been a member of the family.

But family members didn't screw your fiancée.

He had to remember the betrayal hadn't just affected him. His sisters lost someone, too, when he cut Adam and Grace out of his life. They'd suffered so much loss, he wasn't ever going to risk putting them through that again.

He grabbed his beer, wishing they were drinking something stronger like gin or scotch. "I'm fine."

"You're not," Gemma insisted. "We just want to see you happy."

"I am happy." He was. Most of the time.

Did he miss the companionship of a relationship? Someone he was able to come home to and share his day with? Someone to connect with, celebrate life's up and downs with? Sure he did. But all that comfort turned into embarrassment and pain when you found out it was all a lie. Why the hell would he put himself through that again?

"I don't need to start dating again, I'm happy being alone, and I'm just helping Lexi with the DYC repairs. Nothing more. Got it?"

He speared each of his sisters with a look he'd perfected when they were teenagers and used the "you're not dad" excuse on him when he told them to do their homework. Back then it got him a glare, reluctant obedience, and a middle finger when his back was turned. (They always forgot windows are reflective when they did that one.) Now the look got him two heavy sighs and a few muttered agreements.

"Good." He nodded, satisfied his pseudo-parenting mode still worked. "It's settled then."

Macy scoffed under her breath. "That's what you think."

"What?"

His sister graced him with a brilliant, but completely fake, smile. "I said, cake time!"

She most certainly did not, but a shake of Gemma's head had him letting it go. Over the years he'd learned to pick his battles with his sisters. They could pester him all they wanted to about this, but he wasn't changing his mind. After all, what were his sisters going to do? Sign him up for a dating site to hook him up with a new girlfriend?

He laughed to himself at the thought, but a quick glance around the table, at the sneaky looks his sisters were sharing, that silent communicating thing they always had with each other, had him taking a terrifying gulp.

Shit.

That's exactly what they were going to do.

Chapter Three

"Hey Lexi, your sexy firefighter is here."

Lexi glanced up from her desk to see a grinning Zoe in her office doorway.

Her heart rate kicked up, pounding in her chest the way it did after she'd run five miles or saw a really cute pair of shoes. Hoping to cover her reaction, she shuffled through some of the paperwork on her desk.

"He's not my firefighter."

"I don't blame you for thinking he was a stripper." Zoe laughed.

She held back a groan. Why did her friend have to bring up that embarrassing moment again?

"Zoe!"

"What?" She shrugged. "He's good lookin' for an older dude."

Older dude? Dyson couldn't be a day over thirty-two by her guess. How old did Zoe think *she* looked? Scratch that, she didn't want to know. Sometimes the six-year difference between her and Zoe felt more like six decades.

Standing, she moved in front of her desk and ushered the other woman into her office, peeking around the corner to make sure Dyson hadn't started down the hallway yet. The last thing she needed was for him to hear Zoe talk about how hot he was. What if he got uncomfortable and decided not to help with the repairs?

"Please don't say anything like that in front of Dyson." She considered Zoe a friend, which led to a lot of fun teasing and joking, but Lexi was still the center's assistant director. She had to make sure the center came first. "His help is vital. We can't afford for him to decide this isn't worth his time. I need him."

"You need him?" Zoe smirked, a devilish glint filling her dark eyes.

"*We* need him." Lexi corrected. "The center. He promised to help fix our code violations. That's all I meant. I didn't mean it like 'Oh I need Dyson to take off all his clothes and ravish me until neither one of us can walk straight again.' I mean, yes, the man is attractive—"

The clearing of a throat behind her made her freeze. Deer-in-the-headlights freeze.

Silence filled the air for a solid three seconds before she silently mouthed to Zoe, *Is he behind me?* Zoe nodded, eyes wide, and slapped a hand over her mouth to hold back laughter as her body vibrated, tears forming in the corner of her eyes from the force of her restraint.

Shoot!

Without turning, she spoke loud enough for him to hear, "I don't suppose the possibility of sinkholes in this area has gone up in the past few days?"

A soft chuckle sounded behind her. "No, I'm happy to say it hasn't. Sinkholes are very dangerous."

Just as well. The thought of the ground opening up at any moment and swallowing her whole was terrifying. Except for, you know, when she said completely inappropriate things about a person who was offering his help in a *professional* capacity.

Knowing she had to face the embarrassment sooner or later, she turned. "Hi, Dyson."

He dipped his chin. "Lexi."

How was it possible that the man had become even more attractive since she'd seen him last? It wasn't, right? But there he stood, all sexy and strong, with a tiny smile at the corner of his lips. Inside she let out a huge sigh of relief. At least he didn't appear to be upset by what he overheard. Maybe he hadn't heard that much. Maybe she got lucky. Maybe she heard only the last part.

"Any chance you had invisible earbuds in and didn't hear anything I said before now?"

The tiny smile widened into a full-fledged grin, and holy cow was the man sexy when he smiled. It wasn't fair really. No one should be allowed to be that devastatingly handsome while wearing faded jeans and a dark blue T-shirt. If she ever saw him in a suit, she might explode from lust.

Silly, why would she ever see Dyson in a suit? The only time she was ever going to see him was when he was here, working. There was zero chance he'd ever do that in a suit. A woman could dream, though.

"Oh, were you all talking before I got here?" He lifted a finger to his ear and jiggled it slightly. "My ears must have been plugged or something because I didn't hear a thing."

He winked and yup, explosion from lust was imminent.

Handsome, helpful, sweet, and he was willing to overlook her faux pas? He was her sexual kryptonite.

"I better get out of here," Zoe said, moving toward the door.

Zoe held up a hand, blocking her face from Dyson as she mouthed to Lexi, *he is so hot!* Yeah, because that wasn't obvious. Lexi sighed, ignoring the wink and thumbs-up Zoe gave her on her way out.

Dyson's brow raised once they were alone in the office.

"I'm sorry about that, she's…"

"Don't worry about it." He gave a soft chuckle. "I get it."

"You do?"

"Yup." Nodding, he lifted one shoulder in a small shrug. "I have sisters."

"Really? How many?"

"Two."

"Oooh, only boy?"

"Yup."

Now it was her turn to chuckle. "Same for my brother. He's right in the middle of my sister and me. We used to practice our makeup skills on him."

"That sounds familiar. Lucky for me, I look amazing with a sharp wing." He tapped the corner of his eye with a finger.

Would this man stop melting her heart? She had to find something repulsive about him and soon, or she was going to fall hard. Any guy who let his sisters put makeup on him without complaining immediately jumped the ranks from just bangable to boyfriend material. She wasn't allowed to have a boyfriend at the moment, but there was always time for a sex buddy. That wasn't breaking the rules of the bet, right? Hmmm, she better talk to Jordan about it.

"So where would you like to start?" Because as much as she wanted to jump him right now, Dyson was here to help fix the center's issues, not her lack-of-sex issues.

"I figured I'd start with the easier items first and work my way down the list."

"Great!" Oof, that sounded too loud, was she overcompensating? Probably. "Do you need anything, tools or…"

He lifted a large red metal case he held in his left hand.

"I'm all set. I've got the proper tools needed to ensure the repairs are done to the correct specifications. Not that I mean to insinuate you don't have the proper tools," he rushed to say. "But some of these repairs require specialized equipment."

"I understand, and I appreciate the help." Even if he had a less than tactful way of saying he doubted the center had a working hammer.

"The right tools make the job easier."

And she'd bet this man always used the right tools. For everything.

Dyson might be sweet and sexy as sin, but she was coming to learn he had a bit of a straight edge to him. Probably one of those kids who never colored outside the lines. Meanwhile, her entire life was thinking outside the box to make things work. She bet if Dyson had to spend one day in her shoes, the poor man would have a breakdown.

"Perfect. Well, I guess I should let you go do me." She sucked in a sharp breath, face burning. "It! I mean let you go do it, the repairs, the stuff for the fixing and the… I'm just going to go crawl under my desk and hide for the next hour, okay? You just…yeah."

Heat flared in Dyson's eyes for half a second. There and gone so quickly Lexi was sure she'd simply imagined it. Then his smile dimmed a bit, the hand not holding his tool case came up to rub the back of his neck as he grimaced. Uh-oh. Whatever he was about to say, she knew she probably didn't want to hear it.

"Look, Lexi."

Yup, nothing good ever came after a sentence like that.

Please don't take back your offer of help because my brain and my mouth don't always connect.

"I should probably mention that I don't date." He paused, dropping his hand to his side. "Ever. I have a personal rule about relationships."

Okay, fair enough. Most people had rules about their relationships.

"No long-term, no girlfriends."

Oh. Well, that was a bit of a weirder rule. Was the guy a commitment-phobe? Or did he just like sleeping around? At least he was honest about it, but she wouldn't lie and say his rule wasn't a bit disappointing.

"I also don't get involved with people I…work with."

Were they working together? She supposed so. In a way.

"I'm not a good long-term bet. A night or two is all I can offer. I just…don't have time for more."

Why did she feel that that wasn't the real reason? The way he said it, maybe? Dealing with kids who lied on a daily basis, sometimes for fun, sometimes for their survival, Lexi had honed her bullshit detection skills fairly well over the past few years. She could tell Dyson wasn't being one hundred percent honest with his reasoning. But it wasn't like she could date right now, either—thank you Jordan and the bet from hell—and she didn't want to lose his help because he feared she was trying to nab herself a boyfriend, so she didn't press him on it.

"Me either. If I'm not here, I'm at home thinking about how I should be here trying to chip away at my endless to-do pile that never seems to get any smaller."

His skeptical expression made her pause. She could tell him about her "no dating" bet with Jordan, but she didn't want to bring up that mortifying situation in front of Dyson. She'd already embarrassed herself around this man one time too many. She had to say something to save face.

"I'm kind of on a…dating hiatus right now myself." She laughed, and he joined in with a small chuckle of his own.

"Great, I just didn't want any misunderstanding, you know?"

"Of course!" Yikes, that was too loud again.

"Good." He nodded.

"Good."

"Good."

Oh dear, they were stuck in a loop of awkwardness. Where was a DYC emergency when she needed it? A kid who forgot their backpack at school, paint spilled in the art room—heck, she'd even be grateful for a fight to break out right about now.

A small one.

Verbal only.

Maybe just a shouting fit.

Physical altercations were strictly forbidden at the center and the kids got only three strikes before they were banned. She hated banning anyone. No fight distraction, then, but what she wouldn't give for something, anything to dispel the level of discomfort in the room right about now.

"Well..." she said after an uncomfortable silence. "I should probably get back to..." She motioned with a hand behind her.

"Oh yeah, right, right." He vaguely waved with his own hand out the door. "And I should get to...yeah."

"Yeah."

"Good." He nodded, dipping his chin again before he headed out her office door. "Okay then."

Then he was gone. Down the hall off to fix their fire code violations.

"Wow, I think that was the most awkward interaction between two people I've ever seen," Zoe said as she appeared in the doorway, staring after Dyson's retreating form. "And I once went to a wedding where the groom was the ex-boyfriend of the bride's twin sister. You know those family holidays have to be weird."

"Zoe," Lexi sighed, heading back to her desk and sinking into her chair. "Were you standing around the corner eavesdropping again?"

"I would never!" Zoe stepped into the office, shutting the door behind her. "It's my Arbor Day resolution to stop eavesdropping."

"Arbor Day resolution?"

Zoe smiled, coming to sit in the chair across from Lexi's desk. "It didn't stick for New Year's, so I'm trying again. I just happened to be turning the corner and caught the tail end of that painful exchange where you both tried to convince the other you didn't want to bone your collective brains out."

A long, loud groan escaped Lexi's lips. Slouching forward, she gently smacked her head on her desk, wishing it would dislodge the events of the past fifteen minutes. *Ouch!* No such luck. They were still replaying over and over again in her mind in vibrant, vivid detail.

"Why am I so socially inept?" You'd think with her job, being around people all day, she'd be better at social interactions, but "cool" had never been Lexi's thing, sadly. Dork Martin hadn't been her high school nickname because she liked the shoes.

"I don't know, but I love you the way you are, and if it helps any, Dyson seems to be as socially awkward as you." Zoe shot her a look of amusement.

It did help a little. At least she wasn't alone in this vortex of embarrassment. With a sigh she turned to her scribbled to-do list; she had a pile of grant proposals to write today. Nothing like trying to convince a bunch of moneymakers that investing in your nonprofit is a good idea to take one's mind off things. Instead of focusing on how she basically offered herself to Dyson and was swiftly shot down, she could focus on offering the center to donors and getting shot down by them instead.

The ol' self-esteem twofer.

No, she couldn't think like that. True, they probably wouldn't receive most of these grants, but some of them might choose the center for their donations. It's why she applied to every single one they were eligible for. A handful of approvals were better than none, and every penny helped.

"Are we writing more proposals today?" Zoe reached out to take the stack of papers Lexi held to her.

"Yup." One of the reasons Zoe got the internship was due to her excellent grant-writing skills. Since she'd started, the center had doubled their grant approvals. She was hoping they'd receive enough funds to hire Zoe on as the full-time grant writer when the young woman graduated this spring, but Lexi wouldn't hold her breath.

The women worked for the next two hours before Lexi called for a break. Technically, her stomach was the one that called, with a loud growl.

"Lunchtime?" Zoe asked.

"Lunchtime," she agreed.

"Great, want me to grab sandwiches?"

There was a fantastic locally owned sandwich shop a block away that gave all the employees and volunteers at the center a nice discount because the owner's kids stopped by for homework help regularly.

"Yes, grab me a club please." She started to reach for her purse, but Zoe waved her away.

"My treat." The younger woman gave Lexi a sly smile. "Why don't you go see if Dyson wants anything."

"I'm sure he brought his own lunch. Or left already." Okay, so she was purposely avoiding the man in case she embarrassed herself further by forgetting her inside voice and talking about how much she wanted to take a bite out of his luscious backside.

"Go check in with Dyson." Zoe left the office, calling over her shoulder, "And text me if he wants something."

Fine, she'd check in on Dyson. But only because she *should* see if he needed anything. For center-related purposes.

Not because she wanted to watch the man work to add some sexy fantasies to her spank bank later.

She ended up finding him in the far back hall by the small kitchen, standing on a chair. His arms were above his head, one hand holding the exit sign to the ceiling while the other worked a screwdriver to affix the sign back in place. A working sign, she noted, as it now lit up the way it was supposed to.

"We have a stepladder," she said, coming farther into the room. "I'm sorry, I should have mentioned that before."

He glanced down at her with a smile. "No worries. The ceiling isn't too high. Chair works just fine."

"No safety rules about using chairs instead of ladders being hazardous?" she said with a small smile.

Dyson glanced at her over his shoulder with a slight frown. "Are you teasing me?"

She lifted one shoulder with a small giggle. "You *are* kind of a stickler for the rules. A bit strange to see you breaking them by using unauthorized equipment."

He chuckled softly. "I've been called worse. But no, using a chair instead of a ladder isn't breaking any safety rule. Not when it's this low to the ground."

Fair point. She often used chairs herself. Being taller than the average woman at five-nine had its perks in the reaching high places world, sadly not so much in the dating world. If she had a nickel for every man upset when she'd wear heels, placing her slightly taller than them on dates, her student loans would have been paid off years ago.

Dyson stepped down from the chair and she noticed he was only a few inches taller than her in her flats. If she wore heels on a date, would he mind? Irrelevant. They weren't going on a date. They'd discussed that already. He had his weird rule, and she had her bet with Jordan.

"Yup."

She sucked in a breath. Oh no! Had she spoken out loud again? What was with her lately? Usually she was better at controlling her odd habit.

"That seems to have fixed the issue. Just a small wiring problem." Dyson stared at the lit sign. "Easy peasy."

Oh thank goodness. She let out a sigh of relief. He had been talking about the sign, not her verbal outbursts.

"It's fantastic, thank you. Do you want lunch?" Quickly, so he wouldn't think she was offering to take him out after their earlier, painfully awkward conversation, she stipulated, "Zoe went to grab some sandwiches and she wanted me to ask you if you wanted anything. The place makes amazing food and they even have vegetarian and gluten free options if you need."

He smiled, squatting down to pack his tools into the red case. "I'm good, thanks. I actually have to go. Got some stuff to do before dinner with my sisters tonight."

He had dinner with his sisters? That was nice. She wished her siblings lived close enough to meet for dinner.

"Thank you for coming in today, then, and I hope you enjoy your dinner with your sisters."

"Thanks. I can come back in a few days and pick up where I left off."

"Are you sure? I don't want to monopolize too much of your free time."

He let out a rough laugh. "Trust me. The more my free time is filled, the less time my sisters have to meddle."

Okay, she had no idea what that meant but, since the center still needed work and it also meant she got to see Dyson more, she wouldn't argue.

"Okay then, see you soon."

"Bye, Lexi."

"Bye, Dyson."

He stared at her, his gaze filled with something that made

her heart race and her skin flush. She wanted so badly to wrap her arms around his neck and pull him to her. See if those lips tasted as delicious as they looked. Said lips curved as he lifted a hand toward her and…

"I, um, just need to get by," he said, pointing over her shoulder.

That's when she realized she was standing in the middle of the hallway, effectively blocking his exit.

Oblivious, thy name was Lexi.

"Ohmygosh," she mumbled the words all together while taking a huge step to the side and smashing her shoulder into the wall. "Ouch!"

"Are you okay?" His brow furrowed in concern.

"Yup." She rubbed the small smarting spot. "Nothing hurt but my pride. And maybe my shoulder a bit, but it's mostly pride." This man was going to wonder how she ever got the job running the center the way she'd been acting today. *Get it together, Lexi!*

"See you later."

Not if she died of embarrassment first. And with the way she acted around Dyson, that might be a very real possibility.

Chapter Four

After an afternoon of laundry and errands, Dyson headed up the steps to his sisters' place. Family dinner would be short tonight because he had his twenty-four-hour shift starting this evening. They were supposed to have dinner last night, but Gemma had a work emergency and Macy had been frantically trying to finish grading a bunch of late homework she'd allowed her students to make up.

He knocked on the front door, chocolate chip cookies in hand. Gemma answered with an overly bright smile on her face. He knew that smile. It never meant anything good for him.

"Dyson! Good, you're here."

"What's going on?"

Her smile dropped, gaze focusing on everything but him. "Wow, suspicious much?"

"Gemma."

Macy could out-silence anyone, but Gemma was crap at lying and even worse at hiding secrets.

"Fine!" She threw her hands up in the air, glancing over her shoulder before leaning in close to whisper, "Don't get mad, but Macy brought company tonight."

Company to family dinner? They did that only when one of them was dating…

Oh *no*.

He had a sinking feeling he knew exactly what kind of person his sister had brought tonight.

"Gemma, please tell me you two didn't set me up on a blind date for family dinner."

She grimaced, twisting the end of her long brown braid around one finger. "*We* didn't. But Macy might have. She's a new teacher at the school. It might just be a welcoming dinner for a fellow staff member, but… If it helps, Marissa is really nice, she's pretty, and she's—"

"No."

"Oh, come on, Dyson. You haven't even met her yet."

"Don't have to." He loved his sisters, but he'd been very clear with them about his no-more-dating rule. Gemma might be right—this could be just a friendly dinner to welcome a new coworker—but when it came to his sisters, he always had a healthy dose of suspicion.

"Hey, Dyson, you're here! And just in time to meet Marissa."

And there it was. Suspicions justified.

Macy sauntered up behind Gemma with an angelic smile. Yeah, right. He wasn't buying it.

"Macy, I hear you brought company to dinner."

"I did." His sister's smile tightened, gaze sharpening with a warning fire. "And you're going to be nice."

"When am I not nice?"

"Okay, fair, but you will give Marissa a shot."

"No, I won't because I told you I don't want to be set up on any dates."

"It's not a date. I'm simply welcoming a new friend to the area and if anything should spark between you and her…"

"It won't."

"Calm down, you two," Gemma placed a hand on each of their shoulders, glancing into the house. "If you keep bickering like that, she'll hear you. Now, Macy, it wasn't fair of you to spring Marissa on Dyson like this and Dyson, Macy was only trying to help. We all want to see you happy again, so forgive us if we get a little…"

"Pushy?"

Gemma glared. "I was going to say *involved*."

Involved? The only way they could be more involved is if they set him up on dating sites. Now that would be true hell. He snorted out a frustrated laugh. Still, it wasn't this Marissa person's fault his little sisters tried to run his life on their timeline. He'd come in, eat dinner, be nice, and try to convey to Marissa his non-interest in a polite way. Hopefully tonight's dinner wouldn't be too painful.

It turned out to be excruciatingly painful.

Dyson was so glad he had to cut out early for his shift. Poor Marissa had been as uncomfortable as he'd been. Obviously, Macy forgot to tell her friend she was setting Marissa up with her brother. The woman had been nice and, like Gemma said, pretty, but they had absolutely nothing in common. Even if Dyson had been on the market for a girlfriend, he and Marissa were clearly not a match.

Luckily when she mentioned superheroes, Macy had started the discussion of who was better, DC or Marvel. Since he never really jumped on the superhero bandwagon, he excused himself, thanked Marissa and his sisters for a nice dinner, shot a warning glare at Macy, who waved goodbye to him with her middle finger, and headed to work.

"O'Neil," Díaz called as he walked into the common room of the station. "Your shift's just starting, why do you look like you just got out of the red zone?"

He groaned at the familiar term thrown around Station

42. Whenever someone looked like hell warmed over, they likened it to the intense pressure of wandering around in an extreme fire danger zone holding a lit match. One tiny slip up and whoosh, wildfire raging out of control.

"I just left dinner at my sisters' house."

Her head tilted. "So? Your sisters are awesome. You love hanging out with them."

True, normally he did, but, "Macy brought a blind date." At her continued confusion he explained, "For me."

Light dawned in her eyes, the corners of her lips tilting. "Dude, we told you your sisters were going to get more persistent about you dating again."

"Dude?" He chuckled. "You're starting to sound like Ward."

Her dark eyes narrowed. "Take it back."

He mimed tossing out a fishing rod and reeling the observation back in.

"Smart-ass." Díaz smiled. "Look, your sisters love you. They aren't going to get off your back until you find a girlfriend."

"But I don't want a girlfriend."

"Then make one up."

Yeah, like they wouldn't see through that in a hot minute. First off, it'd be entirely too suspicious if he suddenly had a girlfriend. They'd be asking him to bring her to dinner the second the words were out of his mouth and then what would he do? Claim she wasn't from around here? She lived in Canada? The old "she goes to a different school" trick hadn't worked in middle school and it wouldn't work now.

"Or hire a fake one."

He started in surprise. "People do that? Hire fake significant others to dupe their families?"

She shrugged. "Dupe families, lie at reunions, take to weddings. The rent-a-partner business is booming, according to an article I read."

Okay, that was one option, but Dyson didn't think it was for him. It'd be too...awkward, trying to pretend intimacy with a stranger he was paying. More power to the people who could pull that off, but he wasn't that comfortable around people he didn't know.

"Or you could ask a friend to be your fake girlfriend for a while. Just to get your sisters off your back for a bit."

Now that sounded doable. The only problem was...he didn't have very many female friends. There was Díaz. And he shouldn't discount Torres, the other female firefighter at Station 42. He didn't work with her as much, but he knew her, was comfortable around her. But his sisters knew both women. No way would they believe he suddenly started dating one of them, especially since he worked with them. Dating someone he worked with was against the rules of Dyson.

"Okay, but who could I ask?"

Díaz's brow furrowed in concentration before a smile lit her face. She snapped her fingers. "What about that woman you were talking about the other day? The one who runs the DYC?"

"Lexi?"

"Yeah, Lexi. You do her a favor, she does you a favor."

Ward suddenly popped his head into the room. "Who's handing out favors? Because my washer broke and I am down to my novelty holiday Christmas boxers. Help a friend out?"

"Ward!" Díaz scowled at the other man. "Have you been standing there listening to our conversation like a creeper?"

"No, I was walking down the hall like a normal person. Jeez, Díaz. Suspicious much?"

She rolled her eyes. "With you? Always."

Ward brushed her off with the shake of his head. He propped his shoulder against the wall, staring at Dyson. "So, you need a fake girlfriend."

He nodded. "Gotta get my sisters off my back."

"Sometimes I'm glad I have only brothers."

Dyson often wondered what it would have been like to have a brother, but he wouldn't trade his sisters for anything. He loved them, even if they did drive him out of his mind some days.

"As much as I love you, dude, there's no way One-Night O'Neil could ever convince his sisters he magically fell in love overnight."

"He doesn't need to be in love," Díaz argued. "He just needs a girlfriend. He could fake it enough for that."

Ward laughed. "Are we talking about the same guy? Dyson, who has never broken a rule in his life, is somehow going to be able to magically lie to his sisters about dating someone?"

"Hey!" He was right here. They didn't need to talk about him like he wasn't. Besides, "I've broken a rule."

Ward gave him a skeptical glance.

"Name one, dude."

He stared at his friend, drawing a blank.

"Whatever, I could convince my sisters if I needed to."

"And it sounds like you need to," Díaz chimed in. "So you better make it convincing."

Make it convincing? He wasn't even sure he was going with this outlandish plan.

"You can do it."

"No he can't," Ward scoffed.

Díaz grinned. "Wanna bet?"

"Hold up, time out." Dyson held up his hands, both of his friends' heads turning in his direction. "I'm not fake dating Lexi."

"Not yet," Díaz stated before turning her attention back to Ward. "If he convinces his sisters he and Lexi are for real, you have to clean and detail my car."

"That piece of crap?" Ward laughed. "I'm worried one

spray from a hose will cause the poor thing to collapse in on itself."

"Bite your tongue when speaking about my baby," Díaz warned.

Ward shook his head. "Fine, but if Dyson can't convince his sisters for a whole month, then you have to eat an entire meal from start to finish...that I make."

Oh shit. Everyone at the station knew how bad Ward's cooking was. They'd all suffered the effects too, gathered around the toilet bowl.

"Hang on now, guys, I don't think—"

But his friends weren't listening to his protests. The disgust on Díaz's face morphed into determination as she stuck out her hand toward Ward.

"It's a bet."

Ward shook her hand, sending Dyson a sly grin. "Oh dude, this is gonna be so good. I can't wait to bust out the ol' cookbook."

"O'Neil, if you lose this for me, I am going to short sheet your bed for a month and tell your sisters you got over your fear of needles and want your nipples pierced."

His hands automatically went to his chest. Shit, Díaz could be super scary when she wanted to.

"But I haven't agreed to any of this. I haven't even talked to Lexi to see if she'd be willing to—"

"I believe in you, One-Night O'Neil. I believe in your complete inability to fake a relationship," Ward said with a laugh.

"And I believe in you, too, O'Neil," Díaz added as the two of them started heading out of the room. "You can fake it till you make it."

And then they were gone, completely ignoring his protests over the bet they made about his life. Leaving him alone to wonder what the hell had just happened.

Chapter Five

"Dyson, over here!"

Dyson stepped into 5280 Eats the day after his shift ended. He hadn't been able to talk Ward and Díaz out of the ridiculous bet they made about his damn life. Díaz even threatened him again that he better win it for her. But how in the hell was he supposed to ask Lexi to be his fake girlfriend?

He spotted Gemma waving enthusiastically from a booth to the left. His eyes widened in shock. Pulling his phone from his pocket, he glanced at the time. Yup, ten minutes early. He was used to waiting at least twenty for his perpetually late little sister.

"This is a surprise," he said as he slipped into the booth across from Gemma. "Since when are you on time?"

"Actually, I'm early," Gemma beamed, a slight smugness curling the corner of her mouth.

He chuckled. "Have I finally instilled the importance of being on time into that head of yours?"

Her nose wrinkled as she shook her head, smugness slipping when she admitted, "No. I'm early because my boss sent me to lunch early so I could drop off a package at the post office and the line was nonexistent so here I am, finally arriving to something before you."

"Enjoy the one and only time it will ever happen." He smiled, grabbing the water glass set out before him and taking a healthy gulp.

"Oh, I plan on holding this over your head for years. Dyson O'Neil being late to something, the scandal!" She gasped dramatically.

Dyson arched one eyebrow, staring at his baby sister across the table. "I wasn't late. I was ten minutes early for our appointed meeting time."

"Yes, but I was fifteen minutes early, so that makes you late."

"That's not how time works, Gemma."

She stuck her tongue out at him. "Just admit defeat. Let me have this one, Mr. Perfect."

"I'm not perfect."

He drank straight from the carton. Forgot his laundry in the washer half the time. Hadn't changed his sheets in a week and a half. His penchant for being early annoyed a lot of people, but it saved him big-time once. And his insistence on not breaking the rules lost him more than one friend growing up. Some days he felt one mistake away from complete failure. Especially when he'd been raising his sisters.

There was the time Gemma failed chemistry. Or when Macy broke her ankle on the school ski trip. Logically he knew those things were not entirely in his control, but he'd been responsible for his sisters. After their parents passed it had been his job to raise them, guide them, help mold them into confident, capable adults.

He supposed he did all right, but sometimes he wondered if he could have done more. Been a better parental figure. No way to know now.

"Close enough, sisterly bias." Gemma waved away his protests. "Anyway, so why I invited you to—"

"Hey, Dyson!"

He glanced up at the bright voice and smiled when he saw his buddy's fiancé, Tamsen, standing there in her waitress uniform, long dark hair pulled back into a sleek ponytail, eyes bright and happy.

"Hey, Tamsen. I didn't know you were working today." He motioned to Gemma. "You remember my sister, Gemma?"

"Of course, she comes in all the time." Tamsen winked. "Friends and family discount, right, Gemma?"

Dyson turned his head to stare at his sister, eyebrow raised. Gemma's face pinkened, her lips rolled in as a guilty expression crossed her features.

"Gemma."

She grimaced at his use of what his sisters complained was his "dad voice."

"What? You always say the firehouse is family. Tamsen is marrying Kincaid—stellar pull, by the way," she said to Tamsen, who winked back. "That makes her family and, since I'm your sister, I'm family. Plus the burgers here are really good."

"She's right," Tamsen said with a small laugh. "Ty makes the best burgers in town and don't you frown like that, Dyson. As day manager I now have the authority to give out discounts at my discretion. Plus Gemma worked it out so 5280 Eats can put flyers up in the library as advertisement, so it's an exchange of favors, a win-win."

Win-win, huh? Sounded more like both of them were using this situation as an excuse to get what they wanted without admitting what they were really doing. A bending of the rules if he ever heard one.

Dyson hated bending rules. It was one small step away from breaking them. He tried to avoid it as much as possible.

"Now, what can I get you both?"

"My usual," Gemma said with a smile.

"One western bacon cheeseburger deluxe with fries and an iced tea." Tamsen nodded, turning her attention to him. "Dyson?"

Leaning back against the cushioned booth he sighed. "The same."

"Wonderful, I'll put those right in and be back with your drinks." Tamsen gave him a soft pat on the shoulder, turned, and headed back toward the kitchen.

"So, what did you want to talk about?"

Gemma shifted in her seat, leaning forward and placing her hands on the table. "First I wanted to apologize for the other night. It wasn't fair for us to spring Marissa on you like that."

No it hadn't been. But he hoped his sisters learned their lesson and were going to drop this whole dating thing now. Then he could back out of this ridiculous bet between Ward and Díaz.

"And second, hear me out before you say no."

That didn't sound promising. He was already regretting agreeing to this lunch. Whatever came out of her mouth next, Dyson could guarantee he wasn't going to like it.

"Macy and I think you should try out some dating apps."

Bull's-eye. He knew he'd hate it.

"No."

"Dyson! I said hear me out."

He had. He heard her say he should try dating apps. His answer was no. End of conversation. What had she expected him to say?

"Look," Gemma held up a finger, not deterred by his one-word response. "I know what happened sucked, but it's been three years."

"So I should be over it, right?" It's what everyone kept

telling him. Hell, it's what he told himself in the darkest of the nights when his bed felt huge and empty. It wasn't like he wanted to be alone forever. Just seemed to be the card life dealt him, and he was trying to work with that.

Gemma reached over and placed a loving hand on his. "No. Not over it, but maybe starting to move past it? Macy and I are worried about you."

He shook his head. "I'm the big brother. It's my job to worry about you."

She rolled her eyes. "Just because you have a few years and dangly bits between your legs does not preclude me and Macy from worrying about you. And just so you know, she'd be here if she didn't have lunch monitor duty today at school."

Fantastic. Thank the school schedulers or he'd have two loving but annoying nosy sisters to deal with on his day off.

"Dyson, I—"

Gemma's words were cut off when Tamsen arrived back at their table with two tall glasses of iced tea.

"Here we are," Tamsen said with a bright smile, setting the glasses before them.

As she moved her hand away, Dyson noticed a large, beige bandage covering Tamsen's palm. He reached out and gently grasped her hand, turning it over as he examined it.

"Tamsen, what's this?"

"Pfft." She pulled her hand free and waved it in the air before tucking it behind her back. "It's nothing. I might have had a tiny mishap in the back while opening the box of to-go containers."

He arched one brow, staring at the woman he knew to be sweet but clumsier than a bull in a china shop. "How bad is it?"

"Barely a nick, I promise." She pointed a finger at him with her uninjured hand. "And if you tell Parker I swear I'm going to text Díaz and tell her to put a rubber snake in your bed. One with big, long, sharp, pointy plastic fangs."

He shuddered at the thought. Everyone at the station knew he hated snakes. Their fangs reminded him of needles. Dyson had a massive needle phobia ever since he was a kid and passed out after a doctor gave him a shot. He'd rather run into a burning building without his bunk gear than have a needle within ten feet of him. Give him all the creepy crawly six- and eight-legged bugs in the world, he could handle that, but tiny teeth needles that sank into your skin and filled your body with venom? No thank you.

"How are you going to hide that from your fiancé?"

Those two were so lovey-dovey, practically glued to each other anytime they were together. He doubted his buddy wouldn't notice an injury on the woman he loved. Especially since Kincaid was well familiar with Tamsen's...incidents. It was how they met, after all.

"I will tell him when he gets off shift, no need to worry him unnecessarily. But if you see him first." She mimed zipping her lips and pointed with a narrowed stare.

Dyson chuckled, holding up his hands in surrender. "Mum's the word, I promise. Besides I'm not on shift until tomorrow."

"Okay then," Tamsen nodded. "I'm going to go check on your meals."

She smiled and headed off again. Dyson turned back to face his sister, who was staring at him with a half smile, half frown, shaking her head.

"What?"

"See, Dy, that right there is what I mean."

Huh? No, he didn't see. What was she talking about?

"What right where?"

Gemma took a sip of her tea before answering. "You are like the sweetest guy ever, and I'm not being biased because I'm related to you. It's a fact. You're kind, helpful, you care about people. Some of my friends made the horrifying mistake of telling me you're hot and, after I threw up a million times I realized since we're related it must be true, because I'm a snack."

He laughed; leave it to his baby sister to compliment and insult him at the same time.

"The thing is"—she grasped his fingers in her hand and squeezed—"we love you, Dyson. And we just want to see you happy. Now if being alone makes you happy, that's fine, but I don't think it does. I think deep down, you want that connection again. You want to have someone to share your life with. Someone to love and to love you."

"Gemma I—"

"Just try the dating apps," she pleaded. "One, start with one. It's doesn't even have to be a find-your-soulmate one. It can be a hookup one. Get you back out there."

He could inform his sister he had no problem hooking up with willing partners when he wanted, but that was a conversation he was going to have with his baby sister at, oh, about never o'clock.

"You don't even have to activate it until you're ready, just set one up."

"I..." Panic rose in his gut. Throat tightening as the walls closed in. His palms ran slick with sweat as he searched his brain for a reason, any reason, to turn his baby sister down. He didn't want to hurt her, but no way in hell was he going to sign up for the hellscape that was a dating app.

Darkness swam in his vision and his mouth opened without permission, spewing forth words he had no business saying, "I can't because I'm already dating someone."

Gemma frowned, her eyes narrowing as she stared at him. "Oh really?"

"Yup." Nope.

"Who?"

He threw out the first name that came to mind. "Lexi."

Shit, he was in it now. No going back. Looked like Díaz and Ward would be getting their bet settled after all.

"Lexi?" Gemma frowned. After a second her lips slowly curled upward. "Oh, the woman from the teen center?"

He nodded, swallowing down the bile of the lie turning his stomach. "Yes, that's her."

"Dyson, that's wonderful!"

No, it wasn't. Shit! Now he had to ask Lexi to play his girlfriend. Maybe he could frame it like Díaz said, a favor for a favor. Did that make him an asshole?

"Dy, you have to invite her over to dinner soon." Gemma was practically bouncing out of her chair. "I can't wait to meet her—"

"Here we go, two of Ty's best burgers!" Tamsen announced as she arrived at the table with plates full of delicious-smelling food.

Dyson let out a grateful breath at the interruption. He dug into his meal along with Gemma, nodding along as she talked about how excited she was to meet his girlfriend and feeling like the biggest jerk in the world.

Chapter Six

The past few days of work had been hectic, to say the least. Lexi had to deal with a missing school bag accused of being stolen, which turned out to have just been left under a chair in the art room. Two grant rejections they really, really needed. A meeting with her boss regarding possible budget cuts—how they were going to slash an already bleeding budget she had no idea—and a call to DCFS regarding one of her kids who needed help out of a bad home situation.

She. Was. Drained.

Life always took turns, though, and today was looking up. One of the grants she thought they had no chance of getting actually came through, no arguments had broken out between anyone yet, Brenna called to thank Lexi for her help and let her know she was safe at her grandmother's house now. And the coffeepot actually worked this morning.

Yup. Today was going to be a good day.

A quick glance to her calendar reminded her of something else good that was happening today. Lexi opened her desk drawer, pulling out her emergency stock of makeup: the small bag she kept in here in case of long nights that turned into early morning meetings requiring a little freshening up. She grabbed the tube of berry pink lipstick. As she started to apply, her office door popped open and Zoe stepped inside.

"Hey, Lexi, Mateo and Brycen want to..." Zoe's head tilted. "Are you primping?"

Lexi quickly palmed the lipstick. Unfortunately, it was still open so now her hand had a giant pink blob mark on it.

Shoot!

She put the cap back on the tube and pushed it away. "No. Why would I be primping?"

Zoe's eyes narrowed, searching Lexi's face. Her gaze came to rest on something behind Lexi and her lips turned upward in a wide, knowing grin. "Oh hey, isn't Dyson coming by today?"

"Hmm? What? Um, maybe, I'd have to check my schedule."

Zoe snorted. "Yeah right, like you don't memorize the schedule every week."

She liked to be prepared. No, she had to be prepared. Too many variables when dealing with teenagers. There were a million things to do in a day and having a schedule helped mitigate any problems. Well...most problems.

Zoe eyed the lipstick tube by Lexi's hand and pointed a finger in triumph. "You *are* primping!"

"Okay, fine!" No sense in trying to play innocent with Zoe. The woman was like a human lie detector. Came in very handy most days when dealing with unruly teenagers, but Lexi wasn't appreciating the skill at the moment. "I might be touching up my makeup. A little. Because my lipstick wore off at lunch."

"And because Dyson is coming by and you want to see his fire hose."

"Zoe!"

The younger woman shrugged. "What? It's true."

Maybe, but they were at work. One of the kids could walk by and hear.

"Don't worry, they're all in the gym." Zoe stated, reading Lexi's worried expression. "Mateo and Brycen wanted to watch a movie—actually they want to marathon the new Spiderman movies—so I was just coming to grab the DVDs."

Lexi bent down to reach into her bottom desk drawer where she kept the case of DVDs people donated to the center. She pulled it out and passed it over to Zoe.

"Here you go."

"Thanks, and you look great, by the way."

"I'm not..." She tried to protest, but at Zoe's arched eyebrow, she gave in. "Fine, I'm primping for Dyson. A little, but it's not like that."

"Like what?"

A heavy sigh weighed down her chest. "He says he doesn't date, and you know I have that bet with Jordan."

"So? The bet was for dating. You don't have to date him to do him, right?"

True. She supposed she could see if he would be up for being sex buddies and it wouldn't be breaking any rules of the agreement. Jordan even said as much the other night. But that was always an awkward ask.

How did she propose to a man she barely knew that they should hook up occasionally? It'd be easier if they met at a bar or something. Somewhere the social situation lent itself to that kind of thing. The fact that he was doing a favor for the center made what she wanted tricky. She wasn't his boss, so there was no inappropriate power imbalance. He was volunteering his time. He could leave whenever with zero repercussions.

For him.

If Dyson left because she propositioned him, that would

leave the center in a bad spot. She couldn't do that. No matter how much she wanted Dyson, the center came first. She'd have to put her hormones on hold and continue with her empty-bed streak. For now.

Maybe when he finished the repairs, when there wasn't a risk of him leaving, she could ask him. She just had to make it from now until then without accidentally opening her big mouth and propositioning him.

"I'm going to set up the movie for the kids, then finish stuffing the flyers for the fundraiser next month."

"Thanks, Zoe. You're a lifesaver."

"I know." Zoe winked, heading out of Lexi's office, leaving her to her endless inbox.

Zoe really was a lifesaver. She'd had a handful of interns and volunteers over the years, but none had been as helpful as Zoe. She knew the college woman would most likely leave after graduation. On to bigger and better things. But what she wouldn't do to be able to keep her here, have the funds to pay Zoe what she was worth.

Ha!

Lexi didn't even get paid what *she* was worth. This job wasn't about the money; it was about the kids. Providing a safe space for them. Making the world a little bit better. Hopefully having some kind of positive impact.

"Knock, knock."

Lexi glanced up from the paperwork she was going over to see a tall, sexy firefighter in dark blue jeans and a tight gray Henley standing in her open doorway.

Dyson.

Speaking of positive impacts. Not only did the man make her smile just by thinking of him, her heart rate sped up at the sight of him, her mood improved when he was near, and his presence at the center was the most positive thing to happen to the DYC since last year's big donation from the Lemmens

Foundation.

"Hi, Dyson."

"Lexi." He dipped his chin. "I thought I'd start today with replacing all the smoke detectors."

She winced. "Oh, we don't actually have any new ones right now. I have some extra batteries—"

Her words died as he held up a plastic bag. He opened it to show her a pile of brand-new smoke detectors, still in their packaging. The fancy kind that detected carbon monoxide too. A gasp left her lips, heart beating faster at the generosity of the gift.

"Dyson...where did you..."

He lifted one shoulder in a small shrug. "We have a bunch at the station. Always on hand for people who need them."

And the DYC needed them. She was fairly certain the smoke alarms here were older than she was.

"That's amazing, thank you so much."

His cheeks darkened a bit, blushing a charming shade of pink. Holy cow, Dyson O'Neil was blushing because she thanked him, and it was absolutely adorable.

Danger! Danger raging hormones! We can't jump him yet.

"Do you need any help today?" She had a million things to do, but he was volunteering his time and expertise, so she'd offer whatever assistance he needed. For the center, of course. No other reason.

He shook his head. "Don't think so, but I will need a ladder, though, if you have one."

"We do. It's just back in the storage room. Follow me."

She moved out from behind her desk, making her way toward the door. Dyson stepped back into the hall to let her pass.

"This way." She lifted a hand to point.

"Lexi, are you okay?" Dyson frowned, dropping the

bag of smoke detectors and grabbing her hand in his. "What happened to your…wait, what is this?"

It took her a second to understand what he said. The moment he grabbed her, touched her skin, thunder cracked in her ears. A bolt of pure white-hot desire shot straight from her palm right down between her legs. She'd heard of hot flashes, but could people get horny flashes? Because if so, she was experiencing a doozy. Her body screamed for her to push Dyson back against the wall and claim his mouth with hers. Rub herself against all that hard muscle teasing her underneath those clothes. Wrap her legs around him and—

"Lexi, what is this?"

His words finally broke through her fog of lust.

"Huh? What?"

He lifted her hand, his palm still cupping her wrist. "This. I thought it was blood or a bruise or something, but it looks like—"

"Shit!" The lipstick!

"Um, no, it doesn't look like that."

She groaned. Why hadn't she cleaned her palm? The smudge from when she grabbed the lipstick had smeared and it did indeed look like a faint bruise. This is what she got for being silly and primping instead of focusing on important things. Like how Dyson was here only to fix the inspection issues. Nothing more.

"It's lipstick."

The corner of his mouth turned up in a small smile. "Doesn't that usually go on your lips?"

He knew very well it did. She huffed. "Yes, but I was startled when putting it away and accidently got some on my palm. Zoe needed something for the kids, then I had paperwork to handle, and I guess I forgot to clean it off."

He lifted the bottom edge of his shirt, giving her a tantalizing sneak peek of a set of delicious ripped abs.

Yummy!

"You do too much," he said as he wiped the makeup off. "It's no wonder your mind is a million places at once."

Change the horny flash to horny flash flood, because this man was drowning her in his appeal. Who used their own clothing to clean up someone else's mess? Who did that?

"The work never ends around here, but I'm happy to do it."

He stared at her, pale hazel eyes roaming over her face, taking in every inch. Normally she squirmed when someone looked like they were trying to laser eye into her soul, but his thumb stroked her palm, right over where the lipstick mark had been. He nodded, as if he'd seen something deep within her. Something he approved of.

Warmth radiated through her body. She shouldn't give a rat's butt about what Dyson thought of her, but his silent approval made her pleased in a way she couldn't explain.

"It takes a special kind of person to do what you do, Lexi Martin."

She couldn't contain the smile at his words. "I could say the same about you, Dyson O'Neil."

Again he blushed and again she had to stop herself from throwing her arms around the man and kissing him senseless. She had no idea a guy blushing could be such a turn-on, but on Dyson, it totally was.

He dropped her hand, taking a small step back and bending down to grab the fallen bag. "Uh, I should probably get to work."

"Right, right, and I should show you that ladder."

She started off down the hall, hand still tingling from Dyson's touch. So soft, yet so strong. He had strength, but he knew how to be gentle with it. She wondered if that was a skill he learned as a firefighter or if he'd always been that way?

They passed the gym, where Lexi took a moment to peek

in. The teens were all sufficiently distracted with the movie, bowls of popcorn being passed around. More empty soda cans than there should be for that many teenagers, but she wasn't there to monitor their sugar habits, and an extra soda treat or two wouldn't hurt them.

Zoe glanced up from her spot in the large, old, and well-loved beanbag chair she sat in while stuffing flyers into envelopes. She waved at Lexi, noticed Dyson, and smiled slyly. Lexi tried to communicate to Zoe to keep her mouth shut. Zoe's grin widened, but thankfully she didn't say or do anything more.

Satisfied that everyone was okay, Lexi continued down the hall into the back storage room where the ladder, among other things, was kept.

"Will this be tall enough?" she asked, placing her hand on a six-foot stepladder that once was green, but had been so used, dinged, and scratched over the years that most of the paint had come off. At least the steps were still there.

"Should be fine." Dyson started forward to grab the ladder when his phone chimed.

"Do you need to get that?"

He pulled his cell from his pocket. "Yeah, it might be work. Sometimes there's an emergency and we get called in…"

She hoped not. And not because she was enjoying time with Dyson here and the center needed him, but because an emergency for a firefighter sounded dangerous, and the thought of Dyson in danger made her stomach clench. Silly. He was a firefighter. He ran headfirst into danger for a living.

A frown marred his brow as he stared at his phone. "Dammit."

She tensed. "Something wrong? Is it work? Is there a fire? Some kind of accident?"

What else did firefighters respond to other than fires?

She had no idea.

"Yes, I mean no." He shook his head, his expression more angry than worried. "There's a problem, but it's not work. It's my sisters."

"Your sisters?" Oh no, that was even worse. Just thinking about her brother or sister in trouble had Lexi's heart racing. "Are they okay?"

"They're a pain in my ass is what they are."

"Beg pardon?"

He sighed. The heavy sigh of a sibling about to kick another sibling's ass for something stupid they did. Like the time her brother "borrowed" her car for a date and drove it into a snowy ditch, messing up the axle and costing her thousands in repairs.

He shook his head, staring at his phone as if it were a foreign object. "They've been trying to get me to start dating again since…for a while now. Last family dinner my youngest sister Macy even set up a blind date for me."

But he said he didn't date. Why were his sisters pushing him when he didn't do relationships? Did they know about his no-girlfriend rule? They must not if they were trying to get him one. It wasn't like she talked to her brother about her dating life or preferences.

Lexi swallowed past the uncomfortable lump in her throat. "Oh? How did it go?"

"It was a disaster." He glanced up from his phone, a guilty expression filling his face. "And then I, um…"

A heavy sigh left his lips as his eyes turned toward the ceiling. Everything in her ached to rush over and sooth his distress. See what she could do to help.

No.

That was old Lexi, doing everything for everyone without getting anything in return. She wasn't supposed to solve everyone's problems. Whatever Dyson was dealing with she was sure a man as capable as him had it in hand.

"I'm really sorry, Lexi, but I need a favor."

A favor? From her? Unless he needed help organizing a fundraiser benefit or learning the latest slang the kids were using these days, she probably wouldn't be much help.

"A favor?"

"I kind of, maybe, accidently told my sisters I couldn't do any more blind dates or sign up for any dating apps because I was already seeing someone." His face turned bright red, gaze glancing everywhere but directly at her. "Um, you... I told them I started dating you."

"Me?" She blinked, shock causing a small bubble of laughter to escape her lips.

Finally, his eyes came to focus on her. "Yes. Your name just kind of popped out of my mouth. I guess I panicked and... I'm really sorry, Lexi. I'm a total ass and feel free to say no, but I was wondering if you could help me out and..."

While her brain tried to wrap itself around what Dyson was saying, he let out a frustrated groan. He looked so uncomfortable and awkward. Her heart pinched with empathy. She knew that feeling, she lived it daily every time her brain to mouth synapses stopped working. Poor guy.

He glanced back at his phone. "They're already texting me about meeting you..."

"They want to meet me?" His sisters, who thought they were dating. She blinked, brain still clouded with confusion at the strange situation she suddenly found herself in.

"I don't even know how to say this without sounding like a total ass, but, Lexi, would you please help me out here and pretend to be my fake girlfriend? It'll be for only a little while, a month tops. You'll probably have to meet them only once anyway. One dinner. Then I can just talk about you and stuff."

"A favor for a favor?" He was helping out the center, after

all, so playing his fake girlfriend wouldn't be doing something without getting anything back. It'd be repaying someone who was helping her first.

"Shit, that does sound bad." Dyson shook his head. "I'm sorry, forget it. I am a total ass. I'll figure something else out."

"No!" She cleared her throat as the word left her a bit too loudly. "I mean, actually it would make me feel a lot better about using up all your free time. I'd be happy to return the favor by playing your fake girlfriend."

A wave of relief relaxed his features. "Seriously?"

"Yeah, I minored in theater in college," she chuckled. "Nice to get some use out of it."

He glanced down at his phone, cheeks burning red as he slipped the thing back into his pocket. The flustered look on his face was so adorable, she couldn't help but smile.

"You're an absolute lifesaver, but…" He rubbed the back of his neck, hesitating, lips rolling in as he seemed to carefully choose his next words. "It would strictly be for show. Pretend. I don't want to give you the wrong idea or confuse anything between—"

"Dyson," she cut him off. "You've been very clear about your non-relationship rule. I respect that, even if your sisters seem to be a little…"

"Pushy."

She lifted her hands and grinned. "You said it, not me."

He chuckled softly. "Thank you, Lexi. I really appreciate it."

Warmth filled her chest. Not many people thanked her for favors. True, she was just doing this one to return the favor Dyson was doing for the center, but still, it felt good to be appreciated.

"They'll want to meet you. Know how we met when we started dating. I'm…I'm not very good at lying. Especially to my sisters."

A very commendable trait and not surprising, considering his penchant for rule following. "Then we keep it as close to the truth as possible. We met when you came for the inspection. We hit it off. There's a spark and we decided to give it a try and see where it goes."

All the truth for her. Except the last part.

"You sure you don't mind?"

Mind? No. Possibly too excited for it…yup.

"Not at all."

He smiled, a wide, relieved grin crinkling the corners of his eyes. "Great."

"Great!" Oops, too loud. Clearing her throat, she tried again. "Great, then I'll just get back to work and let you…"

"Sure, and um, we should probably meet up to go over our story and stuff. My sisters will demand a dinner invite soon. I think we should do some prep work beforehand. Would, um, tomorrow night work? We can grab dinner."

A meal with Dyson where they concocted a story about being romantically involved? Count her in.

"Works for me."

She gave him her cell so he could text her later with details and left him to his work, knowing she'd either just made the best decision of her life, or the biggest mistake.

Chapter Seven

"Jordan," Lexi called from the floor of her closet. "Have you seen my black strappy sandals?"

At his muffled response, she stuck her head out of the closet door. "What?"

Five seconds later, Jordan appeared in her bedroom doorway, arms crossed over his broad chest. "Lex, you have to stop asking me questions when you're head deep in Narnia."

"Sorry," she winced.

Her closet did slightly resemble a magical kingdom. It was full to the brim with school supplies, extra clothing, board games, and anything else she found for free or at a supremely discounted price. Anything she thought the center might need, she grabbed and kept it here until they had a need or room for it at work. What could she say? She was very devoted to her job.

"And your shoes are in the hall closet, under the picnic blanket. Remember?"

Oh right. Jordan and Angel had invited her to go see a concert in the park last week. There had been snacks, dancing, and many libations. When they got home, she'd tossed everything, including her sandals, into the hall closet.

"Thank you." She stood, rushing out of the closet and patting his cheek as she moved past him on her way out of her room. "What would I do without you?"

"Nothing but work, work, and more work."

"Hey!" She shot him a grimace over her shoulder. But he was right. Without her bestie encouraging her to go out and have fun every now and then, she'd probably spend most of her time consumed with work. It was hard not to give her all when the center needed so much. Well, not the center itself, but the kids.

"And why are we all dressed up like a dime tonight?" Jordan asked as she made it to the closet and started rummaging. "The center having another fundraiser you forgot to tell me about?"

"No." She shoved aside a volleyball, the blanket, and moved the picnic basket she was sure, by the rancid smell, still had some leftover cheese in it, out of the closet. Bingo! Her black strappy sandals with the small kitten heels. "These are perfect for tonight's date."

"Back up a sec, you're going on a date?"

Standing, she slipped the shoes on and turned to face her roommate and best friend.

"Does this mean I get to order the red nose and big floppy shoes?"

"No!" She shifted on her bare feet. "It's not a real date so it doesn't count."

"Explain."

She launched into the events of yesterday with Dyson learning of the predicament his sisters put him in and asking her for a favor by being his fake girlfriend. Once she was finished, Jordan stared at her for a full minute.

She squirmed under his intense stare. No one could stare

like Jordan. Finally, she couldn't take it anymore. Crossing her arms over her chest, she cocked a hip and met his stare with one of her own. Albeit far less potent. "What?"

"Lex, are you sure you know what you're doing?"

"Um, yeah. I just explained it to you. I'm having dinner with a friend to discuss our plan to fool his sisters with a fake relationship so they'll get off his back. And, since it's not real dating I'm not breaking the bet, so don't go buying a clown costume just yet. You're going to need that money for moving boxes."

His sigh was heavy and weighted. "Okay, I'll give you that loophole, but you're pretending to be the girlfriend of a man you're attracted to because you can't see a person in need and not help them—"

"I'm paying back the favor he's doing me by helping the center." A favor for a favor seemed fair to her.

"You're treading into dangerous territory. This is the exact reason we made the bet in the first place. To protect your...overly generous nature from consuming you."

She laughed, but a small sharp pain in her gut whispered that her bestie might be on to something.

"Getting involved with a man when you have real feelings for him is a slippery slope. One that slides right into the disaster zone."

"It's all fake," she insisted. "Besides, I don't have *feelings* for him beyond wanting to *feel* all of him against me."

Dark eyebrows rose. "So this fake dating includes sex?"

"N-no," she sputtered. "I mean, we haven't really discussed anything like that. We both agreed neither of us is looking to date anyone right now, but as Zoe so colorfully pointed out yesterday, I don't have to date him to do him. If we decided to add benefits to our deal, it makes the lie only more believable, right?"

Jordan shook his head with a sad smile. "Oh honey."

She made a squeak of protest. How dare he "oh honey" her!

"I know what I'm doing, Jordan."

"You really don't," he rebutted. "Haven't you ever seen a romcom before? Scratch that, I know you have, because we binged all Ms. Bullock's greatest hits last month."

She did love a feel-good romcom and Sandra made some of the best.

"You know how it goes, two people decided to fake date, but end up doing the nasty and falling face first into feelings. Cue the big dramatic breakup and equally big grand gesture and boom, happily ever after." He stepped forward, taking her hands in his. "Only life isn't like a movie."

"I know life isn't a movie, and I'm not breaking any rules of the bet."

His gaze came back down to her, concern filling his dark brown eyes. "I'm not worried about the bet, Lex. I'm worried about you. If you wanna hop in the guy's bed for a night, go for it—you *should* do something for yourself for once. But pretending to date the dude might muddle things all up. I just…I just don't want to see you get hurt again."

Knowing all her friend's objections were coming from a place of concern warmed her heart, even if his insistence that she didn't know what she was doing irritated a bit. Stepping into his arms, she gave him the tightest hug she could. "You worry about me too much."

"Yes, well, that's my job as best friend. I give hard truths to you—and ass-kickings to anyone who hurts you."

She laughed. The thought of Jordan, the biggest pacifist she knew—who was vegetarian because he once accidentally stepped on a ladybug and cried about it for a week—hurting anyone was absolutely hilarious.

"I promise to keep my heart out of it."

"See that you do, or Lexi the clown cleaning the

apartment will be the highest viewed video on the net."

"Keep dreaming. I am winning that bet and you're going to have to deal with your own issues."

Jordan frowned. Her lips curled in a grin at the small sense of pride welling inside as she reminded her bestie that she wasn't the only one with skin in this game.

"You have to give Angel an answer eventually Mr. Fraidy-cat and when I win—*ack*!" Lexi screeched as a big ball of black fur launched itself at her from the top of the hall closet. "Lucifer!"

She snuggled her fur baby to her chest, pounding heart steadily falling back into rhythm after the scare her cat gave her.

"How the hell does he even get in there?" Jordan asked, looking up at the high closet shelf that held their hats and winter gear.

Who knew? Cats were wicked smart like that. The real question was how did her sweet little devil kitty always know when she was leaving to go on a date? Even if this one wasn't technically real, she didn't want to show up covered in cat fur. Her dark dress hid most of it—the reason most of her closet contained dark clothing—but Luci still shed like the devil. Pun not intended.

"Why do you always get so cuddly the second I have to leave, huh?" The cat meowed in response, wiggling out of her arms and leaping to the floor with a grace only felines possessed. Tail high, he marched into the kitchen, apparently done with her now that he'd sufficiently covered her in his hair.

"If I didn't know better, I'd say he's jealous and just marked you as his territory."

She shook her head at the idea. Mostly because Lucifer did own her, far more than she owned him. She loved her cantankerous cat with all her heart.

"Just pass me the lint roller, please."

Jordan handed it over. Lexi did a quick but thorough brush to get all the cat hair off. Nothing spoiled a date like cat hair in your food.

Fake date.

Right, fake date.

She gave Jordan one last hug and headed out, grabbing a ride-share to the restaurant because it was only six blocks away and she didn't want to spend half an hour looking for parking. They'd agreed to meet at 5280 Eats. Lexi had been a few times, but truthfully anything above fast food was a once-in-a-while treat on her budget.

She arrived at the restaurant to find Dyson waiting for her at the host stand.

"I'm not late, am I?" She glanced at her watch.

Dyson smiled. "Nope. I'm just early. Sorry, it's a habit."

"A good one. Nothing to be sorry about." Especially when he looked so good in his pressed slacks and dark blue button-up shirt. This wasn't a real date, but you couldn't tell from the way he was dressed. She shouldn't read anything into that.

"You look beautiful."

He blinked, looking very much like she felt when she accidentally spoke her inner thoughts.

"I mean, that's a nice dress...um, you look nice."

Don't read into it, Lexi. Don't read into it!

"Thank you. Um, you look good, too."

Oh shoot, this was awkward. Not in a first date kind of way, but in an I-really-wanna-do-you-but-I-can't-because-it's-all-fake kind of way.

"Mr. O'Neil, your table is ready."

Saved by the host.

The tall host with neon green hair and more tattoos on his forearms than Lexi could count led them to a small table in the back corner of the restaurant and left, stating their server would arrive shortly. Private, secluded, completely perfect for a date. Too bad this wasn't a real one.

Dyson held out a chair for her, waiting until she sat before taking his own.

"Wow," she chuckled softly. "Such manners, I think I'm going to like fake dating you."

"Wait until you hear about the fake presents I bought you." He bobbed his eyebrows.

She laughed, the tense knot in her chest releasing as the awkwardness turned into friendly banter.

"So," she started. "How do you want—"

"Dyson?"

Lexi turned at the soft feminine voice. A small dark-haired woman stood at their table, dressed in the same manner as the restaurant staff, but with the exception of a black shirt instead of white.

"Tamsen!" Dyson rose from his seat to give the woman a hug.

Lexi bit back a pang of jealousy. Silly. They weren't even on a real date. What did she care if Dyson hugged another woman?

"Lexi, this is Tamsen. She's engaged to my buddy Parker Kincaid who works at the station with me."

Hoping her face wasn't as red as it was hot, Lexi swallowed her embarrassment and smiled, offering Tamsen her hand.

"It's nice to meet you."

"Likewise." Tamsen glanced back and forth between the two, an assessing glint in her eyes. "I'm just heading off shift, but I saw you and had to say hello. Parker didn't tell me you were bringing a date here, Dyson. If he had I would have made it extra special. Had Ty whip up something in the kitchen to knock her socks off."

Tamsen held a hand up to block Dyson's view of her lips

and mouthed to Lexi, *he's a great guy.*

She placed a hand over her own mouth to smother her laugh when Dyson rolled his eyes to the ceiling. It seemed everyone in his life was trying to hook him up. She wondered why? Seemed to her a guy as great as Dyson wouldn't have any trouble with women. What made this man so averse to dating?

Not her mystery to solve. She was just here to fulfill a favor.

"You don't have to make me look good, Tamsen." Dyson shook his head.

"So how did you two meet?" Tamsen asked with an eager smile.

"Lexi is from the DYC," Dyson quickly answered. "I was there to do their inspection and…"

His face paled as the words seemed to get stuck in his throat. A small pang of sympathy hit her right in the chest. Poor guy really couldn't lie very well. She reached over to pat his hand and turned a megawatt smile on Tamsen.

"We just sort of hit it off and here we are," Lexi finished for him with a small laugh, earning a silent *thank you* from Dyson.

"Oh, I heard you were helping with some repairs there." Tamsen turned to face Lexi fully. "Hey, do you need any volunteers?"

She laughed. "We *always* need volunteers."

"I'd be happy to come by a few hours a week and do some art projects with the kids. I'm kind of an artist. Well, I mean, not an artist in the way that I make millions of dollars or anything, but I have sold a few pieces lately and they've made a sizable dent in my student loans, but I'm not claiming to be an expert, though I do have a degree and I'm happy to—"

"Tamsen is being modest," Dyson interrupted the other woman's rambling. "She's a fantastically skilled artist the kids would be lucky to learn from as long as she doesn't have them make body castings."

"Oh my God, Dyson, why would you bring that up?" She smacked him on the arm.

Okay, there was a story there. One hopefully she'd be able to get the other woman to tell her one day. But for now, she pulled one of her cards from her small clutch and handed it over.

"That sounds amazing, Tamsen. We'd really appreciate any time and instruction you'd be willing to give. We have a few very gifted kids who would love your guidance. Just shoot me an email with your availability when you get a chance."

Tamsen smiled, slipping the card into her pocket.

"Will do, and you two have fun tonight." Her gaze slid between them again.

Tamsen left and Dyson retook his seat.

"She seems nice."

"She is," Dyson nodded.

"So, are we keeping this ruse up for everyone?" Because he'd insinuated to Tamsen that they were dating. She just wanted to be clear on who they were and weren't faking it to.

He frowned. "Probably for the best, though I should mention…"

His words trailed off, a frustrated sigh leaving his lips. She was pretty good at reading people's emotions, had to be in her job with kids who were experts at hiding them, but she was having a real tough time figuring out the man in front of her.

"Dyson?"

"Full disclosure." He let out a deep breath. "Two of my crewmates, Díaz and Ward, know this is fake and they…kind of placed a bet on whether or not I could keep it up. Convince my sisters for a full month."

"Oh." She sat back in her chair, not sure how to process

that. On the one hand it was kind of weird, coworkers placing a bet on your love life—*fake* love life. One the other hand she herself had a weird bet with her bestie about her love life so she wasn't one to talk.

"Okay well, if we're being completely honest, my roommate Jordan knows, too, because of our bet." Since he shared about his bet, she supposed it wouldn't be so bad if she informed him of her own. Honesty would be paramount if they were going to go through with this thing.

"Your bet?"

No backing out now. "It's silly, really."

Grabbing her glass of wine, she took a healthy swig before explaining. "Um, so I don't have the best track record for…putting myself first in a relationship."

A grin tugged at his lips. "You don't say."

She laughed softly. "Okay, I'm a giver and sometimes over the years I may have given too much. A month ago Jordan became my accountabilabuddy. No dating for six months so I could focus on me and what I want."

"And if you do date in that time?"

"I have to clean the entire apartment."

He frowned. "That doesn't sound too bad."

"In a clown costume."

At his confused expression, she explained, "I have a huge clown phobia. I think it's the makeup. The distorted face or whatever. Creeps me out."

"We all have things that terrify us," he said, nodding with understanding.

She tilted her head, grinning at him. "Like being five minutes late to an appointment or accidently breaking a rule?"

His eyes narrowed, but a playful smile curled his lips. "Now that would be truly terrifying."

A laugh escaping her lips, she took a sip of her water

and continued. "Anyway, if I lose the bet, I have to put on a horrifying clown costume and clean the entire apartment and Jordan's even threatened to film the whole thing and put it on the internet. Do you know the amount of endless teasing my kids at the center will give me if that happens?" She shuddered. "No, no way am I losing this bet."

Dyson's smile slipped into a frown. "Lexi, you don't have to do this if—"

"No, it's fine." She waved away his concern. "I explained everything to Jordan. This is fake so it doesn't count. Plus, by fake dating you, it will help me not real date anyone else and I'm sure to win."

"How long left?"

"Five months." Not that she was counting or anything. She never realized how much she missed dating until she hadn't been allowed to do it.

"Well then," Dyson lifted his glass. "Glad to be of service."

They clinked and shared a drink.

The server came by and took their orders. Once he left, Lexi decided to get to the heart of tonight's dinner.

"Shall we go over our story? We're sticking to what really happened, right? You coming to the center for the inspection?"

"Right." He tapped a finger on the table. "Best to stick as close to the truth as possible."

She agreed with that. "Can we please leave out the part where I thought you were a strip-o-gram?"

Dyson snorted out a laugh. "Please let's. My sisters would never let me live that down."

She joined in his laughter. "They sound really fun."

Grabbing his drink, he took a sip. "Don't let them fool you. You're going to get the third degree at dinner. They can be sweet as sugar or as cunning as foxes. But they do it all out of love."

The way he spoke of his sisters melted her heart. Her brother called her Fart Face until he was twenty-five. He still called her Fart Face whenever he wanted to get under her skin. Dyson almost seemed like a proud father rather than a big brother who lived to annoy his sisters.

"You all are really close?"

He nodded. "Yeah. We've always been a close family, but when my parents…" He hesitated, sucking in a sharp breath. Pain filled his eyes, his jaw tightened as he stared down at the tablecloth, finger absently twisting his napkin. "When our parents died, I had to drop out of college to come back home and take care of my sisters. They were both teenagers. Still in school. You could say that experience bonded us pretty strongly."

"Oh, Dyson." Her heart cracked, the pain in his voice when he spoke of his parents reaching inside and squeezing her chest like a vise. She reached over, placing her hand on his. "I'm so sorry."

"It's okay. It was a long time ago."

He tried for a smile, but it was dim in comparison to the ones she'd seen on him before.

"It must have been hard raising your sisters when you were barely more than a kid yourself."

He shrugged but turned his hand so it grasped hers. "We made do. In part thanks to the Sundale youth center. My sisters went there a lot while I was working. They even helped Gemma and Macy apply for scholarships to Metro. Shame when it closed."

She remembered that center. Sadly, a lot of nonprofit centers closed all the time for numerous reasons, but mostly it was due to lack of funds. Now she understood a little more about why Dyson had been so willing to help do the repairs for free.

He knew better than most how desperately help was needed.

Their food came and they ate while discussing their plan. They settled on going with more or less the truth. They met, he offered to help, they got to talking, connected and bonded during his time at the center, and decided to give this chemistry between them a go.

She shared a bit with him about her family, but they didn't delve too deeply, since their supposed relationship just started. It actually worked out pretty well to fool his sisters. They were only just getting to know each other so the hard questions wouldn't likely come out over a family dinner. Hopefully.

They finished their meal and Dyson insisted on paying. Claiming it would help him stay closer to the truth with his sisters if he paid for dinner, the way a real date would go.

"I'll walk you to your car," he said as they left the restaurant.

"I took a ride-share."

"Oh." He glanced around the busy city streets. "Can I take you home then?"

"Sure, that'd be great." A real boyfriend would need to know where his real girlfriend lived, right? Of course. That was the reason she accepted his offer. Not because she wanted to spend more time with him.

They headed to his car and she directed him the six blocks back to her place. Since her building had tenant only parking, he pulled up at the front entrance to let her out.

"Thanks for dinner, Dyson."

"I know I already said it, but I want to thank you for playing along with this...whole thing." He shook his head as if he still couldn't believe they were going through with it. "So, um, the crew goes to pub quiz every week."

"Pub quiz?" That sounded like fun. She hadn't been to a

pub quiz night in forever.

"Yeah, and, um, I was thinking we could go. Ya know, like practice some more being…"

"A couple?" she finished for him when it was clear he couldn't. It seemed Dyson had as much of a problem with fake relationships as he did real ones.

"Yeah," he nodded. "If we can convince my friends, I'm sure it will be easier to convince my sisters."

"Okay."

"Really?"

She smiled, pushing down the tiny voice in her head that warned her more time with Dyson was a bad idea. Fake or not.

"Sure, besides, I haven't been to a pub quiz in ages, sounds like fun."

Dyson let out a breath of relief. "Thanks, Lexi. I really owe you for all this."

"Just make sure the center passes inspection and we're even."

She grabbed the door handle, but paused, a thought striking her. His sisters and friends would probably expect a little PDA. Not much, but new couples were often very touchy. Every time she touched Dyson, sparks raced along her skin. Which she supposed was a good thing, for their lie and all. Still, touching hands and touching lips were two very different things. Would his sisters expect them to kiss in their presence?

"Lexi?" Dyson stared at her with concern. "Something wrong?"

"What? Oh no, I was just wondering…um, should we, I mean will your sisters and friends expect us to, ya know…kiss in front of them?"

His eyes widened, mouth dropping open but no sound escaping. He blinked a few times, cheeks reddening. Great, and now the night was back to being awkward.

"Right, um, I suppose people will expect us to...yeah." He nodded before straightening his shoulders. "But we should have some rules along with this."

Rules? For kissing? She guessed that was a good idea, but seriously, did the guy have to make a rule for everything in his life? She wondered if he had a list of them taped up to his bathroom mirror so he could study them every morning to make sure he didn't step out of line.

"Physical contact in the presence of friends and my sisters should be limited to appropriate displays of affection."

"Appropriate displays of affection?" She arched one eyebrow. "Wow, with sweet talk like that, it's a wonder you don't have a girlfriend."

He frowned and she couldn't help the small giggle that escaped her.

"I'm teasing you, Dyson. Rules are smart." Reaching out, she patted his thigh, immediately pulling her hand back when the contact sent a spark of awareness through her. "So, um, what type of displays? Kissing? Hugging? Hand-holding?"

He nodded. "Yes, those all sound acceptable."

"So just to make sure we're a hundred percent clear on the rules..." She hesitated a moment before she queried, "No sex?"

He glanced at her, eye filling, for a brief second, with a scorching heat that nearly burned her panties off. But then it was gone. His jaw clenched and he turned his head, focusing out the windshield again as he nodded.

"Yeah, better not muddle things more than they already are. Safer to keep this thing PG-13."

PG-13?

She stifled another giggle. What she wouldn't do to see this man break loose of his carefully controlled demeanor. Dyson was so sweet, but the guy could stand to lighten up a little.

"Good. I agree." She twisted her fingers in her lap. "So do you think we ought to try it before then, a kiss, I mean. Just so it looks convincing and all."

And because she'd been dying to kiss him all night.

Dyson nodded. He shifted in the driver's seat, turning so his body faced hers. His hand came up to cup her cheek, thumb stroking along her jaw. Her eyelids drooped, closing until she saw only a small slit of the world beyond them. Her breath shallowed, all the nerves in her body focused on the point where Dyson's skin touched her own.

"If you're okay with it?"

She was so much more than okay with it, but all she managed to get out was, "Yes."

There was a moment, or maybe a millennia, she couldn't tell, when Dyson simply held her. Cradled her face in his strong grasp. Then his warm breath whispered across her cheek, followed by the soft press of his lips against hers. It was sweet and simple and over far too soon for her liking, but when he pulled away and she blinked her eyes open, she swore she could still feel him there.

Never had such an innocent kiss impacted her so much. And by the looks of the white-knuckled grip he had on the steering wheel, she wasn't the only one affected. Not sure how to proceed, Lexi did the only thing she could think of: she muttered a quick goodbye and bolted.

She pushed her way through the lobby doors. Luckily the elevators were mere steps away, because her knees had turned to jelly. She didn't know how much longer they would support her. When the elevators doors opened, she stepped inside and turned. Thanks to the large glass doors of the lobby, she was able to see Dyson, sitting patiently in his car as he watched her get inside safely. She lifted her hand in a small wave. He waved back with a smile before driving off.

As the elevator doors closed, she could think of only two things:

There went her fake boyfriend.

And that their kiss had been the most real thing she'd felt in a very long time.

Chapter Eight

Dyson stepped into City Tavern, palms damp with nervous sweat. The bar was already full of people filling the dozen round tables in the middle of the room. The clack of balls smacking into one another could be heard from the far left where he knew a tiny room housed the pool table and dartboard. Way in the back on a raised platform, the emcee was already setting up for trivia. Tall black speakers sat on either side of the small card table the computer was set up on.

A quick glance around the bar showed a couple of his crew already seated in their usual table near the back. Díaz waved and pointed to the bar on the far wall where Ward stood with Kincaid and Tamsen. Dyson headed their way to grab himself a beer, eyes scanning the crowd, but he didn't see the one person he was looking for.

Lexi had agreed to meet him here for trivia so they could practice their dating skills on his friends. Ward and Díaz already knew the deal, but the rest of the crew didn't. And if he wanted to steer clear of Díaz's wrath, they never would. He still couldn't believe his friends made that damn bet.

"O'Neil, you made it." Kincaid smiled. "Need a beer?"

"Yeah." He nodded to the bartender. "Whatever seasonal ale you have is fine."

She nodded and moved to get his drink.

"Dude, don't look now, but the woman at the end of the bar is checking you out."

Dyson turned his head. Ward groaned softly.

"I said *don't* look, jeez, way to be subtle, O'Neil."

He didn't have to be subtle, because the woman at the end of the bar wasn't checking him out. She was waving at him with a soft smile on her lips and a blush warming her cheeks. She was here. Lexi made it.

His heart rate kicked up a notch, like it did when they got a call. That rush of endorphins knowing he was running headfirst into danger, but also the thrill that came with winning the battle. He was a mass of nerves thinking about how they were going to pull this off, but he was glad to see her.

"Yeah, that's Lexi." He cleared his throat. "My, um… girlfriend."

Three audible gasps sounded from his friends.

"Girlfriend?" Kincaid chuckled. "Since when?"

"Yay, Lexi is here!" Tamsen squealed with glee, hopping up and down. "Babe, remember I told you about her. Dyson brought her on a date to the restaurant the other night and I promised her I'd volunteer."

She smiled up at Kincaid.

"Oh, right. That's the woman who runs the DYC?"

"Yes," Dyson said quickly, avoiding the arched brow from Ward. "That's Lexi. We met at the DYC when I was doing the inspection and now…we're dating."

"Wow," Ward deadpanned. "Such a romantic story, dude. I'm really feeling the love. Very *convincing*."

Dyson leaned back so Kincaid and Tamsen couldn't see

him give Ward a threatening gesture. He knew the guy was on the opposing side of him getting this plan to work with Lexi, but he didn't have to actively sabotage the thing.

"If you're dating her, who are those guys she's with?" Ward crossed his arms over his chest with a smug smile.

He turned his head to see Tamsen making her way toward them with two men behind her. One very tall guy who could have been mistaken for Shemar Moore's twin brother and a shorter guy with dark hair.

"Stop being a caveman, Ward." Tamsen gave him a light smack to his arm. "Women and men can be friends."

Very true. He was friends with Tamsen and Díaz and Torres. And considering they were holding hands, he doubted Lexi was either man's type.

The bartender came back with their drinks, and Dyson tore his gaze away from Lexi to pay, leaving a generous tip. His heart raced with each passing second. They could do this. They had to do this. How hard could it be to convince his friends he finally started dating again?

"So, One-Night O'Neil is finally hanging up the towel, huh?" Kincaid said with a smile.

Ward snickered, changing it into a cough when Dyson glared at him.

Shit, this might be harder than he thought if his buddies kept bringing up that ridiculous nickname.

"Hey, Dyson."

He turned to see Lexi standing before him, her friends huddled close behind her. The shorter guy gave him a friendly smile, but the tall guy's gaze raked over Dyson with a hearty dose of suspicion.

"Hey…babe. Thanks for meeting me here."

She arched an eyebrow at his endearment. Okay, yeah. That had come out a little weird. He was rusty. And he'd never been good with pet names anyway.

"Sure, *honey*," she rolled her lips to keep from laughing. "Thanks for inviting me. I hope you don't mind that I brought some friends. They wanted to meet you. This is my roommate, Jordan, and his boyfriend, Angel."

The roommate. That's why the taller guy was glaring daggers at him. The no-dating bet. Lexi mentioned at dinner the other night that Jordan knew about their deal. Why was the guy here? To make sure their fake date was really fake?

How the hell was he supposed to convince his friends they were real dating and her roommate they were fake dating at the same time?

This night was going downhill fast.

"Hey, guys." He reached out to shake Angel's hand first. "Nice to meet you."

Jordan reached out a hand, giving Dyson a firm warning squeeze. One that clearly said *hurt my friend and there'll be hell to pay.*

"I hear my roomie here mistook you for a birthday present she thought I sent." He glanced at Lexi. "Absolutely ridiculous, Lex, you know I'd never send a strip-o-gram to your work."

"Whoa, she thought you were a strip-o-gram?" Ward piped in from behind him. "Dude, you didn't tell me that."

Yeah, and for good reason. Now it would be all over the firehouse in a matter of days and Dyson would have to suffer endless torment about it. Giving one another shit was a favorite pastime at Station 42. He didn't mind giving it, but he hated to be on the receiving end. Hypocritical? Maybe, but it was what it was.

"Oh my, that's worse than our first meeting," Tamsen giggled to Kincaid. "And here I thought being rescued by a sexy fireman who turned out to be my new stepbrother was going to be a weird one to tell the grandkids. Lexi and Dyson might have us beat."

"Hold on," Jordan held up a hand. "I'm gonna need that story by the end of this night."

Tamsen smiled at Jordan while Lexi leaned in close and whispered to him, "I'd like to hear that story later, too. Might make me feel better about my first impression on you."

Dyson chuckled softly, gesturing to his friends. "This is Eli Ward and Parker Kincaid. They work with me at the firehouse. And you remember Tamsen Hayes—"

"Soon to be Kincaid." She stuck her hand out, wiggling her finger with the engagement ring his buddy had put on it a few months ago.

"Oh wow!" Lexi leaned closer, examining Tamsen's right hand. "That's beautiful, congratulations."

Kincaid pulled Tamsen close, kissing her with a sappy smile on his face.

"Break it up, you two," Ward slapped a hand down on Kincaid's shoulder. "We've got a game to win, so the fraternizing ends now."

Lexi glanced over at Dyson with confusion. He leaned closer to her to explain.

"Tamsen is on the opposing team."

She frowned, opening her mouth to ask something more, but whatever she was about to say got drowned out by the emcee announcing the start of trivia in two minutes.

"Oops, I better get to my table." Tamsen smiled, giving everyone a small wave. "Lexi, Jordan, Angel it was nice to meet you, and I'm sorry we'll be crushing your team tonight."

"Don't count on it, sweetheart," Kincaid said.

She blew him a kiss and hurried over to her table across the room.

"Here, Lex."

Dyson glanced over to see Jordan hand Lexi a beer. He hadn't even noticed the guy get drinks from the bartender.

"Dude, you didn't even get your girl a drink?" Ward blew

out a breath, shaking his head. "Not very boyfriendish if you ask me."

He glared at his friend, noting the small smirk on Jordan's face. Great. Now he had two people working against him. This night was going fan-fucking-tastic.

"Thanks, man." He nodded to Jordan. "I've got next round."

Lexi patted his chest. "You are so sweet…honey bunny."

He bit back a groan at the weird endearment. Staring into her wide eyes, reading the clear regret that filled them.

"Let's pub quiz!" Ward announced, heading toward their table.

Dyson nodded to Jordan and Angel, who followed his buddy.

"Honey bunny?" he said softly with a small chuckle.

"I panicked, okay?" she hissed back. "Besides, you're the one who started it by calling me babe."

"What's wrong with babe?"

"I don't know, it's just…weird."

This whole situation was weird.

"How about we stick to the classics? Sweetheart or sweetie?"

She nodded. "Works for me."

"You two coming?" Ward shouted from across the room.

"Shall we?" Lexi asked, a nervous smile playing on her lips.

"Yeah, let's go." He held out his hand, realizing it was his left, since his beer was in his right. "Oh shit, sorry."

Quickly transferring his beer, he wiped his palm on his jeans to get off the condensation from the glass and held it out. Lexi laughed softly, slipping her hand into his. His heart rate kicked up at the contact, but he brushed it off as nerves. The pounding he felt, the heat burning in his gut, the tightening of his muscles. It was all due to his anxiety over lying. It had nothing to do with the softness of Lexi's skin. The warm feel of her touch. How her soft scent seemed to surround him, sweet yet subtle. Intoxicating.

They arrived at the table where Dyson introduced Lexi, Ward having introduced everyone else seconds before they arrived.

"Hey, Lexi," Díaz said with a huge grin. "Nice to finally meet you, Dyson has talked about you so much."

"He has?" Ward scoffed with an arched brow.

Díaz glared at him.

"Yeah, I don't remember you ever mentioning, Lexi," Kincaid agreed with a confused look.

Dyson forced a smile, giving Díaz a quick glance that promised hell later. She winced, mouthing an apology. Lotta good it did him now. He knew she wanted to win the bet. Hell, he wanted to win, but her "helpfulness" wasn't very helpful at the moment.

"Maybe he just talked to me about her because Ward never shuts up long enough for anyone to get a word in."

Jordan leaned forward in his chair, addressing Díaz, "So Dyson has talked to you about his relationship with Lexi?"

The man's suspicious gaze slid over to Dyson. Fuck! This was getting out of hand. How had he ever thought they could get away with—

"So what's your team name?" Lexi asked cheerfully, steering the conversation away from the dangerous path it had taken.

"Most Extinguished."

She chuckled. "Oh I get it, because of the firefighter thing."

He nodded.

"That's a fun name."

Ward leaned across the table, "Yeah much better than the stupid Lumbersnacks."

"The what?"

Dyson pointed across the room where a table full of plaid-wearing people sat, all of the occupants glaring daggers at them. Well, almost all of them. Tamsen stared lovingly at Kincaid.

"Hey," Kincaid smacked Ward on the shoulder. "Stop insulting my future wife's team."

"Stop losing to her on purpose."

"I don't lose on purpose."

Dyson laughed, watching his friends go over the same argument they did every pub quiz night. Lexi leaned in close, her warm breath caressing his cheek, causing his skin to spark and tingle like he'd just received a shock from a faulty outlet.

"Does he really lose on purpose?"

He turned his head to answer—big mistake. She was so close, all he had to do was lean an inch or two and he could press his lips against hers. The memory of their brief kiss from the other night still consumed him. Damn thing had snuck into his dreams last night. Tormenting him with all the possibilities of what could happen if he'd let the kiss go further.

No.

Rule number one. Kissing and hand-holding only. Nothing more intimate or this whole thing might go sideways. Besides, they were trying to convince his friends they were dating. Not gross them out with PDA.

Fighting the urge to cup her cheek and take her mouth, Dyson answered with his own hushed whisper. "Maybe. They like to bet on whose team wins."

Her gaze darted back and forth between the two with avid curiosity. "What does the winner get?"

"Sex."

Her breath hitched, eyes darkening. "What does the loser get?"

"Sex."

The tip of her tongue came out to sweep across her lower lip in a move he knew she didn't intend. Like the habit she had of speaking her inner thoughts out loud. But damned if he didn't feel his body hardening to the point of pain at the sight of that sweet pink tongue.

"Seems like a win-win to me."

She leaned in to him, her eyes darting to his friends sitting at the table watching them with avid curiosity. Knowing he had to sell this, Dyson slipped his arm over Lexi's shoulders, pulling her in to his side. The contact was heaven and hell at the same time. His heart raced, from the thrill of touching Lexi or the nerves of the situation, he couldn't tell.

A quick glance around the table told him things had settled down and they were selling it pretty well. Díaz had a small smile, Ward was looking grumpy, but then Dyson's gaze caught on Jordan's. He almost removed his arm—he didn't want Lexi to lose her bet—but he couldn't. He had to make this look real. Instead, he nodded to the guy, trying to communicate that he would never hurt Lexi or lead her on.

Jordan stared at the two of them for a full minute before giving Dyson a slight nod and snuggling back against his boyfriend. Dyson let out a breath of relief. Maybe things were starting to look up.

"Okay Quizzers are you ready for pub quiz?" The emcee's booming voice crackled over the loudspeaker. A cheer went up around the room.

The first few rounds went by quickly. They took the lead easily with the help of Jordan's massive trivia knowledge. The guy seemed to know the right answer to every question. Lexi even teased him, calling him a human computer. Ward was begging the guy to come play with them every week.

"So, Lexi," Kincaid said during one of the round breaks. "How long have you two been dating?"

He felt Lexi's body stiffen under his arm.

"Oh, um, just a few…"

"Days," Dyson answered quickly.

"Yeah, yup." She nodded her head in agreement. "A few days. It's all really new."

"How'd you two start dating?"

For fuck's sake, when did Kincaid becomes so interested in his friends' love lives? Tamsen had turned the guy into a mushy romantic. Dyson shifted in his seat, noticing the curious look Jordan was giving Lexi. Seemed like everyone wanted to hear the story, or in a few people's cases, the story they made up.

"How did we start dating?" She gave a nervous laugh. "Oh, you know how it happens. You spend time with someone and just…click."

"Leaving out a lot of details there, Lexi," Ward said with a knowing grin. "Ow! Fuck, Díaz, what the hell did you kick me for?"

Díaz smiled, taking a sip of her drink. "Oops, sorry, Ward. My foot must have slipped."

Dyson sent a grateful look Díaz's way. She inclined her head slightly.

The emcee came back on and saved him and Lexi from having to answer any more questions. The rest of the night passed, thankfully, with no more intrusive questions. Tamsen hung out at their table during a few of the breaks, and everyone who wasn't in the know seemed to accept that he and Lexi were an actual couple.

It set his mind slightly at ease. Maybe this would work out. Now all they had to do was convince his sisters.

By the end of the night everyone was in a happy mood. Even Ward. Probably due to the fact that Lexi and her friends had helped them crush the Lumbersnacks. Claiming victory, the gift certificate, and more importantly, bragging rights.

"Please say you guys will come back next week," Ward begged Lexi and her friends. "Please!"

"Ward hates to lose," Díaz chuckled. "He's a big ol' baby about it."

Ward glared at Díaz, pointing a finger at her then himself. "Takes one to know one."

"And on that grade school insult, I'm out." Díaz rose from her chair. "Lexi, Jordan, Angel, it was nice to meet you. Hope to see you again."

"Hold up," Ward stood. "I'll walk with you."

"He needs someone to walk him home after dark or he gets scared," she said in a staged hush to Lexi.

"Yeah, yeah, I'm a baby. Just put on your meanest scowl and protect me from all the drunks trying to bum cigarettes I don't have, okay?"

Lexi laughed as the two left. "Are they together?"

"No." Dyson shook his head. "But sometimes I think they protest too much, if you get my drift."

She nodded, taking another sip of her drink. "I do. We often deny ourselves the things we want the most."

Her voice turned a bit sad as she said that. Made him wonder what Lexi denied herself. Probably any number of things. She seemed to be stretched thin at the center and, according to her bet with Jordan, she gave too much in her relationships. Hell, she was helping him out by agreeing to fake date him. Guilt crawled up his throat at the thought that he was yet another person in her life taking up her time and attention.

No, he was helping her with the center. It was a mutual agreement, she even said so.

"Hey, Lex," Jordan appeared at Lexi's side, holding out his hand. "You ready?"

She nodded.

Jordan stared at Dyson, his gaze assessing. "Good, then

say goodbye to your *boyfriend* and let's go."

Lexi smiled through her teeth at her friend. "Okay."

"Thanks for coming out tonight, Lexi." He rose as she stood, glancing around to see half of his team was still at the table, gathering their things.

Jordan stood behind Lexi, staring directly at him.

"Um…" He had no idea what to do. His friends would expect him to kiss her goodbye, right? She was his girlfriend. That's what he would normally do with someone he was dating.

Leaning in close, he brushed his lips across hers. A spark of fire burned low in his gut at the contact. His hands gripped her hips, pulling her closer. Her head tilted, deepening the kiss. For a moment Dyson lost himself in the smooth warmth of Lexi's kiss, before the clearing of a throat interrupted them.

He pulled back, eyes darting behind her to see Jordan staring at him with a quizzical expression.

"Bye, Dyson," Lexi said softly, her face flushed, pink staining her cheeks.

She turned and headed for the door, Jordan and Angel following her. Dyson let out a sigh of relief. They'd done it. Now all they had to do was get through a dinner with his sisters and everything would be fine.

Chapter Nine

Lexi woke with a small ice pick chipping away at her right temple. Not because she'd had a lot to drink last night. She had one beer. She'd barely been buzzed.

Not from the alcohol, anyway.

Her body had been blissfully tingly, her head fuzzy, all throughout trivia, but it had nothing to do with the libations and everything to do with the man who sat next to her all night, tempting her with his rich scent of pine and the slight smell of campfire. She wondered if all firefighters constantly smelled that way or if it was unique to Dyson?

It had been a roller-coaster of a night. When she told Jordan about her trivia night fake date he insisted on coming to, and she quoted, "Keep an eye on her." She told him she wasn't breaking the rules of the bet, since this was all fake, but he insisted on seeing with his own eyes. She allowed it as long as he promised not to mention anything about their deal to Dyson's friends. The whole point of the night was to convince people they were a real couple.

Other than a few awkward exchanges, she thought they

did pretty well.

Still, an entire night, pretending to be his girlfriend, having their bodies pressed together...kissing him. It had really messed with her. So instead of coming home and drowning her nerves in booze, she'd eaten an entire bowl of double fudge chocolate ice cream. Some might say it was the wiser choice but, since she had a mild chocolate allergy that tended to give her migraines when she ate more than a small square of the stuff...

"Ouch," she groaned, holding her head as she made her way into the small kitchenette in her apartment.

"Lex, I told you not to eat that entire bowl last night." Jordan stood at the sink holding out a glass of water and her headache medication. "I know chocolate is delicious, but no man is worth the headache."

She took the pills and glass, muttering a small thank you before downing the medication. "How do you know it was over a guy?"

He let out a small huff of a laugh. "Please. For one, we've been friends since the fifth grade, you can't hide anything from me."

True. They met on the playground when Tammy Largent made fun of Jordan's nails because he had them painted pink. Lexi put a worm down the back of the bully's shirt. She'd never heard a screech as loud as the one Tammy made. And Jordan had saved her when she got her first period in math class and stained her pants. He'd offered her his large sweater that came down to her knees. Since then they'd been the best of friends. Looking out for each other, supporting each other, calling each other out on their BS.

"And for two," Jordan continued, taking a sip from his coffee cup. "You were muttering all night long about sexy firefighters who didn't need to date you to bang you. Your brain-to-mouth filter works even less when you're on chocolate, Lex."

She sighed, knowing he was right and really wanting a sip of that coffee, but migraines and caffeine did not mix well. Maybe she'd grab a smoothie on her way to work today with an energy boost in it. Too bad the smoothie shop didn't have a stop-spouting-out-your-inner-dialogue-in-embarrassing-situations booster.

"Meow!"

Lexi felt soft fur rub against her ankle seconds before a tiny nip of sharp teeth. She glanced down and glared at her sweet but impatient cat. "Ouch! Dang it, Lucifer, I just woke up. I'm getting to your food. Give me half a second, okay?"

Lucifer stared up at her, his blue and green eyes impossibly bright against his black fur, his expression stating that he didn't care what she was doing, he was hungry, and his bowl was empty. Problem for the human to fix now.

Jordan grabbed a can of cat food from the cupboard and handed it over. "I still don't know why you adopted that devil."

"He's sweet," she argued grabbing the can opener so she could fill her hungry fur baby's bowl. "Besides, I didn't pick him, he picked me."

The second she stepped into the back room where the shelter kept all the cats, Lucifer immediately pressed his face against the cage, mournful dual-colored eyes aching with the need to be loved. When she placed her palm against the wire, he'd licked her fingertips, and then nipped at her with a small angry hiss. But she saw behind the tough cat exterior down to his soft mushy soul just begging for a place to call home.

After three years, he was still grumpy, a bit standoffish, and had a tendency to nip—tiny ones that never broke the skin—but he also knew when she needed a little extra comfort. She was the only person Lucifer would snuggle up with. He wouldn't even sit in Jordan's lap, though he would let her roommate feed him. Lucifer let anyone give him food.

Greedy little devil.

"You and your soft spot for the emotionally unavailable, it's a problem, Lex."

She did not have a soft spot for...okay she kinda did. She couldn't help it. Whenever she saw someone in pain all she wanted to do was help. And yes, it tended to be a bigger problem when it came to relationships.

"It's why we made the bet in the first place."

Ugh, the cursed bet. Why had she ever let Jordan convince her it was a good idea? She'd like to blame it on wine, but she'd been of sound enough mind when they made the bet a month ago after her disastrous breakup with Ted, who had convinced her to give up her tickets to a concert she'd been looking forward to for a year and a half because he wanted her to see the latest superhero movie with him on opening night.

She didn't even like superhero movies.

"And yet you went with him," Jordan said as she accidentally spoke out loud. "Plus you gave up your precious vacation days to help Luke build his deck, you let Dan take his buddy on your vacation to Key West when you had a center emergency and couldn't go, instead of postponing the vacation you helped pay for."

"Okay, okay, I get it!" She didn't need a highlight reel of Lexi's questionable decisions regarding men.

"Lex," Jordan placed a soft hand on her shoulder. "I love you, but you know you bend over backward for people. You give too much and if you keep doing it...I'm worried there won't be anything left for you."

A heavy sigh left her chest. She knew he worried. She did, too. Which was why she'd agreed with this idea in the first place. She knew she'd never be truly happy until she learned to be more assertive, to take what she wanted instead of letting people walk all over her. But it was hard. She hated upsetting people. Making someone smile was the highlight of her day. Even if it came at the expense of her own happiness. But as her bestie pointed out, that wasn't exactly the healthiest of attitudes. And secretly she had to admit to herself, sometimes she felt stretched too thin with the needs of others.

So here she was. Trying to put herself first, learning to place her needs above others. Or, at least on the same level. But her friend knew her too well. Jordan knew she wouldn't stick with the bet unless some pretty high stakes were on the line. He had been the one to put a consequence on it.

"Look, this thing with Dyson is all fake. You know that. You saw it."

Jordan snorted. "Yeah, you two were...well maybe it's just because I knew, but it was like watching two middle schoolers at a dance. All fumbling and fidgeting."

They hadn't been that bad. Sure, there'd been some weirdness, but his friends seemed to buy it. And the kiss at the end of the night...there had been nothing awkward about that.

"You're safe." His eyes narrowed. "For now."

"Thank you oh magnanimous bet maker." She gave him a sarcastic bow.

Her roommate's mouth curved in a knowing smile. "Oh and if you do end up hooking up with Mr. Doesn't Date, remember to keep your heart out of it."

"Who says we're going to hook up?"

He rolled his eyes with a heavy sigh. "The lights at the bar that were overloading with all the sexual sparks coming off you two eye-fucking each other last night."

"Jordan!"

"You know it's true."

"But wouldn't hooking up be against the rules of the

bet?"

"Hooking up and dating are not the same thing, Lex."

She knew that. She didn't hook up often, but she'd had a few moments in her life where sex was for nothing but fun.

"Besides," Jordan continued. "What better way to take care of yourself and your needs? I think a night or two in the sexy firefighter's bed would be good for you."

Maybe, but wanting something and doing something about it were two very different things.

Chapter Ten

"We got a call at Northwest High," Chief Jeffords called out from his office.

Dyson's heart leaped into his throat. Northwest was the school his sister Macy taught at. What was it? A fire? A medical emergency? Fear stopped his heart. Oh hell, he hoped with everything in him it wasn't a shooting.

"O'Neil," Jeffords called to him in a calm voice. "It's nothing serious. Kid got stuck in a chair pulling some stupid stunt."

Dyson let out a breath of relief. As a firefighter, being called to emergencies was par for the course. But it hit different when the emergency involved a loved one. Thankfully this emergency was only loved one adjacent.

"Thanks, Chief." He nodded, heading toward the rig, grateful his chief had given him the heads-up right away. If he would have had to wait to be briefed on the ride over, he would have been a wreck.

"What do we have?" Ward asked as he hopped into the rig.

"Chief said it was a stuck kid."

Turner slid into the driver's seat and tossed over his shoulder, "Yup. Some kid bet another he couldn't fit through the hole in the back of the lunchroom chair. Turns out he couldn't. School tried their best to get him free, but…"

Dyson shook his head. He never understood that type of mentality. When he was in high school, he watched his classmates do stupid shit all the time in the name of "fun." Half the time people ended up in the ER with broken bones. How was that fun?

Then again, his sisters would say he was a stick-in-the-mud who wouldn't know fun if it bit him on the ass. So he was cautious? Nothing wrong with that.

"Stuck in a chair?" Ward chuckled. "I think that happened to me once in high school."

Díaz snorted. "Why am I not surprised?"

"Because you know what a daredevil I am," Ward said, nudging Díaz with his shoulder as Turner started the rig and pulled out of the station, siren blaring.

Her eyes rolled. "Not the word I'd use to describe you."

Dyson chuckled as Díaz placed her hand to the side of her mouth so Ward couldn't see and whispered "dumb-ass." Ward sighed heavily.

"Sitting like six inches away, Díaz. You can't whisper as quietly as you think."

"Wasn't trying to." She leaned back and crossed her arms over her chest with a smug grin.

"Hey, O'Neil," Kincaid said from the front next to Turner. "Doesn't your sister work at Northwest? Macy?"

"Yup." He wondered if it was one of her students who was stuck. They'd find out soon.

Turner pulled into the school lot, parking at the front. Thankfully no one was idling in the emergency zone. If he had a nickel for every time some jackass parked along the red painted line.

They all piled out of the rig. Dyson grabbed the medic kit. Ward grabbed their small handheld mini saw.

"Should we bring in the jaws of life?" Díaz asked. "Just to scare the kid from doing something this stupid again?"

Kincaid shook his head. "Doubt that will work, besides I'm sure his classmates are recording everything and posting it on all the social media. Either this kid will be too embarrassed to ever do it again, or he'll become a viral sensation and we'll have twenty of these exact same calls in the next month."

As they made their way into the school, a teacher's aide met them and guided them to the cafeteria where the stuck boy was. Dyson sighed as he came upon the scene. Kincaid was right. Every kid in the room had their phone out and was recording.

Unlike when he went to school, this cafeteria didn't have the long tables with benches. This room was filled with smaller round tables surrounded by those uncomfortable plastic chairs. The kind that stacked on top of each other and had holes in the middle of the back for some weird reason. No one was sitting in them, though—everyone was standing, some arching on their toes, straining to see.

In the middle of the room was a boy, probably around fifteen or so, halfway through the hole in the back of one of the chairs. He had no idea what genius decided that was a good design—did they not realize kids would see the hole and try to go through it?

He didn't want the kid to suffer any emotional distress along with the physical, but he really hoped this incident didn't inspire others to repeat the action. He did not want to be sawing kids out of chairs for the next month.

"Hey, you're that firefighter who's working at the center."

Dyson glanced over to see two teenage boys, one he

recognized as the kid he met the day of the inspection.

"Uh, yeah, I am. Mateo, right?"

The kid nodded and gestured to his friend. "This is Brycen."

"You here to get Nick the Dick out?" Brycen asked.

"Oh, yes, we're here to—"

"O'Neil, what's up?" Kincaid asked as he came up beside him.

"Hey Kincaid, these are a couple of the teens from the DYC."

"Your girlfriend's work?"

"You're dating Ms. Martin?" Mateo asked, eyes wide.

"Nice pull, man," Brycen added.

Mateo shoved the other teen slightly. "Don't be an ass, Bryce."

"Dyson!"

He turned at the familiar voice and saw his sister running toward him. Macy looked equally worried and pissed. He knew how much she cared about her students, but he'd also heard her swear about the logic of their choices under her breath many times.

Turning back to the teens, he dipped his chin. "Gotta go, guys, see you at the center." Where they would no doubt be spreading around that he was dating Lexi. He wasn't sure if that was a positive or negative.

Kincaid patted his shoulder and rushed over to the rest of the crew while Dyson moved to meet his sister.

"I'm so glad you're here," Macy sighed heavily as she motioned to the boy. "Nick Baker's friends bet him twenty bucks he couldn't fit through the chair backing and as you can see…he can't. Nurse Rivera tried her best to get him out, but nothing worked. We called his parents and they're on their way, but—"

"Macy, Macy, slow down." He gently grasped her arms.

She was near hyperventilating. "It's going to be okay. It's not the first time we've had to saw a person out of a chair."

"Saw?" Her voice went up an octave, fear filling her eyes. "You have to *saw* him out?"

"Did you say saw?" A tall man with a stern expression slid up next to them, addressing Dyson.

"Principal Hill." Macy motioned to the man and then to Dyson. "This is my brother Dyson; he works for Station 42. Dyson, this is Principal Hill."

"Sir." Dyson nodded, holding out his hand.

The principal shook it.

"Thank you and your station for coming. Nurse Rivera has tried just about everything, but it seems Mr. Barker is well and truly stuck." He stepped closer to Dyson, lowering his voice. "Do you really have to use a saw to get him out?"

Dyson glanced over to where his crewmates were inspecting the kid in the chair. Ward looked up at that moment and gave Dyson a subtle nod, lifting the mini saw.

"Yes, sir," Dyson answered. "But don't worry. It's a small saw and we'll be extremely careful with the boy. All of us have EMT training as well, so you're in good hands."

The principal nodded, motioning for Dyson to proceed.

"We good to go?" Ward asked.

Dyson nodded.

"Fuck that shit, man!" The kid shouted, terror blanching his face as he stared at the saw. "You ain't getting that thing near me!"

"Language, Nick," Macy admonished as she came to stand by the boy's side.

"Sorry, Ms. O'Neil," Nick mumbled, eyes still wary as he stared at the saw in Ward's hands.

"You got yourself into this situation," Macy continued. "Now you have to face the consequences."

"I didn't think the consequences would be sawing me the

fu— fork in half."

"Dude," Ward chuckled. "We're not magicians. Not gonna chop you in half and put you back together. We're just going to make a few cuts in this plastic and get you out of this chair. Unless…you like being stuck in there?"

Nick grumbled.

"Nick," Macy softened her voice. "See that guy right there? That's my big brother Dyson, and he's the best firefighter in the world."

Dyson smiled, knowing his sister was trying to comfort the kid. She'd never claim him to be the best at anything. Maybe at annoying her.

"He's going to make sure nothing happens to you and that we get this chair off, okay?"

Nick nodded, eyes still filled with trepidation.

"Can you move at all in there, Nick?" Dyson asked.

The kid squirmed in the seat hole. He was stuck pretty good, but he could wiggle up and down a bit. His hips and ribcage kept him from being able to slip out entirely. How the hell did he manage to get in there in the first place? Fear might have caused his body to swell a bit after the fact. It was known to happen to some people.

"Okay, Nick. We're going to lay you on your side, okay?"

The kid nodded. He and his crew helped lower the kid and the chair until it rested on the ground sideways. The new position forced Nick's body toward the ground, leaving a few inches of space between him and the chair.

"Díaz, can you grab a neck brace?"

Díaz rustled through the med kit Dyson had brought in, coming up with a child-sized foam neck brace. Dyson thanked her, bending down to slip the medical device between the chair and Nick's body, providing a soft cushion of protection for the kid. Ward was good with the saw, he knew his buddy wouldn't cut the kid, but he wanted to give Nick something to feel safer. Sometimes people needed extra precautions even if they weren't strictly necessary.

"Okay, Nick. We're going to go real slow and if you need a break at any time, just let us know."

The kid nodded, eyes wide as Ward started up the saw, flinching as the blade began to whirl.

"Nick, look at me," Macy said in a low, calm voice. "Tell me again about the project you picked to do for the science fair."

"I'm testing out the properties of chemical versus organic fertilizers and their effect on plant growth."

His sister was so smart. Distracting Nick made it easier for him and his crew to do their job. He, Kincaid, and Turner held the chair steady while Díaz helped guide Ward. Dyson heard a few teachers yell for the kids to put their phones away, but he noticed from the corner of his eye a few—not very well hidden—phones still focused on them.

Within a few minutes Ward had cut through the hard plastic chair. He made another cut higher up so they could pull a large chunk of the chair out, leaving enough room for Nick to slide his body loose. The entire cafeteria erupted in cheers once the kid was free.

Principal Hill held his hands up and the room immediately fell into silence. "Students will report back to your homerooms, and if anyone tries to pull this stunt again, it will be an automatic three-day suspension—do I make myself clear?"

A grumble of "yes sirs" filled the air as everyone shuffled out of the cafeteria. Turner moved to the principal to have him fill out some paperwork while the nurse thanked them and took Nick off to her office to await his parents.

"Well, that was fun," Ward laughed.

"You're just saying that because you got to work the saw. Boys and their toys," Díaz muttered with a shake of her head.

Dyson laughed as his crew started to pack their stuff up, ready to head back to the station. He moved to help, but a soft hand on his arm stopped him.

"Thanks, Dy."

He glanced down at his sister. "Just doing my job."

Macy smiled. "I know, but you do it so well and you really set Nick's mind at ease."

No, that was all her.

"So did you ask her?" Her eyes shined brightly as she stared up at him.

"Ask who what?"

"Dyson!" Macy smacked his arm lightly. "Lexi, did you ask Lexi about dinner?"

Oh right. He held back a groan. Gemma had texted Macy about Lexi and both sisters had been bugging him to invite her to dinner. He meant to text her this morning, but then the call came in and—

"Your girlfriend hasn't met your sisters yet?" Ward asked, sliding up behind him like some slimy villain from a kids cartoon show. "Dude."

"They just started dating, Ward," Díaz said, coming to his rescue. "Like you've ever introduced any woman to your brothers. Good thing, too, because they'd drop your ugly ass for the triplets."

Ward scowled. "Which one?"

Díaz shrugged. "Any of them, they're all better looking than you. Smarter too."

"Wait," Macy interrupted their bickering. "You've both met Lexi?"

Dyson cleared his throat. It tightened to the point of suffocation the second his sister brought up his fake girlfriend. "Um, yeah she came to trivia with me the other night."

"Met you at trivia," Ward corrected, leaning in close to Macy. "He's been One-Night O'Neil so long he doesn't even remember you're supposed to pick a woman up for a date."

Macy frowned and Dyson made a silent promise to help Díaz short sheet Ward's bed for the next month. Lucky for him, Díaz didn't like to lose. She swooped in to his rescue, leaning forward with a knowing grin as she spoke softly to his sister.

"You should have seen the two of them. So sweet the way they were...kanoodling."

"Did the word kanoodling just come out of your mouth, Díaz?" Ward asked, his jaw dropping.

"Shut up. It's a word."

He laughed. "Yeah, one octogenarians use."

"You want me to tell O'Neil's sister they were eye fuc—" She snapped her mouth shut, eyes moving around the room still teeming with teenagers shuffling slowly out of the cafeteria. "There're kids around. I was trying to be age appropriate."

Dyson was sure the teenagers around them used much more colorful language than anything heard at the firehouse. Besides, he really needed to get his friends away from his sister if he had a shot in hell at convincing her he was really dating Lexi. Between Ward trying to undermine him and Díaz trying to overcompensate, this whole thing might go south before it even started.

"Still weird, dude."

"Whatever," Díaz shook her head. "She brought her friends to meet him, and you know what that means, One-Night O'Neil is hanging up his title. You don't introduce your friends to the person you're dating if it isn't serious."

Turning back to him, she gave him a pointed look. "Right, O'Neil?"

"Um...yeah." He swallowed hard, wishing like hell he had a gallon of water for his parched throat, or a shot of whiskey. "And I was just about to text her about dinner, but then we got the call and..."

"Well, text her already. Go, you guys saved the day here." Macy made a shooing motion with her hands. "Text Lexi about dinner because Gemma and I can't wait to meet her."

"She's an absolute sweetheart," Díaz said.

Ward snorted. "Yeah, a real, *honey bunny*."

Dyson narrowed his eyes at his friend, But Ward just grinned, until Díaz not so subtly lifted the medic kit from the ground and shoved it into his arms.

"Let's go, guys. I think I heard Turner call us."

Ward let out a grunt, glaring at Díaz before turning and following her. Dyson put an arm around Macy, giving her a quick goodbye hug.

Moving up onto her toes, she kissed his cheek. "So happy for you, Dy."

"Thanks, me too." Lies. He was the furthest thing from happy right now if the tangled mass of cramping nerves in his gut was anything to go by.

"Love you," Macy said, waving as she moved toward the crowd of kids heading back to their classrooms.

"Love you too, see you at dinner."

She waved over her shoulder, calling out, "Don't forget to bring Lexi!"

He sighed, pulling out his phone as he walked out of the school and joining his crew in the truck.

Dyson: *Told you it would be coming.*

Lexi: *What? The end of the world?*

Dyson: *Worse...a dinner invite from my sisters.*

Lexi: *Lol. So doom and gloom. I'm sure it will be fun.*

Dyson: *Are you also one of those people who think the dentist is fun?*

Lexi: *Dental hygiene is very important. Plus you get to sit there while someone else cleans your teeth. I like to think of it like a spa day for my mouth!*

He chuckled. She *would* see the positive side of it. Lexi had a way of looking at everyone and everything with the best of intentions. An admirable trait he wished he could attain, but he'd seen too much of the world's darkness.

Dyson: *You free the day after tomorrow?*

Lexi: *Yup.*

Dyson: *Great I'll pick you up at six. Does that work?*

Lexi: *I'll be ready at five fifty;)*

He chuckled, slipping his phone back into his pocket, hope filling his chest that this ruse of theirs might actually work out.

Chapter Eleven

Dyson checked the time on his car dash once again. It still said he was twenty minutes early to pick up Lexi. Damn his apprehension over being late. His nerves always made him at least ten minutes early to everything, but tonight he'd been extra nervous because tonight he was taking her to family dinner.

This isn't going to work.

Yes it would. It already was working. Díaz and Ward knew what was up, but the others at trivia night had no idea, and he and Lexi seemed to convince them pretty well.

His stomach turned, clenching as a sour taste filled his mouth. He hated lying. Hated lying to his sisters even more. He tried his best never to do it. They all agreed on honesty first when Mom and Dad died. He never wanted them to hide their pain or struggles from him; how was he supposed to help if he didn't know they were in trouble? And he promised to be honest with them, too.

Though he had fibbed a time or two about not being tired or stressed when he was a constant ball of exhausted anxiety trying to hold down a job, finish up his own schooling, and take care of his sisters all at once. He'd managed to handle it. They didn't need any more stress on their shoulders than they had.

So that's all this was. Another small fib to lessen the stress he knew his sisters felt over his dating situation. He'd told them time and again he was fine, but they still didn't believe him. And after that conversation he had with Gemma the other day, he knew all their hounding was just out of concern. If it eased their worry, he'd do it. Or, at least, appear to be dating again because, as much as he loved his sisters, taking another plunge into the world of love was the very last thing he wanted to do. Ever.

Rule number one. No long-term relationships.

Grateful he'd found some street parking in front of her building, he pulled out his phone and opened up his reader app. Never go anywhere without a book was a motto he'd learned long ago due to his penchant for being early. Now that he bought most of his books in e-formats it was much easier to carry them around. Just as he started to read, a knock on the passenger window startled him.

Lexi stood, bent over, smiling at him through the closed glass. He pressed the button to lower the window.

"Hey," She tilted her head, a playful glint in her eyes. "What are you doing out here?"

Her grin broadened and he noticed she had a slight dent in her left cheek, not a dimple, but a tiny crease that for some reason he suddenly wanted to explore with his lips and tongue.

Down boy.

Despite what his dick thought, this was still all fake. True, he hadn't been this attracted to anyone in a long time, but Lexi was doing him a favor. She didn't need him making a move on her and muddying up the waters of their agreement.

Rule number two. Touching is necessary only in the presence of others to cover their lie.

"I could ask you the same question," she said with a small chuckle. "I believe I still have seventeen and a half minutes to get ready for dinner, yes?"

He glanced at the clock again and winced. "Yes, that's why I'm still in my car instead of knocking on your apartment door."

"You could have come up. Aren't you bored?"

He raised his hand, waving the cell currently lit up with the pages of the latest thriller novel he was reading. "I have a book."

She opened the door and slid into the passenger seat.

"And I have wine," she declared, holding up a bottle. "I figured I'd have enough time to pop down to the corner liquor store, grab it, and be back upstairs before you showed up, but I should have known better, Mr. Perpetually Early."

Her cheeky grin had him letting out a sigh of relief. He was coming to discover he really enjoyed it when Lexi teased him. A lot of people found his habit of arriving too early annoying or downright rude. He didn't understand it. Dyson liked being on time. Lateness was one of his biggest pet peeves. And it's not like being early ever hurt anything. In fact, once it even saved him from making the biggest mistake of his life.

He pushed the dark memory away, not wanting anything to risk the success of tonight's venture.

"Good thing I was already ready to go before I left." She pulled the seat belt across her chest and clicked it into place over her dark peacoat.

Summer was just around the corner, but the cool spring night air still held a bit of a chill. Dyson had a jacket himself, but it was tossed in the back. He wondered what she was wearing under the coat. Not because he was worried. She'd looked absolutely beautiful in the sundress she had on at dinner the other night. It fit her like it had been made for her, hugging her curves in all the right places, causing his hands to ache to reach out and grasp the flare of her hips, pull her closer to him until—

Nope! Time to stop that thought train right now. Unless he wanted to start this dinner off in a very awkward spot. Sure, his sisters would expect him to be a little infatuated with his new girlfriend, but he didn't want to be sporting wood at family dinner. Talk about disturbing.

"You look nice," she said as he turned the key in the ignition.

He glanced down at his dark slacks and blue button-up. Nothing fancy, but his sister had threatened him with fish dinners for a month if he showed up in ratty jeans and a T-shirt for this dinner.

He hated fish.

"Thanks, so do you."

She laughed softly. "You can't even see what I'm wearing."

True, her coat was on. It fell past her knees, obscuring whatever she had on underneath, but her dusty blond hair had been pulled up into some kind of intricate bun with tiny tendrils falling loosely around her face like a halo. Her makeup was subtle and highlighted her deep, dark brown eyes, making them sparkle. Plus, she was Lexi. She always looked nice because she was a nice person. Dyson fully believed that beauty came from the inside.

He pulled out onto the street and headed toward his sisters' house. It wasn't far from Lexi's, only about an eight-minute drive. The second he pulled onto their street his heart started to pound. Suddenly he found himself second-guessing everything. He pulled into the small driveway in the back of their house. The one normally filled with their cars, but tonight was free because he was bringing a date and they, quote—didn't want her running scared when Dyson busted a tire trying to parallel park on the street.

That had happened once, dammit.

He turned off the car, sitting back and taking a deep, calming breath.

"It's going to be fine, Dyson."

Lexi's hand enveloped his own, squeezing tightly. He turned his head to stare at her, wondering how he'd managed to get himself in this position.

"I hate lying to them," he confessed.

She smiled gently, as if she understood. "We don't have to do this."

They did. Because as much as he hated lying, he hated dodging dates and the pressure to sign up for dating apps even more. Explaining hadn't worked. The only way to stop his sisters' "find big brother a girlfriend" crusade was to pretend he had one already. Plus, he was terrified of Díaz. If he couldn't convince his sisters and she lost her bet to Ward, he'd have to sleep with one eye open at the station for the next year.

"It's fine." He pushed for a smile. "Are you ready for the third degree?"

Lifting the bottle, she grinned. "Why do you think I brought a peace offering?"

He laughed, some of the tightness in his chest easing. Reaching into the back he grabbed the dessert. "Let's do this then."

Opening the car door, he hopped out and rushed over to Lexi's side, grabbing the handle before she could open it herself.

"What a gentleman," she cooed, stepping out of the car.

"The vultures are already watching."

She frowned, glancing to the side when he nodded to the house where the curtain twitched shut when his sisters realized their peeping was caught. Lexi smothered a laugh with her hand, speaking in a hushed whisper.

"Please tell me you don't actually call them that."

With a grin, he shut the car door and hit the lock button, wrapping an arm around her waist and leading her toward the house. "Not to their faces."

At that she did laugh, loudly and beautifully.

He took them around the side of the house so they could enter through the front door. The front door that was already open and filled with the two women in the world he loved beyond reason and was most annoyed by in equal measure.

"Hello," Gemma and Macy said in unison like creepy witches from some old Shakespeare play.

"Lexi." He started the introduction on the front stoop, since his sisters were blocking the door. "These are my sisters, Gemma and Macy. Weirdos, this is Lexi."

"Dyson!" Gemma admonished with shock.

"Takes one to know one," Macy countered.

"It's okay, I have a brother." Lexi leaned in close to his sisters. "And he's a social ignoramus too."

Macy snickered. "Oooh, I like her already."

"All men are ignoramuses," Macy agreed with a roll of her eyes.

He scowled at the women who were already teaming up against him. "Hey!"

"Oh sweetie, you know I adore you, but it's true." Lexi patted him on the chest with such ease.

He let out a sigh of relief as the endearment rolled off her tongue as if she called him that every day. It was a good thing they did trivia the other night and worked out their nicknames. If Lexi had called him "honey bunny" in front of his sisters, they would have suspected something right away.

"Well." Gemma passed a curious glance between the two of them, but stepped back and motioned with a hand. "And on that note, I believe we should all head inside."

His sisters entered first, heading toward the kitchen. Gemma grabbed the box filled with the chocolate fudge cake. Lexi handed the wine to Macy.

"She brought booze." His little sister winked. "She's a keeper, Dy."

He shook his head, taking Lexi's coat as she unbuttoned it and shrugged it off her shoulders.

"Wow, Lexi!" Gemma whistled. "That is a killer dress."

It was.

Dyson had to grip the coat with all his might to stop himself from reaching out to touch the soft-looking forest green material. Thanks to his sisters, he knew quite a bit about women's fashion. Lexi's tea-length flared dress was stunning. It had a throwback appeal. Vintage-looking, he'd say. And the sweetheart neckline revealed just a hint of cleavage that had his body hardening and his mouth watering.

Dammit! Maybe he should have gotten laid before diving into this fake dating situation with Lexi. He knew having sex with his fake girlfriend was a bad idea; it would muddy the waters too much. But that didn't stop his mind from wandering to dangerous places. He couldn't tell if all these urges he was having were because he found Lexi attractive or because it had been a while since his last hookup.

"Thank you." Lexi smiled at his sister. "I got it at a thrift store on Broadway and the best part is—" Her hands disappeared somewhere in the folds of the dress.

Simultaneously Lexi and Gemma shouted, "It has pockets!"

Growing up with sisters, he knew the magical property that was pockets in women's clothing. He grinned. Hanging Lexi's coat on the rack, he followed the women into the kitchen where the table had already been set. Usually that was his job, but he could see his sisters were trying to impress his date.

They all sat and passed around the meal, a delicious chicken, carrot, and potato slow cooker dish marinated in a lemon Italian herb butter sauce.

"This is heavenly," Lexi exclaimed after a bite.

"Thanks." Macy gave a small shrug. "I like to cook. I find it very relaxing and I seem to have a bit of a talent for it."

"Are you a chef?"

Macy shook her head. "No, just a hobby. Dyson actually got me my first cookbook on my sixteenth birthday. Most people would think that was a weird present for a teenager, but he's always been supportive of our interests and hobbies."

Oh no, he knew where this was going. He did not need his sisters extoling his virtues to his fake girlfriend.

Gemma leaned forward; bright eyes locked on Lexi. "Did you know Dyson worked two jobs while going to school and taking care of two sullen teenagers when he was barely out of his teens himself?"

"Gemma," he warned, but his obstinate sister didn't listen.

Lexi gave him a small smile, patting his hand. "He did mention you lost your parents at a very young age. I'm so sorry."

Gemma's expression faltered, her lips falling from their upturned position.

"Yeah, it sucked. But Dyson was a rock for us. Always has been." She huffed out a despondent laugh. "Also, a bit of a stickler for the rules."

"You don't say." She turned to him with a cheeky smile.

He couldn't stop the grin from curling his lips.

"Oh yeah," Gemma continued, "He's got a ton of rules about life and stuff. So many we can't even keep track."

"I wonder what all these rules are?" Lexi gave him a sassy wink, placing her chin in her hand as she looked adoringly at him as if he were the world's most interesting boyfriend. "Care to share, sweetie?"

"Most of them revolve around fire safety," Macy laughed, but her smile dimmed. "But I guess that makes sense after the fire took Mom and Dad."

Lexi's teasing mood vanished, concern etched deep in her eyes. "They died in a fire?"

Right, he told her his parents died, but he hadn't mentioned how. He rarely did. No need to have everyone wonder if he got into firefighting due to the tragic death of his parents perishing in a house fire. Of course he did. Didn't need the eighteen months of grief counseling he and his sisters took to tell him that.

He turned his palm, grasping her hand. "It was a long time ago."

Not long enough. He wasn't sure it was ever long enough to lose someone you loved, but it was what people said.

The next few minutes they ate in silence, the mood significantly diminished. Of course, it was Gemma who started the conversation again.

"So, Lexi. Dyson tells us you run the DYC?"

Lexi nodded to his sister. "Yes. I'm the assistant director so I am in charge of the day-to-day operations and assist in helping secure funding and volunteers."

"It's amazing all she does for those kids," he added, because it was true and if they were really dating, it's what a proud boyfriend would say.

"What kind of volunteers are you looking for?" Macy asked.

"Any and every kind we can get," Lexi laughed.

She and his sisters talked for a few minutes about the center and what kind of help they could offer. He wasn't surprised. Lexi had this bright energy that just called to people, made them want to help. And his sisters were gems, always willing to lend a hand. Though he didn't know if it was such a good idea, his sisters spending more time with Lexi. He'd kind of been hoping after this one dinner they could continue with their pretend relationship in theory only, away from the prying eyes of his sisters.

"I can drop by after work on Wednesday," Macy offered.

Gemma nodded. "Me too."

Shit. Looks like that plan wasn't going to happen.

"Wow," Lexi smiled up at him. "A fabulous boyfriend and a batch of new volunteers. I must have hit the jackpot."

She leaned over to kiss his cheek, the slight brush of her soft lips sparking a roaring fire of need within him and earning a chorus of "Aws" from the vultures.

Dinner passed pleasantly after that, his sisters inquiring more about how they met and got together. Lexi told the story of him coming to do the inspection—minus the strip-o-gram part—and their time spent together morphing into something more. Since most of it was true, Dyson found himself nodding along in agreement.

Dinner finished and Gemma cut the cake, passing slices around the table. When Macy gave one to Lexi, she held up a hand.

"No thank you."

"You don't like chocolate?" Macy asked, mouth dropping open in shock as if it was the oddest thing she'd ever heard.

"I love chocolate, but it doesn't love me back." Lexi shrugged. "I have a mild allergy that gives me horrible migraines if I eat too much."

Both of his sisters' heads turned to stare at him, their eyes heavy with wariness.

Shit!

Lexi hadn't mentioned her chocolate allergy. They hadn't delved too deep because they were playing this off like a new relationship. Could he be convincing in his lack of knowledge about this? Were allergies something people shared early on while dating? He supposed so, since most first dates were food related. But their first date had been more of a strategy meeting and less of a get-to-know-you date.

"Dyson knows I'm trying to cut back on my sugar because I'm training for the center's 5k Fun Run fundraiser next month so he brought a dessert that wouldn't tempt me." She rested her head on his shoulder, gazing up at him with adoring eyes. "Thanks, sweetie."

Macy nodded as if that made perfect sense. Gemma gave another squeaking sound of approval. Damn, the woman was so convincing, she half had him believing it.

"We don't have to if it—"

"Don't be silly," Lexi cut Macy off, waving at everyone around the table. "Eat, enjoy, and if you still feel guilty you can always sponsor me for the run."

A small chuckle rose from the table as Lexi worked her charms. They finished their dessert, talked more about his sisters' work and the center. Soon it was the end of the night. This time they left through the back door, since it was dark. His sisters each gave Lexi a hug, telling her how nice it was to meet her and looking forward to seeing her again. His gut cramped, wondering how long they would have to keep up this charade. At least a month according to the bet with Ward and Díaz. How much face time did his friends expect his sisters to have with him and Lexi? He had kind of hoped it would be a one and done type deal and then the rest of the month could be spent telling them about his relationship.

I should have known my sisters would butt their way into my relationship.

He'd been so preoccupied with convincing them, he'd forgotten about after.

"I think that went well," Lexi said as they walked arm and arm back to the car. In case his sisters were watching, of course.

"You were amazing, Lexi. Thank you."

"No, thank you. Every time we go somewhere, I get new volunteers for the center." She grinned up at him. "You're like my very own lucky charm."

He laughed, opening her car door.

"Um, Dyson," she said, turning and leaning against the open door.

"Yeah?"

Leaning in, she spoke in a hushed whisper. "The vultures are watching."

From the corner of his eye he noticed the curtain of the back window slightly parted and sure enough, two heads trying and failing to be inconspicuous.

"We should probably make sure they're fully convinced." Her teeth came out to gently bite her bottom lip. "Don't you think?"

He couldn't think. All he could focus on was Lexi's mouth and how much he wanted to taste it again. Grasping the back of her neck, he bent down, pressing his lips to hers. But unlike the two previous times, this was no innocent kiss. No quick and soft press of closed lips. Lexi threw her arms around his neck, pulling him to her until their bodies were flush. Until he could feel every soft inch the dress was hiding.

She moaned, thrusting her hips against him, rubbing against his painfully hard cock. Her mouth opened and he tasted her sweetness. The tart, fruit-forward wine from dinner, the tiny bite of chocolate cake she'd sneaked when she thought he wasn't looking. But really, the most delicious taste was simply her, Lexi.

He'd never wanted anything so badly in his life. For a moment, Dyson forgot he was in the middle of a driveway, in full-on public, with his sisters watching from a few feet away. All he knew was Lexi and the way she made him feel, made him crave. He was two seconds from hiking her skirt up when she pulled away, her heavy, breathy pants matching his own. Their foreheads pressed together as his heart rate tried to return to normal, but the damn thing was running at Mach speed and he didn't see it slowing down anytime soon.

"Well...I bet that...convinced them."

Since he didn't see his sisters at the window anymore, he'd say she was right.

Now all he had to do was make sure this heat between them didn't convince him, too.

Chapter Twelve

Wednesday afternoon, Lexi was refereeing a game of basketball when Zoe texted to let her know Gemma and Macy were waiting in her office. They had an intercom system in the building, but it was so old and outdated, she wasn't even sure it worked. Normally whoever was checking people in at the front desk just texted her or walked the person to her office.

"Sorry, guys," Lexi apologized with a smile. "I have some volunteers waiting for me in my office. I'm going to have to bow out."

"It's okay, Ms. Martin." Mateo gave her a brief smile.

"Yeah, the game will probably go better without your bad calls," Brycen said under his breath.

Mateo glared at the other teen, growling softly. "Dude, shut up."

Lexi smiled and pretended not to hear. Mateo was sweet, but Brycen had a point. Her ref skills were subpar at best. She'd never been a big sports person. She wouldn't have reffed the game at all, but the kids asked her to with their big puppy-dog pleading eyes and of course she caved. Even though she had a mountain of work waiting for her on her desk.

After apologizing again to the kids for bailing on the game, she headed out of the gym toward her office, the whispers of Mateo calling Brycen out on his rudeness warming her heart. He was such a good kid. They all were, even Brycen. He was just a little bit blunter than Mateo. Didn't matter. She loved all her kids.

She arrived in her office to see Dyson's sisters milling about the room. Gemma was staring at the calendar behind her desk. Macy was leafing through one of the center's pamphlets Lexi always left on her desk for visiting donors.

"Hello, ladies."

Both of them jumped, heads turning toward her, cheeks burning red the way Dyson's did whenever she complimented him. So, the brother got embarrassed by praise and the sisters by being caught. Interesting.

"Hey, Lexi." Gemma smiled, big and wide. "We were just—"

"Snooping?" She arched one eyebrow.

"No!" Gemma exclaimed.

"Yes," Macy said at the same time.

Macy laughed while Gemma gave an embarrassed shrug.

"Lexi," Gemma said, turning her attention back to the calendar on the wall. "How the hell do you ever get anything done with this much on your plate?"

Lexi made her way around the desk, studying the large paper calendar filled with so many notes and reminders there was barely any blank space left.

"Honestly, I delegate a lot to our interns and volunteers."

"Yeah, but you're in charge of making sure all this gets done?" Gemma stared in disbelief.

"Sure." Lexi shrugged. "But lucky for me I have wonderful people like yourselves who graciously give their time to help me not drown under the pressure."

"You don't have to butter us up." Macy came to stand by Gemma. "We're already here and willing to help."

"Butter makes everything better."

All the women agreed on this point.

"So." Macy set the pamphlet back down on Lexi's desk. "How can we help?"

"Well, if you want to work with the kids, you'll have to fill out some paperwork and agree to a background check."

"Of course." Gemma nodded.

"But if you have any time today, one of our back rooms needs to be cleaned and set up for an art studio."

"Art studio? Cool."

Very. The center had some art supplies for the kids' schoolwork, but they never had a designated space or teacher. But thanks to Tamsen, who so generously agreed to volunteer three hours a week and get the studio she worked for to sponsor some art supplies, the kids would now have access to legitimate art classes. Once Tamsen's background check went through, they'd be all set. And it should come back any day now, which was why she needed to get the room ready pronto.

"Cleaning, we can do." Macy waved her hands in front of her. "Just don't ask me to teach any art stuff. I can't even draw stick figures."

"Our family lacks any sort of artistic gene," Gemma agreed.

"Lucky for all of us, I already have a wonderful volunteer to be the art teacher. And coincidently I met her through Dyson, too." He was just bringing her all sorts of helpers. He was like a magic, sexy, volunteer magnet.

Macy cocked her head. "Oh yeah, who?"

"Tamsen. Do you all know her? She's engaged to someone at the firehouse. I met him too—"

"Kincaid." Both sisters said at once.

"It was a sad day when that man was taken off the market," Gemma gave a wistful sigh.

Macy snorted, "Oh please, like Dyson hasn't threatened every guy there within an inch of his life from hitting on his sisters. It's fire crew code or something. Don't date the siblings."

The thought of sweet, helpful Dyson threatening anyone made Lexi laugh. She knew he loved his sisters, but she doubted Dyson would hurt a fly. He probably caught spiders in cups and gently carried them outside into the fresh grass. She'd bet he even had a silly rule about it.

"Actually, he scoops them up in his hands, but you're right. Dyson couldn't hurt any living thing."

Lexi sucked in a sharp breath, staring at Gemma who stood smiling, approval clear in the woman's gaze.

"He told us you might do that."

"What?"

"Speak out loud without meaning to."

Macy nodded, the happy grin on her face mirroring that of her sister's. "Dyson said, and I quote, 'She does this adorable thing where she vocalizes her inner thoughts sometimes so don't make a big deal about it and don't embarrass her over it.'"

Too late for that. Her cheeks were so hot, she knew she had to be blushing bright red. Plus her throat had gone dry and her hands clammy. She should be grateful the thing she misspoke out loud wasn't anything to the effect of "this is all fake" but honestly, it was always embarrassing when her strange unconscious habit got caught.

And yet...

Dyson had called it adorable. What did that mean? Did he think *she* was adorable? The adjective had been gifted to her a time or two over the years. She didn't mind it. Though she'd rather have Dyson think she was a smoking hottie he couldn't keep his hands off. Their kiss the other night at dinner sure felt like that. But then the guy had barely spoken the whole drive back to her place. He'd been polite, but stiff, closed off.

She wondered if she took it too far, offended him, but he'd texted the next day to thank her for the night and say he'd be coming by later in the week for more repair work, so she assumed they were good. Dyson was a hard read. The guy was so rigid sometimes. He really needed to let loose a little. Unwind. Relax on some of those rules he loved so much.

"Um...we should probably get to cleaning the room, if you're up for it."

"We are," Gemma stepped forward and placed a hand on Lexi's. "And we didn't mean to make you feel self-conscious. We think it's great how taken with you our brother is. You seem like an amazing person, Lexi, and just who he needs."

She smiled, even though Dyson's sister's words made her feel like garbage in that exact moment. She could call it a fib all she wanted, but Dyson was right, they were lying to his sisters. They were so nice and clearly loved their brother deeply. Her stomach cramped knowing all their hopeful dreams about her and Dyson would one day be crushed.

Hadn't thought that part of this charade through.

Maybe they could work it so they had an amicable fake breakup. Claim the spark died out or they were better as friends. But how long before they were able to do that? Dyson mentioned one dinner with his sisters so he could keep up pretenses. Neither one of them had counted on his siblings being such sweethearts that they actually volunteered at the center. If his sisters were here when Dyson was here, they'd have to keep pretending to be dating, right?

Oof, this was getting complicated. She definitely needed to talk it through with Dyson when he came over this week.

But, for now, they had a room to clean.

Lexi ushered Gemma and Macy to the room they'd be using as an art studio. When she first started working here it had been the music room, but over the years all the donated instruments had been broken or gone missing. As much as she loved each and every kid here, sometimes desperation won over everything else. She would never punish a kid for taking something they so clearly needed, but she did sit them down for a talk and worked out a plan for them to make amends. And sometimes, when she knew it was their last option, she turned a blind eye to missing items. It wasn't like anything in the center was particularly valuable anyway.

"Oh wow," Gemma muttered as they entered the room.

Macy swiped at a cobweb hanging in the window. "When was the last time anyone was in here?"

"It's been a while." Lexi glanced around the dusty, cluttered room with a sigh. "We've mostly been using it for storage and junk that needs to go out to the dumpster."

But now they had a purpose for it. Her heart leaped with glee. The kids were going to be so excited. She couldn't thank Tamsen enough, or Dyson for bringing the woman into Lexi's sphere.

Macy walked around the room. It wasn't very large, but it appeared much smaller because of all the crap in it.

"We should start by separating the stuff you want to keep from the stuff that needs to go to the dumpster."

"Macy's a teacher," Gemma said in a hushed whisper. "She's good at planning things, but that means she always thinks she's the boss even though I'm older."

"I heard that, and I am the boss because I'm the smartest."

"Smartassiest," Gemma muttered.

Macy flipped her sister the bird. Gemma simply laughed. Lexi could see why Dyson cared so much for his sisters. They were so fun. Her heart sank a little as she realized how long it had been since she'd been able to spend time with her own siblings. Maybe she should FaceTime them this week.

They set to work, with Lexi directing which items would stay and which would go. Very few stayed. It made her realize how neglectful she'd been about dealing with all this. Yes, she had a million things on her plate, but that didn't mean she should have kept stuffing junk in here to deal with later. She winced at her failing. She should probably put this on her self-eval this year.

"Don't do that," Gemma argued. "Self-evaluations are for talking about all the amazing things you do and then saying something like 'my only fault is that I work too hard,' which from what I saw in your office is actually true."

"I'm sorry," Lexi covered her mouth, dropping her hand before continuing. "I didn't mean to say that out loud."

"It's fine, Lex." Macy paused, "Can I call you Lex?"

She nodded. "Sure, my friends do all the time."

"Yay, we're friends!" Gemma jumped up and down, throwing her arms around Lexi and giving her a surprisingly strong hug.

She blinked back moisture, touched that these women were excited to call her friend. They'd known each other only a few days, but she'd never met more welcoming and wonderful people in her life. Except for Dyson. Must run in the family.

"And don't worry about the talking out loud thing." Gemma grabbed a box of used glue sticks and placed them in the trash pile. "It's nice that Dyson is with someone who's so honest and forthcoming."

She was honest with him, but with his sisters…there went that stomach cramp again.

"What do you mean?" Because it felt like there was a story behind that statement and not just an unknowing barb that hit Lexi right in the chest.

The sisters shared a look, speaking in that silent way siblings possessed. She and her brother and sister had entire screaming matches with their eyes at the dinner table under the completely ignorant eyes of their parents.

"He hasn't shared anything about his ex with you yet, has he?"

She stared into Gemma's worried eyes and shook her head.

Gemma hesitated, biting her lip. "It's not really our place to share, then, but just know she was… She hurt him. Badly."

"She was a bitch!"

"Macy!"

Macy shrugged. "What? She was."

"It's not our place to judge her," Gemma stated. "But we can say their relationship ended very badly."

That would explain Dyson's no dating rule. A traumatic breakup put a lot of people off of relationships. It was hard to risk yourself again after being hurt so badly.

Gemma stepped closer to her sister, reaching out a hand as if she needed strength to speak whatever was on her mind. Immediately Macy grabbed her hand.

"After our parents died, Dyson dropped everything. He came back from school, handled the funerals, the will stuff, made sure he had everything in order to become our legal guardian. He worked two jobs to support us until I insisted Macy and I could help by getting part-time work after school."

Macy nodded. "It took a year, but we finally convinced him to start taking classes again so he could finish his degree. He insisted we both go to college, but we weren't going to let him give up his dreams, either."

Okay, now the mist had gone into full waterworks. Lexi sniffed and blinked, trying to hold back the tears as Dyson's sisters explained what she already knew. He was an amazing man.

"He provided for and protected us." Macy stared her directly in the eyes. "And we will do anything to protect him, too. So as much as we like you, just know this, Lexi. If you ever hurt our brother, we know how to hide a body without it ever being found."

Silence filled the room as the women all stared at one another, Lexi's palms started to sweat, her tears dried up at the slightly outrageous threat uttered by an obviously caring yet extremely protective sibling. She didn't quite know how to respond, but then Gemma turned to Macy with a baffled expression.

"No, we don't. Jeez, Macy." Gemma shook her head. "Going a little dark there."

"I was going for intimidation."

"Mission accomplished." Lexi nodded.

Gemma dropped her sister's hand and came to Lexi's side. "What Macy meant to say, without sounding like Liam Neeson, is that we love our brother very much and we don't want to see him hurt again. So, if you don't think this is going anywhere, be mature and break it off nicely."

"We just started dating." Fake dating, so his sisters' concerns were baseless. Couldn't break the heart of someone whose heart you didn't have. Not that they knew that, or ever would, hopefully.

"But," she continued at their insistent looks. "I promise I would never do anything to hurt Dyson."

And that she could say with one hundred percent honesty.

"Great!" Macy declared. "Then let's finish cleaning and go grab a pizza, I'm starving."

The center was open for another forty minutes and Lexi tended to stay for another hour or two catching up on things, but she could take a dinner break for some pizza. Then again, she wondered if spending more time with Dyson's sisters was a good idea. She liked them. A lot. They were fun and sweet and hilarious. When she and Dyson fake broke up, could she still hang out with them? Maybe if they went with the "better as friends" story, it was a possibility.

The only problem was, judging from the kiss the other night, the way her heart raced whenever Dyson was near, the fact that he was constantly in the back of her mind and often directly front and center, and he was starring nightly in her dreams—her very erotic dreams—she was worried pulling off "just friends" with Dyson might be trickier than she imagined.

Maybe if she could convince him to work off this sexual awareness between them, that spark would die, burn out, and they really could be just friends. It was worth a shot. What did she have to lose? After all, it wasn't like she was going to actually fall for her fake boyfriend.

Chapter Thirteen

Dyson finished up the rep of squats and sat down on the weight bench. Working out wasn't his favorite thing in the world to do, but his job required him to maintain a certain level of fitness. The station had a small gym with free weights, a bench press, a few stationary bikes and treadmills, and a rowing machine. Ward was currently on the rowing machine while Díaz was using the free weights. Everyone made time for fitness in their downtime during shifts.

Grabbing his water bottle, he tilted it up and took a thirst-quenching drag. A drop of sweat rolled down his temple; he wiped it away with the back of his hand.

"I'm out, guys," he said to his crewmates. "Gonna grab a shower."

"Cool," Ward replied.

Díaz simply grunted.

He grabbed his cell where he left it on the floor next to his water bottle. The second he touched it, it chimed with an incoming text.

"A firefighter *and* a psychic," Ward joked. "Man of many

hats."

He ignored his friend, glancing down to see he had a new text from Lexi. The uptick in his heart rate was simply due to his strenuous workout. Not receiving a text from his fake girlfriend.

Oh yeah, then why was he smiling as he unlocked his phone?

Lexi: *Your sisters are so sweet and fun...but kinda scary too.*

He groaned.

Dyson: *I am so sorry. I'd like to claim they were raised by animals but, since I kind of raised them...*

She sent back a laughing emoji.

Lexi: *They're fine, just being protective, which I totally get. And they're here, so I can take whatever they dish out.*

Right, it was Wednesday—the day his sisters promised to help out at the center. He was proud of them for volunteering, but also worried. The more time Lexi spent around them, the more likely their charade would fall apart. Also, as much as he loved his sisters, they could be total pains and ridiculously overprotective—family trait. He cringed, imagining what they'd said to Lexi.

"What's up, dude?"

Pointing to his phone, he answered Ward, "My sisters are helping Lexi at the center today and they're being..."

"Barracudas?" Díaz offered without even breaking her reps.

"Yeah, pretty much." He had no idea what was going on, but he bet his sisters read Lexi the riot act about treating him well or some shit. Silly when *he* was the big brother. As oldest, it was his job to warn off their partners. And besides, Lexi wasn't even a real girlfriend.

Not that they knew that.

Díaz stopped her reps. Her dark, curly hair was contained in a high ponytail, but the small wisps in the front clung to her forehead, matted by sweat. She grabbed one of the workout towels folded neatly on a shelf and dragged it across her face and the back of her neck. "So the dating thing is working? Your sisters think you're legit?"

He nodded.

"Nice, you all did a good job of convincing the crew at trivia night." She smiled at him. "I knew you could do this. Get your soap and bucket ready Ward, my baby needs a car wash."

"What are you talking about?" Ward scoffed. "Were we at the same night? They were awkward AF."

She glared at him. "Only because you kept trying to screw them up. That's cheating, Ward."

"Is not." Ward glanced back and forth between the two of them and shook his head. "Besides, it won't last—you'll screw it up."

"Thanks for the vote of confidence, Ward." He scowled at his supposed buddy.

"Ignore him," Díaz said with a taunting smile. "He's just pissed because he knows he's going to have to strip down to a banana hammock and wash Baby."

"Whoa, time out!" Ward stopped rowing and dropped his arms over his knees. "We never agreed on a banana hammock."

Díaz shrugged. "I'm adding on."

"You can't do that! O'Neil, tell her she can't do that!"

Dyson shook his head, smart enough to know not to get into the middle of a Ward and Díaz argument. "Hey, this is your bet, not mine."

Ward glared. "You're just siding with her because you want her to win."

Yeah, of course he wanted Díaz to win. For multiple reasons. One, because he really needed to convince his sisters this thing with Lexi was real and two, he didn't want to be on Díaz's bad side. No one did.

"This is some bullshit, dude."

"Leave him alone," Díaz said. "Dyson knows what he's doing."

Ward frowned.

"What?"

"Telling your sisters you have a girlfriend is one thing, but them actually spending time with your fake girlfriend is a whole other can of worms that will not be pretty when it cracks open and explodes all over you." He rose, coming to stand beside Díaz, facing Dyson. "I know we said a month, but I thought you were just going to tell your sisters about Lexi and do one dinner. Not have them get all chummy."

That's the way it was supposed to go. One dinner. Proof he wasn't just making someone up and they could all leave him alone. But that wasn't what happened.

"That was the plan, but when Lexi mentioned the center they both jumped in to volunteer. What was she supposed to say, no?"

The DYC needed all the help it could get.

"Aren't you worried about your sisters finding out it's all a lie?"

"Of course I am," he answered Ward. "But I couldn't exactly tell them not to volunteer, they'd want to know why, plus Lexi needs help."

Díaz arched an eyebrow. "Lexi?"

"The center," he corrected himself. "The center needs help and my sisters offered just like I did."

Shoving down the uncomfortable knot in his stomach, Dyson took another swig of water.

Ward grabbed his own water bottle and took a drink. "Yeah, but the more they all spend time together, the more the cracks in your story will start to show."

Why the hell was Ward harping on this? Eli Ward was one of the most fun-loving, devil-may-care, happy-go-lucky guys he ever knew. Where was all this doom and gloom attitude coming from and why?

"We stuck as close to the truth as possible." Really the only lie they'd told his sisters was that they were dating. Their meeting, hanging out, getting along well, all true. He really did enjoy hanging out with Lexi. She was fun and she made him smile, even when she was teasing him. Especially when she was teasing him. It had been a long time since he'd been friendly with anyone other than the men and women of Station 42. After Adam's betrayal…making new friends just didn't seem worth it anymore.

"Sticking close to the truth and the actual truth are two different things, my dude."

Had he woken up in an alternate dimension? Did a meteor hit earth last night and they were all in some weird purgatory state? Did aliens land and start inhabiting people like body snatchers? Because there must be something wrong with the universe if Ward was giving him moral advice.

"Leave him alone, Ward. You're just pissed you're losing the bet. Besides, O'Neil shouldn't take dating advice from a man who hasn't had a date in…" Díaz turned to smirk at Ward. "Come to think of it, have you ever had a date?"

"Very funny, Díaz."

"No, I'm serious, you talk a big game, flirt like it's going out of style, but I don't think I've ever seen you with someone in the four years I've known you." Díaz laughed, heading back over to the free weights to grab her water bottle.

Ward's gaze followed her. Dyson saw so many emotions cross his friend's face, longing, desire, regret, resignation. Huh, who knew Ward had that many emotions. When his buddy's eyes came back to him, Dyson raised a brow, but Ward shook his head. Okay, guess they weren't talking about that little glimpse into Ward's soul he just saw. Very interesting, though. Dyson now felt like he understood a lot more about Ward and why he acted the way he did.

Unrequited love was a bitch. Though he wondered if the man ever simply told Díaz how he felt, he might be surprised by her reaction.

Then again, what the hell did he know? He was lying to his sisters about a fake relationship with a woman he was far too attracted to. He didn't have the right to tell anyone what to do when it came to matters of the heart.

"Thank you for your concern, but it's fine." Walking over to the shelf, he grabbed a towel and wiped the sweat from his brow. He'd like to claim it came from his workout, but it was totally due to nerves. He already felt shitty about this situation, and Ward wasn't making it any better. "Lexi is great, and my sisters have no clue. Plus…"

"Plus what?" Díaz asked when he trailed off.

He rubbed the towel over the back of his neck and tossed it into the hamper in the corner. "Plus it's pretty easy to pretend to be with Lexi. She's…we're…there's a…" How the hell did he say this without sounding like a major skeevebucket?

"There's a shit ton of sexual tension between you two that makes the relationship lie believable because you both want to rip each other's clothes off and do the nasty?"

Leave it to Ward to tell it like it is in the basest way possible.

"Something like that," he muttered.

"Then just date her, dude."

"Admitting defeat already, Ward?" Díaz chuckled.

"No, I'm trying to look out for my friend's happiness, which is a little more important than a bet, Díaz."

She waved away his argument.

"I don't do relationships. Rule number one, don't get involved." Never again. Plus, Lexi had that whole "no dating" bet thing with her roommate so there was no chance of them accidently falling into real dating.

Ward sighed. "One day you're going to have to get over what your ex and that dick of a former best friend did to you. And by the way, dude, breaking the rules can be fun sometimes. You should try it."

Sometimes it really sucked being close to the people you worked with. The firehouse was basically his second family, so of course they all knew about Grace and what she'd done. Scratch that, what she and Adam had done. It was only three years ago, so they'd all had a front-row seat to his heartbreak and utter humiliation.

But they'd also all had his back, which meant more than he could ever say.

"You could ask Lexi if she wanted to be fuck buddies," Díaz casually tossed out, like it was a thing people asked each other all the time.

Dyson blinked, staring at his friend. He glanced over to see Ward's jaw open so wide, the man looked like a cartoon.

"What?" Díaz shrugged. "It's clear you wanna bang each other, and adding intimacy to your agreement would just heighten the reality of your lie. I mean, technically you two would be doing all the things people in real relationships do, but without the actual relationship part."

"Exactly, Díaz!" Ward argued. "That's why it's a bad idea. Waters will get muddied, emotions involved."

She laughed. "Stop being such a prude, Ward. People can have sex without getting their hearts involved. That wouldn't be breaking your precious rule, right?"

Not his personal rule, but he and Lexi had made a PDA guideline for this whole situation and sex was out.

But some rules could be bent slightly...

Could he and Lexi do that, add a sexual element to their fake relationship? Would that help relieve all this...tension surrounding them or just add more problems?

Something he should probably talk to her about if he wanted any kind of answer. But how did he ask without sounding like a jerk? He didn't want her to think he asked for her help just to get into her pants.

What should he do? Ask and risk upsetting her or forget it and try his best to shove the primal attraction he had for this woman as far down as possible?

Both options seemed fraught with danger.

"Hey guys." Kincaid popped his head into the workout room. "Dinner's here. Tamsen brought over some extra burgers and fries Ty made us."

Ward practically ran for the door. "Kincaid, have I ever mentioned how much I love your fiancée?"

"Yes, and as I've said before, she's too good for you."

"Too good for you, too, but somehow you convinced her otherwise."

"Luckiest day of my life." The man grinned.

Ward and Kincaid headed out to the kitchen. Díaz passed by Dyson on her way out, but paused before leaving, turning to face him with a serious expression on her face. Which wasn't anything new. Díaz was always serious. But the worried glint in her eyes did cause him to pause.

"Spit it out, Stephanie. You know you want to."

She cringed at the use of her first name. Using last names was kind of a thing around the station. Their crew was fairly small and regular but, since everyone's last name was stitched on their gear, it just became a thing to use them. Whenever anyone used first names, you knew they meant business.

"Fine. As much as I hate myself for saying this, I kind of agree with Ward that you need to be careful with the whole Lexi fake girlfriend situation."

He chuckled, trying to lighten the suddenly tense mood. "Agree with Ward? Did you die a little inside saying that?"

"Shut up." She flipped him off and continued, but some of the graveness in her voice dissipated. "Look, I know you—you're a good person. You're not going to trick her or let her believe anything you don't feel."

True. He might be fibbing to his sisters, but he'd never lie to a woman he was involved with. Even if the involvement was a lie in itself.

"I say go for it. Tell Lexi what you want, ask her what she wants. Be completely open, honest, and upfront. Come up with some of those rules you love so much so nothing gets confused. Who knows? She might be as game for it as you are."

With that, she left, leaving Dyson alone with his thoughts.

Knowing his friends might eat his burger if he didn't hustle his ass, he pushed thoughts of Lexi and sex out of his mind. Okay, to the back of his mind. For now.

After dinner and a quick shower, he headed to the room where he was sleeping tonight. The station had four, and everyone bunked together except Díaz. She shared a room only when Torres was on shift, but the two women rarely had shifts together.

He lay in his bed, going over the requirements for his EMT recertification. He still had a few months before he had to complete it, but he liked to be prepared.

Just as his eyes started to droop, his cell phone rang. Reaching over to the small night stand, he glanced at the caller and smiled.

"Hello, Gemma," he said as he answered his baby sister's call. "How'd it go at the center today?"

"Wonderful! Lexi is fantastic. I really like her, Dy."

He did too. Which was kind of the problem.

"What'd you call for?"

"What? Can't I simply call my big brother because I miss him and want to hear his voice?"

He snorted, shifting in the bed to lie back against the pillows. "No. You're allergic to talking on the phone. You do it only when you're trying to convince me of something. Otherwise you text."

"Rude, but true."

He heard some clicking and knew his multitasking sister was working on her computer as they spoke. Gemma never could focus on one thing at a time.

"I wanted to finalize the plans for the Estes trip this weekend."

Every year since his parents died, the siblings had taken a small family vacation in Estes Park up in the Rockies. They rented a cabin, went hiking, ate out, played board games. Nothing fancy, but it was bonding time. Family bonding time.

"Everything is good to go. Made sure of it weeks ago."

"I know, but are we adding another person to the trip?"

He frowned, even though his sister couldn't see his confusion through the phone. "Another person? Who?"

Gemma laughed. "Lexi, of course."

He swallowed down a ball of nerves and anticipation at the mention of her name. "But that's family time."

"Well yeah." Gemma swore slightly as he heard her typing increase and she muttered something about stupid new log-in systems. "But girlfriends and boyfriends have always been welcome."

True. Over the years, his sisters had brought whomever they'd been dating at the time. Kind of a trial run to see if their significant other fit in with the family dynamic. Grace had come a few years. All but that last one. The fatal year when—

He shook his head, pulling himself out of the past.

"It's not a big deal, I was just wondering if I should grab more coffee and snacks for the cabin. I think it'd be really fun to have Lexi along. She's so sweet."

She was. Sweet, kind, generous, funny, beautifully tempting. Honestly, his sister's question made sense. If he was really dating Lexi, he would have invited her to their Estes trip without hesitation. His heart rate kicked up just thinking about an entire weekend with Lexi. Hiking the trails, dining out, playing silly games with his sisters.

Sleeping together...

Right. The hitch in the plan.

If Lexi came along, his sisters would probably assume that they'd want to sleep in the same room. The same bed.

His body tightened at the thought. His mind filled with images of Lexi, warm and naked in his bed. Her hair spread out on the pillow as he rose above her—

"Dy? Are you still there?"

Oh what the hell!

The phone almost slipped out of his grip. Had he seriously been fantasizing about his fake girlfriend while on the phone with his baby sister? He shuddered. Hot mental fantasy sufficiently squashed. He needed to get his head in the game and stop being so distracted by a woman who was simply helping him, out of the goodness of her heart.

"I'll ask her, but she has a lot on her plate right now." Not a lie. "I don't know if she'll have the time."

Gemma sighed. "I know. She works so hard. Have you seen her calendar at work?"

He had. There were far too many tasks on it for one person to accomplish. Lexi worked too damn hard. She deserved a break.

A break like a weekend away in the mountains.

The corner of his mouth ticked up as the thought popped into his head.

Yeah. Lexi did deserve a break. And what better break than a free vacation provided by her fake boyfriend? It wasn't like he was asking her up so they could fall into bed together. He just wanted to offer her the rest she so clearly deserved. And he guessed Lexi would never take it unless it was being framed as a favor. He was coming to discover she was good at taking care of everyone but herself.

Well, as her fake boyfriend, it was his duty to make sure her needs were met.

He sucked in a sharp breath as his logic went to a dangerous place.

Emotional needs, not physical ones.

So yes, asking Lexi to come on his family's trip with him seemed like an excellent idea. They could keep up their ruse, and she would get some much needed downtime. And if he was looking forward to spending more time with her, it was only because he enjoyed her company.

Not for any other reason.

Chapter Fourteen

"Ms. Martin?"

Lexi stopped short of running directly into Mateo. The sixteen-year-old was nearly an inch taller than her, but her head had been down, reading the latest "sorry but we've picked another applicant" rejection from one of the grants the center applied to. *Dang it!* She really shouldn't be reading while walking.

"Hi Mateo, what is it?"

"Is your boyfriend coming in today? The firefighter guy."

She opened her mouth to say "he's not my boyfriend" but he kind of was. At least that's what they were telling most people and, since Dyson's sisters were coming to the center on the reg now, she supposed she should let everyone there think they were in an actual relationship.

"Yes, he is. In fact"—she pulled her cell out of her pocket to look at the time—"he should be here any minute. Why?"

Mateo shuffled on his feet, his gaze falling to the worn gray hallway carpeting. "I just had a question for him, no big deal or anything."

Lexi wasn't a parent, but she knew when one of her center kids said "it's not a big deal" it was usually in fact a very big deal. She hoped Mateo wasn't in any kind of trouble. As much as she told her kids to come to her when they needed something, some of them were too embarrassed or too scared to ask for help. She had no idea what sort of help Dyson could give Mateo, but she'd do anything in her power to make sure the kid got it.

Her phone buzzed in her pocket, but she ignored it.

"As soon as he gets in, I can send him your way."

Mateo shrugged. "If he has work to do first, that's fine. I just have a question for him."

"Okay, but I'll leave it up to him what he wants to do first. After all, he's volunteering, so if he wants to talk to you before he gets to work, that's fine with me."

She didn't want Mateo to feel guilty if Dyson decided to talk to him before addressing the center's repairs. Mateo was such a sweet boy, and he knew how much this place needed help, but often these kids were so busy looking out for their family and friends, they forgot they were important, too.

"I'll let Dyson know you have a question as soon as I see him."

"You have a question for me?"

Lexi started, turning at the smooth, familiar voice behind her. Her heart rate kicked up as Dyson stood there, dark blue jeans, heather green T-shirt, dirty blond hair slightly tousled, like he was in need of a haircut and couldn't quite get it styled properly in the interim. Her stomach dipped, butterflies taking flight as her entire body fell in sync with a common mission.

Doing Dyson.

"Uh, Lexi…"

Dyson's eyes widened and he nodded toward Mateo. She turned her head to see the kid blushing bright red. Slapping a hand over her mouth, she prayed to every deity in the world that what she assumed just happened did not in fact happen.

"Oh no," she whispered around her cupped hand. "Please tell me I didn't just say that out loud?"

"It's fine, Ms. Martin. I've heard worse." Mateo shrugged.

Dropping her hand, she cleared her throat and faced the young man with as much dignity as she could muster. "Regardless, I shouldn't have let that inappropriate thought slip out."

"He's your boyfriend, I assume you guys fu—do it." Mateo corrected his language at her raised eyebrow. "I mean, I have a girlfriend, too."

Oh crap, this was not a conversation she wanted to have in front of her fake boyfriend.

"Mateo, do you remember when we had the health expert in last month?" They'd had a nurse come in to talk to all the kids—who'd gotten permission from their parents—about sex, consent, protection, STDs, and pregnancy. Very necessary, since a lot of the local schools were abysmal about their sex education.

"Yes, Ms. Martin."

"And you're being…safe?"

He slapped his hands over his ears, cheeks reddening. "Yes, can we stop talking about this, please?"

Poor kid. She knew he was embarrassed, so was she, but these kinds of things were important.

"You have a question for me?" Dyson asked, blessedly driving the conversation back around to a safe topic.

Mateo dropped his hands, straightening his shoulders and looking Dyson directly in the eyes. "Yeah, I mean, yes sir."

"You can just call me Dyson."

Mateo nodded.

"Go for it, Mateo."

"I was wondering how you became a firefighter."

What? Lexi didn't know Mateo wanted to be a firefighter. Just last week the kid was talking about how he had no idea what he'd do after high school.

"You thinking about becoming a firefighter?" Dyson asked.

Mateo nodded. "I like the idea of helping people."

Her heart melted. Mateo was such a sweet kid. Yesterday he spent two hours helping a freshman with their math homework just because the kid needed help.

Dyson dipped his chin. "Good answer. But it's a really tough job, long hours, rough calls, dangerous."

"I can handle it." Mateo puffed his chest out, lifting his chin high.

She watched as Dyson studied the boy, admiration gleaming in his eyes. "I think you can. Tell you what, my station participates in the National Junior Firefighters program. It's kind of like a pre-firefighter training camp. Education, some training, lets you know if the job is really something you want. If you're really serious, I'll be your sponsor and mentor. Here's my number, shoot me a text and I'll help you fill out all the paperwork. And we'll need your parents' okay."

Mateo took the card Dyson extended with a huge grin. "Thank you, sir—Dyson. I'm sure my mom will say yes. I'll text you as soon as I talk to her."

Mateo gave a small wave and rushed down the hallway toward the gym where most of the kids were hanging out. Lexi turned to Dyson.

"That was nice of you."

Dyson shrugged. "He seems like a good kid."

"He is." A very good kid. "And I'm sorry about before with the…"

Dyson chuckled. "I think you embarrassed Mateo more

than me."

She groaned. Just thinking about it had her wanting to crawl into a cave and hide for a week, but Mateo seemed to move on to the firefighter thing pretty quickly, so that was good. But wow, she really needed to stop letting her mouth speak about how much she wanted Dyson when those thoughts were supposed to stay safely locked away in her brain.

"So, what are you working on today?"

"Wiring." He lifted the tool case in his hand. "I might need to turn a few breakers off if that's okay."

She glanced at her phone again. "The kids will be leaving in an hour, should be fine to flip the switch soon."

He nodded. "I have a few minor repairs I can work on until then." He shifted on his feet. "Um, I also had a favor to ask."

"Another one?" When he didn't smile, she laughed. "I'm kidding, of course I'm happy to help. What do you need?"

He rubbed the back of his neck. "My sisters and I have this tradition—kind of like a mini family vacation type thing. We go to Estes Park every year, rent a cabin, go hiking, just kinda chill."

"That sounds lovely." She'd been to Estes a few times. It was only about an hour away from Denver at the entrance to Rocky Mountain National Park. Lovely little tourist town. Great for wildlife viewing.

"Yeah, it's really fun. And, um, usually we include significant others so..."

"Me?" She blinked, understanding settling in. "You want me to go?"

"Think of it as a free vacation."

He smiled, cheeks reddening slightly with that blush she found so adorable.

"You deserve some time off, Lex."

She did. Everyone was always telling her, including her boss. But it was hard to leave when the center needed so much. There was always work to do, always tasks to finish.

"I would love to, but I have so much work to do…"

"It'll be here when you get back," Dyson said. "Everyone needs a little R and R. And I think you've earned a few years' worth."

She laughed, touched by his sweetness and concern. Remembering how she was supposed to be taking more time for herself, taking her needs into account, she smiled and nodded.

"Sounds like a blast. When are you all going?"

"This weekend. We're leaving after my shift is over Friday afternoon."

Lucky for her, she had the weekends off and she had some personal time. She was sure her boss would let her duck out early on Friday. Zoe was here that day, too. Things would be fine.

"Okay. I'm in."

"Thank you so much, Lexi. I really owe you now." He smiled, tapping the case in his hands. "Well, I better get to work."

He passed her, walking down the hallway. She watched him go—correction, she watched his ass as he went and no one could blame her. It was a spectacular ass.

Once Dyson was busy working, she emailed her boss about the PTO and received word back almost immediately with approval. She wasn't surprised, she rarely took any time off. This wasn't the best paying job in the world. Her boss was happy to keep her happy. He promised he'd get the weekend director to come in Friday afternoon and relieve her early.

Next Lexi checked in on one of the volunteers who was helping a group of kids with their homework. Everything ran smoothly that afternoon and before she knew it, all the kids and volunteers had gone home. Lexi locked up and went to find Dyson to let him know it was safe to turn the breakers off now.

She found him in what the kids liked to call the "chill zone." It was a room filled with older donated bean bags, some of them leaking their stuffing, pillows and throws, and three shelves filled with books, manga, comics, and magazines. All donated or bought from secondhand stores.

It was Lexi's favorite room.

"Hey," she said as she leaned against the open doorframe.

Dyson looked up from the comic he was reading, that adorable blush tinting his cheeks.

"Oh hi, sorry I came in here to check and make sure the detectors I installed last week were all working and got distracted." He held up the battered copy of Sandman Volume 1. "I'm a huge Neil Gaiman fan."

"You and Jordan would get along then." She pointed to the comic. "Those are actually his. He donated them when his boyfriend bought him a signed first edition copy last year for his birthday."

Dyson whistled. "That's a keeper."

"That's what I told Jordan."

"Have you read any Gaiman?"

She nodded. "Jordan wouldn't get off my back until I did. I liked Stardust and the one he did with that other author, Good Omens."

"Terry Pratchett, I've read his Discworld series, too. Great books."

"Nerd," she snorted with a laugh.

"Totally." He grinned. "So, what kind of books do you like to read?"

"I like cozy mysteries, memoirs, and romance." Whenever she had the time to read, that is, which wasn't much. What she wouldn't do for a book vacation where all she did was read on the beach, or in a hammock, her bed, anywhere really. Her TBR was a bit out of control.

"I like romance."

She blinked, used to people mocking her whenever she uttered the *R* word.

"Does that surprise you?" He tilted his head.

"Yes, actually." Stepping into the room, she walked over to stand beside him. "You don't really seem like the happily ever after type. You know, with the whole no dating thing."

His smile fell, the happy light in his eyes extinguished, replaced with something...sad. She wished he would open up about what his ex did. It obviously still affected him.

"I think," he started, speaking slowly as if each word had valued importance, "I know that life has its ups and downs. Happily ever after doesn't really exist, because you can't be happy all the time. Bad things happen, that's just life. And some people do find that person who makes the bad things... less bad, or bearable if you want to put it that way. It's a nice thought. The hope there's someone out there for everyone..."

"But?" she asked when he trailed off.

Dyson scowled down at the book in his hands. "But sometimes the hope is all we get."

What a conundrum this man was. He read a genre dedicated to hope and love, yet he didn't want to seek out that love for himself. She knew not everyone needed romantic love, but the way Dyson spoke, the pain she saw in him sometimes, the yearning, it almost seemed like he wanted it, but was too afraid, too wary, to seek it out.

What the hell had his ex done to him?

"Are the kids gone?"

Clearly a subject change. That was fine. She understood exposing yourself emotionally to others was difficult for most people.

"Yes. I just came to tell you it was okay to turn off the

breakers now. I can show you where they are."

He placed the book back on the shelf. "Lead the way."

She took him to the furnace room where the water heater and HVAC system were. Pointing to the box on the far wall, she said, "Right there."

Dyson made his way to the box and she followed. He might need help after all. He set down his case and opened it, pulling out a flashlight and handing it to her.

"I'm going to shut off the electricity so when I fix the wires, I don't electrocute myself."

"Yes, let's keep that from happening, please. I don't want to go on the run from your sisters."

He laughed. "Okay, it's about to get dark in here, so turn that thing on."

She turned the flashlight in her hand, finding the button to click it on and pointing it down so she didn't accidentally shine it in Dyson's eyes and temporarily blind him. He couldn't fix the wiring if he couldn't see.

Dyson opened the breaker box, taking a look at the labeling before turning off half of the switches. The small room plunged into darkness, the only light coming from the flashlight's beam pointed directly at her feet. Lexi wasn't particularly scared of the dark, but that didn't mean she liked it. Zoe was a horror movie buff and made her watch all kinds of spooky things. She knew ghosts and serial killers liked to hide in dark corners.

There's not a serial killer or a ghost in the DYC, Lexi. Get it together or Dyson will think you're a total baby.

"Nothing wrong with being scared of the dark," Dyson chuckled. "And babies aren't scared of anything. I once saw a six-month-old try to hug a tiger like it was a stuffed animal at the zoo. Sweet kid was hugging that glass, screaming, so mad it couldn't get to the actual tiger."

She glanced up at him. The dim light from the flashlight

casting a soft glow, allowing her to see just a hint of his face, his smiling lips, those beautiful hazel eyes.

"I really need to stop saying what I'm thinking, or I might just slip and tell you how much I want to kiss you again." She could try to blame that on her strange habit, but honestly, she needed him to hear it. It was getting harder and harder to keep this attraction inside, and if they were going to spend an entire weekend together? Forget it. No way could she pretend she didn't want to make at least one aspect of their fake relationship real.

Dyson turned to face her, his smile slipping. "Lexi...I—"

"I know," she interrupted before he could go on. "You have rules. You don't want a real relationship and that's fine. As you know, I can't really risk dating right now anyway."

He gave a soft chuckle at the reminder of her bet with Jordan.

"But, rules can be bent a little. I'm not asking you to break your no-girlfriend rule. I was just thinking...we do have chemistry. I mean, there's attraction here."

He said nothing and the bravado she'd been building up all afternoon faltered.

"Right? Please tell me it's not all one-sided or I might actually have to go find a cave to live in for the next century."

He chuckled, a small hint of a smile returning. "It's not one-sided. I feel it too. But your bet?"

"Sex isn't dating. Jordan said so himself." He also warned her to be careful about getting into bed with her fake boyfriend, but she left that part out. She knew what she was doing.

She had no illusions that this thing would turn real. She just wanted to know what it was like, and she needed to burn off this lust before it killed her or worse, made her spout out more inappropriate things in front of the teenagers.

"Just think about it," she said. "No rush, no pressure.

And if you want to bend the rules a little and add sex buddies to our fake arrangement, let me know."

She leaned forward until their lips were a hairbreadth apart. "Hey, Dyson."

"Yeah?" His warm breath caressed her lips.

"I'm going to bend the rules a little and kiss you now."

His nose nudged hers slightly, a tiny rub that sent shivers down her spine, bringing his lips even closer, so close she swore she could taste them already.

"Okay."

Silently cheering her success, she placed a soft and brief kiss on Dyson's lips. His hand reached out to grasp her hip, pulling her closer and deepening the kiss. She opened for him, brushing her tongue against his, reveling in the taste that was unique to Dyson. She wanted nothing more than to pull him to the floor and ride him until she couldn't see anything, hear anything, feel anything, but Dyson.

But this floor was disgustingly dirty, it was already hard to see because the lights were out, and she was being honest when she told him she didn't want to pressure him. So instead of jumping him in the dark, she pulled away, regretfully, handed him the flashlight, and took her cell out to light the way back to her office.

She worked on paperwork by the light of the battery-operated lamp she kept in her office for emergencies. When Dyson was done, he turned the lights back on and headed out, but not before walking her to her car after she locked up.

He was so sweet, and she knew it wouldn't take more than an invite to get him to come back to her place and seal their new arrangement, but she wouldn't do that to him—he needed time to make his decision, and she needed to go home and take a shower.

A *very* cold shower.

Chapter Fifteen

Dyson headed into the DYC. It had been a few days since Lexi agreed to accompany him on his family weekend. A few days since she proposed a change to their deal. A few days since that kiss that started out so innocent but then turned his body inside out.

There had been something about that kiss in particular. It hadn't been to practice. It hadn't been for show. Lexi had kissed him because she wanted to. And he deepened the kiss because *he* wanted to. So what the hell was he going to do about it now? Could he really bend his rules enough to go along with Lexi's plan? Díaz had suggested he float the same deal. Was that a sign he should?

"Hey, Dyson, I didn't know you were fixing things today."

Zoe's cheerful voice interrupted his thoughts. He glanced up at the woman manning the front desk and smiled.

"I'm not. I'm actually here to meet with Mateo. I got some paperwork for him."

A bright smile lit the woman's face. "Right, Lex told me you were helping him out with some junior firefighter program thing. That's really nice of you."

He shrugged, feeling heat rise up his face. "It's nothing. Seems like a good kid."

"He is." She nodded.

"Is, um, Lexi here?" He wasn't here to see her. In fact, he'd be picking her up in just an hour for their weekend trip, but that didn't stop the question from pouring from his lips. Or stop his body from tightening with the desire to catch a glimpse of the woman who'd starred in far too many of his late-night dreams these past few days.

Zoe smiled and gave a small shake of her head. "You just missed her. I practically had to shove her out the door so she could pack for your trip this weekend."

Zoe knew? Oh course she knew, Lexi probably told her coworkers why she was leaving early for the day. And from what he gathered, Zoe was more of a friend. Made him wonder just how much Zoe knew about his and Lexi's arrangement.

"I hope you all have fun up in Estes."

"I'm sure we will."

"It's nice of you to take Lexi. Everyone knows she needs a freaking break." Zoe sighed. "I even caught her sneaking some paperwork in her bag as she was leaving. Can you believe she was trying to take work on her vacation?"

Yes. He could totally believe that.

"You make sure she relaxes and has fun this weekend, okay?"

He nodded. "I'll do my best."

"Good." Zoe smiled and pointed down the hall. "Mateo is in the study room. Third one on the right."

He thanked her and set off, sparing a glance at Lexi's dark, closed office as he passed it. When he entered the study room, he saw Mateo sitting at a table with a boy who looked a few years younger. They were hunched over a paper. The younger kid was frowning as Mateo pointed to something on the paper and explained in a calm voice.

"You forgot to flip the denominator here. See?"

"Crap, I did." The kid vigorously erased and scribbled again on the paper. "I always forget to do that. Stupid!"

"You're not stupid. We all forget stuff. Math is hard, but you got this. You're doing better already."

"Thanks to you." The kid smiled. "Thanks, Mateo."

"Anytime."

Dyson felt a sharp pinch in his chest. This kid was a good one. Spending his free time to help another kid, explaining instead of talking down. For a brief moment he was transported back in time to when his dad used to sit patiently and help Dyson with his math homework.

He didn't want to interrupt, but he was on a timeline. Reaching out, he knocked softly on the doorframe. Two heads popped up as both of the teens looked in his direction.

"Hey, sorry to interrupt, but I got some paperwork for you, Mateo." Dyson smiled, holding up the folder in his hand.

"Oh, hey Mr. O'N—Dyson." Mateo turned his attention back to the other teen. "Is it cool if we finish this up later?"

The kid nodded. "I think I got it now, but can you check my work before school tomorrow?"

"Sure, no problem."

The kid smiled, gathering his things and moving past Dyson with a smile as he left the room.

"It's nice of you to help with homework," Dyson said as he moved into the room and took the chair across from Mateo the younger teen just vacated.

Mateo shrugged, avoiding eye contact. "Not a big deal."

He thought it was, but Mateo was clearly embarrassed by the praise—something Dyson could identify with—so he dropped it. Setting the folder on the table, he opened it and took out the paperwork.

"Okay, so here's everything you need to fill out to apply. I also grabbed a scholarship form. Then there's some stuff for your parents to sign. You said your mom and dad were okay with you doing this, right?"

"My mom is." Mateo dipped his head, gaze falling to his hands, and his fingers tapped the table absently. "My dad died two years ago. Heart attack. Just me and my mom now."

Dyson sucked in a sharp breath. "I'm sorry."

Mateo lifted one shoulder in a halfhearted shrug.

Discomfort roiled in his gut. Dyson didn't like opening up to anyone, but he could practically see the hurt coming off this kid. Like looking into a damn mirror of days past. He remembered the grief, the anger, the deep yawing despair. The hole he swore was eating him alive after his parents died. Some days he feared it would never close up. And it didn't, not really, but it did get easier to deal with.

He couldn't sit here, knowing what the kid was going through, and not say anything. Even if he'd rather face a shot with a six-inch needle than be vulnerable, he knew Mateo needed this. Taking a deep breath, he opened his mouth and tried to connect with the kid.

"Sucks to lose a parent."

At that, the kid's head lifted.

"I lost both my parents. A while ago, but I still miss them. Every day."

Mateo sniffed, rubbing his eyes with the back of his hand. "Yeah, it does suck. And I'm sorry too…about your parents."

"I'm here if you ever…" He shifted uncomfortably in his seat. "Want to talk or anything."

Mateo nodded silently, covertly rubbing at his face again.

The room fell into an awkward silence for a few moments before Mateo cleared his throat, sat up straighter, and reached for the paperwork. "So, what do I need to fill out?"

Clearly the kid was done talking about their crappy

shared experience. Fair enough. It wasn't a happy topic one wanted to wax on about, but he hoped the teen knew he wasn't alone in his grief.

They spent the next twenty minutes going through all the paperwork. Dyson answered all of Mateo's questions, showed the kid where his mom would need to sign and helped him fill out the scholarship application. He wasn't worried about that going through. Most of the kids in the program were on scholarship. Thanks to a generous donation from the Kincaid Foundation, they rarely had to turn anyone down.

"Okay, I think we're good." Dyson gathered all the paperwork back into the folder and handed it over. "Just get your mom to sign where I notated and mail it in. There's a stamped addressed envelope in there so all you have to do is put it in and drop it in a post box."

"Cool." Mateo grabbed the folder and carefully put it in the backpack hanging on his chair. "You working on the center today?"

"No, um, I'm actually about to head out for a trip with Lexi."

"Ms. Martin?"

"Yeah."

A small smile curled the teen's lips. "You guys going on some romantic weekend getaway?"

"My sisters are coming, too, so I don't know how romantic it will be." More nerve-wracking because they would have to spend the entire weekend playing boyfriend and girlfriend while his sisters watched their every move.

Mateo leaned back in his chair. "Hey, at least you're taking her away. Ms. Martin deserves a break."

Even her kids could see she needed time off.

"Ms. Martin is really nice and she's always making sure we get…the stuff we need. She never talks about it, but I know she's had some real asshole boyfriends."

Dyson arched his brow, but Mateo didn't apologize for his swear.

"How do you know that?"

He lifted one shoulder in a halfhearted shrug. "Me and Brycen heard Zoe talking to one of the other volunteers a while back. She said Ms. Martin gave up her vacation because of some center emergency and her fuckwad of a boyfriend took his buddy on it instead even though she paid for it."

Now both eyebrows climbed his forehead.

"Hey, she said it, not me," Mateo said holding up his hands.

Dyson didn't blame Zoe or Mateo; that guy did sound like a fuckwad. Damn, is that what Lexi had to deal with when it came to dating? Jerks who didn't appreciate her? She deserved so much more. She deserved to have everything she wanted.

She wants you.

The thought whispered in his mind.

She did want him, and he wanted her. Her proposition the other night still hadn't left his head. The offer to bend the rules. He wanted it, she wanted it. So why not go for it? Why not take what he wanted and give Lexi what she wanted? As long as his main rule stayed in place, everything would be okay. No one would get hurt.

"Dyson."

He glanced up at Mateo, realizing he'd been lost in his own thoughts for a moment.

"Yeah, what's up?"

Mateo frowned, a serious expression filling the teen's face as he stared Dyson directly in the eye.

"Ms. Martin is awesome. She's really…she's a nice person and works real hard."

He agreed, but he didn't know where the kid was going with this.

"I really appreciate all your help with this firefighter stuff, and I know I'm just a kid to you, but if you hurt her..."

Holy shit, was he really getting threatened by a teenager? Judging by the warning light in the kid's eyes, yes, he was.

"Don't worry, Mateo. I promise I'm not going to hurt Lexi."

Mateo nodded, standing and slinging his backpack over his shoulder. "Cool. Then have fun on your weekend and make sure Ms. Martin smiles a lot."

With that the kid headed out the door. Dyson felt a smile curl his lips as he watched the teen leave. It felt good to help Mateo, connect with him. He and Grace had talked about having kids in the future after they got married, but once it all fell apart...he hadn't really given much thought to his future and kids. He'd help raise his sisters so he wasn't afraid of parenthood, but most of the time that required a partner and Dyson was done with that.

Still, he didn't realize how much he'd missed this. Guiding a young mind, offering help to someone who needed it. He didn't see fatherhood in his future, but maybe he could do more of this. More mentoring, helping kids like Mateo.

He tucked the thought away to examine later.

Dyson stood and made his way out of the center, waving goodbye to Zoe as he left. It was time to head over to Lexi's and pick her up for the weekend. A million thoughts swirled in his head, but one in particular kept flying to the forefront.

"Make her smile a lot."

He grinned as he slid into his car and started the engine. Yes, they could do this. The rules could be bent a little.

And he was damn sure going to make Lexi have a big, satisfied smile on her face. All weekend long.

Chapter Sixteen

Lucifer twined his way through Lexi's legs as she walked toward her bedroom door. She nearly tripped, almost dropping the suitcase she held in her hand.

"Lucifer!" She scowled down at the cat. "I know you hate it when I leave, sweetie, but I promise I'll be back Sunday night."

"You know he's just trying to make you feel guilty so you'll give him extra catnip."

She glanced up to see Jordan standing in her doorway. "Oh, like you weren't going to give him some the second I left."

"Hell yeah I am. Luci and I have a deal. He doesn't destroy my shoes and I supply him with enough catnip to keep him mellow while you're out of town."

"You're a terrible influence on each other."

She made her way out into the living room, double-checking her mental list to make sure she hadn't forgotten anything for this weekend.

Charger for my phone. Check

Toiletries. Check.

Clothing. Check.

Sexy underwear just in case... Double check.

She hadn't spoken to Dyson since their conversation—okay, her proposition—in the furnace room. They'd texted back and forth a bit about the trip and such, but he hadn't mentioned her proposal and she wasn't going to pressure him by bringing it up. But she really, really hoped he agreed. She was so wound up with need for Dyson not even her bedside drawer of fun could do anything to take the edge off. And she'd tried. So much she had to grab new batteries at the store the other day.

"Got everything you need?" Jordan asked.

She set her suitcase down by the front door and scooped up Lucifer, rubbing her face in the soft black fur. He nudged his head into her face, giving her a mouthful of cat hair.

"I need a snuggle from my fur baby before I go."

Lucifer meowed and nipped at her nose. His way of saying "I love you and I'll miss you, but I'm done now." She put the cat down and accepted the lint roller from Jordan.

"Thanks, don't want to get into a car covered in cat hair. I'm still trying to impress his sisters."

"If they don't love you, they're clearly awful people."

Dragging the brush over her blue T-shirt and down her jean shorts, she laughed. "You have to say that because you're my best friend, but don't worry. I think they like me, and I like them."

"And you like Dyson." Jordan leaned against the coat closet door.

"Sure, what's not to like? He's handsome, sweet, caring, generous—"

"And he's not your real boyfriend," Jordan interrupted.

"I know that." She scowled, rolling the brush over every spot of her clothing even though she'd already removed all the cat hairs.

"Do you?"

With a sigh, she handed the brush back to Jordan, who opened the closet door and put it in its spot on the shelf before closing the door and leaning against it again. This time with his arms crossed over his chest.

"Yes I do. Besides, my mental health knows what's at stake. I will not be scarred for life by your twisted need to get me to face my clown phobia."

"They're literally children's entertainers. I don't know why they scare you so much."

"Hey! A lot of people have clown phobias." She waved a hand over her face. "It's the exaggerated makeup. You can't tell what they really look like. Also, the fact that my brother made me watch *IT* when I was like eight."

She shuddered at the memories of a white-faced Tim Curry, mouth agape with razor-sharp teeth.

"I'm not letting anything get real." Except the sex, Dyson willing. "I love you for caring about me, but I'll be fine. I got this."

"Famous last words."

She stuck her tongue out at him then pulled him in for a hug. A chime sounded from her pocket. She pulled out her cell and read the text from Dyson that said he would be there in five minutes.

"I gotta go, but I love you and thank you for taking care of Lucifer this weekend. Love you, baby!"

The cat flicked his tail, turned, and headed toward his favorite sunning spot on the living room windowsill.

"Yeah, I'll miss you, too," she snorted.

Jordan opened the front door, scooping up her suitcase and handing it over. "Be good."

"No promises." She grinned back, grabbing her bag and heading out the door.

Since she had her suitcase, she skipped the stairs and headed to the elevator. The doors opened just as Dyson's car pulled up. She hurried out of the elevator and through the front doors. He parked and popped the trunk, getting out of the driver seat and moving over to her.

"Hi," he smiled, reaching for her bag. "This it?"

She grinned back, a swarm of butterflies taking flight in her stomach at the sight of him.

"Yup."

Gently taking the suitcase from her hands, he placed it in the car and shut the trunk. "See, that's how it's done," he muttered under his breath.

"What?"

He came back over to her side, opening her car door and motioning for her to enter.

"One suitcase."

Was she supposed to have more? As she slipped into the car, she stared up at him in confusion. "It's a weekend trip. How much was I supposed to pack?"

A small chuckle left his lips. "Oh no, you got it right. I have only one suitcase, too. So does Macy, but Gemma…let's just say my sister likes to be prepared for any eventuality and therefore overpacks every time. I think my last count had her at three."

Three suitcases for a two-night stay? Seemed excessive, but she supposed being overprepared was better than underprepared. Maybe Dyson's sister had a good reason for bringing everything along with her. And speaking of his sisters, she noticed with a quick glance in the back seat that they weren't in the car.

"Where are Gemma and Macy?"

"They took Gemma's car up. Gonna meet us there. I always drive separately in case there's an emergency I need to get back for. Doesn't happen often, but I make it a rule to always be prepared."

She laughed. "You need that on a T-shirt. I think it's your life's motto."

His cheeks reddened and for half a moment, she feared she'd upset him, but then he rubbed the back of his neck and sheepishly answered.

"Um, yeah, Gemma might have gotten me a shirt that says almost exactly that for my last birthday."

She burst out laughing. Dyson rolled his eyes with a smile, shutting her door and moving around the car to retake his seat on the driver's side. He pulled out of her apartment complex and onto the road. Within ten minutes they were out of the city and on the highway, heading toward the mountains.

"It's so great that you and your sisters get to spend so much time together."

Dyson kept his eyes on the road as he asked, "You don't get to see your siblings much?"

"Sadly, no." She stared out the window at the passing scenery. The homes getting sparser, the trees getting thicker, the mountains in the distance reaching higher as they moved closer. "My sister lives in Ohio and my brother moved to Washington a few years ago."

"What about your parents?"

"When my brother and his wife had their son, Mom and Dad decided to retire near them so they could spoil their grandbaby with all the love in the world." She missed them terribly, but she knew they all had their own lives to live. They couldn't stay in Colorado just because she missed seeing them all the time.

"Sounds wonderful," Dyson's softly spoken words echoed in the car.

Lexi turned from staring out the window to glance at the man beside her. Guilt washed over her as she remembered Dyson's parents were gone. He would never get to see them again. They'd never get the chance to spoil any future grandchildren Dyson or his sisters might give them. She mentally smacked herself for her insensitivity. How could she have forgotten?

"Oh Dyson." She placed a hand on his thigh, giving it a comforting squeeze. "I'm so sorry. I didn't mean to bring up any—"

"It's fine." He spared her a quick glance with a soft smile before turning his attention back to the road. "I'll always miss them, but it's been a long time."

Yes, but she imagined the pain of losing a loved one never disappeared entirely.

"Do you go out to Washington for the holidays?"

She sat back in her seat, knowing he was turning the focus of the conversation back to her. She understood. Loss was a hard thing to talk about. She was happy to drop a painful subject if that's what Dyson wanted.

Jordan might say she was doing it again, bending over backward to see to the needs of others. But it wasn't like she wanted to drag up and dissect Dyson's pain. He'd share if he wanted to. She had no need to pull it from him.

She launched into stories of past family get-togethers. The few and far between trips where she went out to see her family. She'd been lucky enough to sneak a quick two-day trip to visit her nephew a few months after he was born. They usually gathered at her brother's house for the holidays, but last Christmas she hadn't made it because the center had been understaffed and she couldn't get the time off.

Talking about her family with Dyson made her realize how much she missed them.

"Hopefully this weekend will be proof that you need to take more time for yourself." He reached out a hand, grasping hers and rubbing his thumb along the back of her hand. "You do too much for others, Lexi."

Her heart pounded in her chest at his touch, the butterflies moving from her stomach all the way up her throat, threatening to burst from her lips on a nervous giggle. But she held it in and instead replied in a teasing voice, "Says the man I'm currently doing a favor for."

He winced and she couldn't stop the laughter from escaping.

"I'm teasing, Dyson. And don't worry. I do have a trip planned for the end of the summer. An entire week for our family reunion. We're going on a cruise."

"Sounds fun."

They spent the rest of the drive talking about their favorite movies and books. He told her some funny stories about the learning curve of suddenly raising two teenage girls. She laughed when he shared the sweet, but clearly embarrassing story of the first time his sisters had to send him out for feminine hygiene products and he came back with one of everything just in case. Before she knew it, they'd arrived in Estes and were pulling up at the cabin. His sister's car was already there, but they must have been inside because Lexi didn't see anyone.

Lexi whistled as she stared at the car in the driveway. "Think your sister has enough bumper stickers?"

The entire back was covered. All different shapes, sizes, colors. Each with a different saying or slogan. She laughed as she read one that stated the elevation of Estes followed by THIS WHOLE TOWN IS HIGH with a pot leaf underneath it. There were so many the only thing visible on the back of the car were the taillights and the license plate.

"Yeah," Dyson shook his head with a sigh. "Macy has a thing for bumper stickers. You know how some people collect postcards or those tiny spoons? My sister collects bumper stickers."

Lexi laughed. Everyone had their thing, she supposed,

though all that clutter would make the car a pain to resell if Macy ever wanted to.

"Shall we?" Dyson asked as he opened his car door and motioned to the cabin.

Lexi stared at the log cabin before them. It was beautiful. It had an older type of aesthetic with the natural logs forming the outside of the cabin like those Lincoln logs she and her siblings used to play with at their grandparents' house. A porch appeared to wrap all the way around the house and there was a large porch swing next to the front door. She remembered Dyson saying something about a hot tub in back.

Her good bits perked up at the thought of sharing a hot and steamy soak with Dyson.

Huge pine and aspen trees surrounded the property and Lexi could barely see the neighboring cabin. A strange concept being so far away from a neighbor. She was used to the Portmans pounding on the wall whenever she and Jordan watched a movie with the volume above twenty.

She got out of the car and took a deep breath, sighing when all her muscles relaxed as the scent of fresh air and dirt filled her nostrils. She might not be the best at camping, but she did appreciate getting out into nature once in a while. Felt good to unplug and unwind.

"I can put your suitcase in our room if you'd like."

She turned to see Dyson holding her suitcase as well as his own. At the words *our room* her thighs clenched. Right, they would be sharing a room, because they were adults in a relationship—according to his sisters—and so why wouldn't they share a room?

Because if I get into a room alone with this man, I might rip my clothes off and beg him to have his way with me.

"About that," Dyson glanced over to the closed door of the cabin. He tilted his head down, placing his lips next to her ear. "I've been thinking, and if you're okay with adding benefits, then so am I."

She pulled back in shock. Sure, she'd been hoping he would agree, but a part of her had feared he wasn't feeling this as much as she was. "Really?"

He nodded, a hungry light in his eyes. "As long as we're on the same page? No relationship. My rule still stands, but I'm okay with…bending it a little."

Him and his rules. She had to admit, they got a bit frustrating at times. But she supposed, since he was bending this one, she shouldn't complain.

"No relationship," she agreed. She glanced back to the house, but his sisters hadn't come out yet. "Except the fake one, of course."

He frowned. "Yeah…are you sure? I don't want to… confuse anything if we add sex into the mix. And your bet with Jordan…"

He had a valid point, but her logical brain had been overtaken by her horny demon brain days ago.

"Trust me. I'm not about to clean that entire apartment. Jordan has been known to leave plates of food under his bed and I'm pretty sure he's created botulism in there. No way am I risking it. I can stay clear if you can. What happens in Estes stays in Estes."

He chuckled. "I think that's Vegas."

"Tom-ay-to, tom-ah-to."

He laughed, setting down the suitcases and cupping her face in his hands. He gently pulled her to him. She went willingly. *Very* willingly. She missed the feel of his lips so much.

This kiss was different from the others, still as hot, still as delicious, but now they were kissing because they wanted to. Not to convince his sisters, not to convince each other. This was a kiss of desire simply because they both wanted it. And it was bliss.

"Hey, you two, stop making out and get in here," Gemma called from the open doorway. "We want to get settled and grab some grub so save the hanky-panky for later. We gave you the downstairs bedroom and I brought my noise cancelling headphones so I don't have to be scarred for life."

Dyson grinned against her lips, his breath caressing her mouth as he spoke. "We better get in there before Gemma picks the restaurant. She has terrible taste."

"I heard that, jerkface! And just for that I'm voting for Cowboy Burgers."

Lexi hadn't been to Estes in a while, but the name sounded familiar. "Is that the kitschy place that all the tourists go to?"

"Yes," Dyson answered. "And their food is fine, but it's always super busy and loud. She knows it's my least favorite restaurant here."

Laughing, she grabbed her suitcase and his hand and tugged. "We better get in there, then."

Chapter Seventeen

Lexi leaned against Dyson as they made their way inside, reveling in the feel of his warm strength. This weekend just went from potential torture fest to—no, wait, it was still torture because now that he said yes, they had to wait until later tonight. His sisters wanted to go into town and window-shop, have dinner, do tourist things. Which meant she couldn't get naked with Dyson for another few hours.

Yup, still torture.

"Wow," she smiled, eyes widening as she took in her surroundings. "This place is amazing."

It was amazing. The cabin was small but clean, and the large windows in the living room area gave the illusion of a bigger space. A tiny kitchen with stainless steel appliances was off to the right. There was a staircase leading to an upstairs area and a hallway beside it which she assumed led to the bedroom Gemma spoke of. Their bedroom.

Shivers of anticipation shook her knees at the thought.

"Let's drop our stuff and head into town," Macy said, dragging her suitcase up the stairs. "We have only an hour and a half until most shops start closing and I want to get in some shopping before dinner."

"No more bumper stickers!" Gemma called out, following her sister up the stairs, arms full. "You have too many on that car already."

"I'm going to find one that says my sister is an annoying bit—"

"Children, behave," Dyson called up to them.

Lexi covered a laugh as both the women raised their middle fingers, calling down to Dyson in high-pitched voices, "Yes, *Dad.*"

He sighed heavily, rolling his eyes. "Sorry about them."

"I think they're wonderful." She rose up to place a soft kiss to his cheek. "And so are you."

He grinned, a hungry look heating his gaze. "We should go to the bedroom."

Her thighs quivered, core tightening with need.

"To unpack," he finished with a cheeky smile.

"Tease," she accused.

Dyson grasped her hand again, tugging her down the hallway to an open doorway. She admired the decent-sized bedroom with the large bed, imagining all the things she was going to do to Dyson later under those covers, when the door slammed behind her. She turned to see Dyson leaning against the wall, his eyes burning with desire as he stared at her.

"Dyson?"

"We don't have much time, not nearly enough for what I want, but you accused me of being a tease and I have to defend my honor."

He stalked toward her, a wild look she'd never seen before on his face. Oooh, she really liked rule-bending Dyson.

Her suitcase slipped from her hand, falling to the carpeted floor with a soft thud. Within seconds, Dyson was standing in front of her, stark need etched on every line of his face. He cupped her cheek, slamming his mouth down on hers in a hungry, desperate kiss.

Lexi sucked in a sharp breath, moaning when his tongue came out to taste hers. Dyson was potent. Her head swirled, floating away on a cloud of lust as the man backed her up until she was flush against the wall. His lips left her mouth, trailing down her neck. His hands moved over her chest, gently cupping her breasts, his thumbs rubbing the stiff peaks of her nipples, hardening them almost to the point of pain.

She bit the inside of her cheek to keep from crying out. His sisters were directly above them. She had no idea how much time they needed to unpack. No clue how long she and Dyson had with their stolen moment, but she knew if he stopped now, she might literally die.

Thankfully, he didn't stop. His hands continued to move down, unsnapping the button of her shorts and pulling down the zipper. He pushed the jean shorts off her hips along with her underwear. It should have been strange standing in front of him with her shirt still on and no bottoms, but it wasn't. She was so turned on, she didn't even care she was straight up Donald Ducking it.

"I'm sorry," Dyson said with a laugh. "Did you just say you were Donald Ducking it?"

"No, yes, I don't know. Ignore me and keep defending your honor."

He chuckled, his fingers stroking through her curls as he pressed soft kisses to her hips. She felt the gentle brush of his thumb against her center. Her thighs tightened in response. A warm palm on her inner thigh made her glance down. She sucked in a deep breath at the sight of Dyson on his knees before her.

"Open for me, Lexi. Please."

Letting out her breath, she widened her stance, making room for Dyson between her legs. The wicked grin he gave her made her heart skip a beat. But it stopped altogether when he leaned forward, eyes still locked on hers as his tongue came out to swipe against her.

She shoved her hand in her mouth to keep from crying out as Dyson used his mouth to turn her body into a quivering ball of want. He licked and sucked, using the exact right amount of pressure to have her body tightening with the need for release. When he slipped two fingers inside, she nearly fell over, her legs turning into useless jelly. Dyson used his free hand to tug one of her legs up and over his shoulder. The position opened her even more to him.

"Dyson," she panted, trying with all her might to keep her voice down. "I'm close."

He kept up his ministrations, working her body as if he'd known it his entire life. His fingers curled inside her, hitting that sweet spot that made her eyes cross while his mouth still devoured her until she felt herself cresting over a wave of bliss.

She did her best to muffle her cry as her orgasm hit. Muscles giving out, she sank back against the wall, heaving breaths coming from her chest. A faint chuckle reached her ears. Dyson placed one more soft kiss against her and rose.

"So, did I defend my honor?"

She tried to lift her hand to his cheek, but her energy was spent. The best she could do was a soft pat to his abs. "I'd call that an arousing success."

He laughed at her silly joke.

Glancing down, she saw the hard bulge of Dyson's erection straining his jeans. A pop of energy sparked within. Her mouth watered. She reached down, cupping him in her hand through his pants.

Dyson hissed. "Fuck, Lexi."

Yes, she was hoping they would get to that very soon. His hips pushed into her hand. She squeezed gently, rubbing her

hand up and down his impressive length. His mouth found
hers again. She could taste herself on him. An intoxicating
aphrodisiac she'd never thought of before. Never, before
Dyson.

Her fingers fumbled with the button of his jeans. If luck
was with them, they'd have a few more minutes to play—

"Dyson! Lexi! You two ready yet? Macy's getting antsy."

Dyson groaned—not a happy groan. Pulling away from
her, he glared at the door.

"We should get going."

She glanced down at the strain in his jeans. Much more
prevalent now than it was a minute ago. "But—"

"Trust me, I know." He took a large step back, adjusted
his pants with a small wince. "But if we continue, I'm going to
strip you completely naked and spend hours worshiping your
body on every single surface of this room."

"Sounds fantastic to me."

He grinned. "Later, I promise, but Gemma tends to get
hangry if she doesn't eat. So, dinner first, worshiping your
glorious body after."

How could she be so turned on and turned to absolute
mush at the same time?

Dyson was so kind and caring and, if this little preview
was anything to go by, a very generous lover. As much as
she liked his sisters, a small part of her wished they were
anywhere but here right now.

"Okay, I just need to…" She motioned to the small door
where the attached bath was. "Freshen up and change."

Dyson nodded. "I'll go tell my sisters you'll be right out."

With another soft kiss to her lips, he turned and headed
out the bedroom door, closing it softly behind him. Lexi
sighed, sinking against the wall for half a second. Letting her
body wind down from the absolute soul-destroying power
of the man. She couldn't remember the last time she'd had

an orgasm that powerful. And that was just a taste of what he could do. Her mouth watered just thinking about what tonight would hold.

"I might not survive." She giggled at the idea. What a way to go, though.

Knowing time was ticking, Lexi moved to her suitcase, opening it up to grab a fresh pair of underwear. She dug around until she came up with the red lace panties she bought specifically for this trip. After half a second of thought, she grabbed the matching bra as well. Dyson deserved a treat. She didn't match her underwear and bra for just anybody.

She stood, heading to the bathroom to clean up, grabbing her discarded shorts on the way. After cleaning up and dressing, she dragged a brush through her hair and fixed her lipstick, hoping there weren't any signs of "your brother just went down on me in the bedroom" on her face for Macy and Gemma to see.

As she stepped into the living room area, she saw the siblings standing around arguing. Correction: Gemma and Macy were arguing. Dyson was standing against the wall near the front door, staring at his sisters with an exasperated but loving smile on his face. When he spotted her, his smile went from sweet to heated. A flush rose up her body as his eyes locked on her, filled with carnal knowledge of her body and promises of more to come.

"We should shop before dinner," Macy said.

"I'm starving!" Gemma complained. "Eat first."

"But then all the stores will be closed." Macy countered. "This is Estes not Denver. The sidewalk rolls up at seven."

"I have a protein bar in my purse," Lexi offered, hoping to hurry this evening along. Selfish? Maybe, but that small stolen moment with Dyson hadn't been nearly enough to quench her thirst for the man. "You can have it to tide you over until dinner. It's a really yummy one too, blueberry almond."

Gemma grinned. "Lexi, you are just the sweetest."

Dyson's sister came over and linked arms with her.

"So…shopping first?" Macy asked with hopeful eyes.

Lexi pulled the protein bar from her purse and handed it to Gemma, who gave her a small squeeze, then ripped the package and bit into it.

"See," Dyson chuckled. "Hangry."

"Stuff it, Dy," Gemma said around a mouth full of blueberry bar bliss. "Mmmmm, ohmigaw, Lexi this is amazing! What's the brand?"

She laughed as Gemma inspected the wrapper, bringing out her phone and snapping a pic as she talked about ordering the bar in bulk. Dyson grabbed her hand as they left the cabin. Her skin tingled with the memory of what that hand did not ten minutes ago…body tense and ready for another round.

As he opened the car door for her, his hand left hers to slide down her arm, over her hip, where his fingers lightly caressed the round curve of her ass. She held back a moan, cursing the need for dinner and towns that closed at eight p.m.

Once they were all piled into the car, they headed into town for what Lexi was sure to be the longest night of her life.

Chapter Eighteen

This was the longest night of his life.

After an hour wandering the main drag of Estes—honestly it was the only drag—they decided to grab some dinner. Dyson suggested Poppy's, a family favorite pizza place. Dinner was delicious, as always, but he was having trouble concentrating on the food when his mind was obsessed with the woman sitting next to him.

He never should have started their little interlude in the bedroom. He hadn't been able to take the time he wanted with Lexi. But once they'd agreed to add benefits to their deal, he hadn't been able to stop himself from touching her the way he'd been dreaming about for weeks. He could still taste her on his tongue. A delicious, intoxicating sweetness that was unique to Lexi.

He wanted more. He wanted all of her.

It was all he could think about. Dammit! He should have waited to mention it until after dinner. Maybe then he would have been able to control himself earlier. Now he had to sit through hours of his sisters telling the most embarrassing childhood stories they could remember to his fake girlfriend while he smiled and rolled his eyes, when what he really wanted to do was take Lexi back to the cabin and test the soundproofing of the first floor.

She wasn't helping matters, either.

When he'd left her to freshen up, she'd said she was going to change, but when she came back into the living room...she hadn't changed her clothes. At least not the ones he could see. Which made him wonder just what she had changed and when he would be able to see them. He was pretty sure it was some kind of sexy lingerie. His imagination ran wild during dinner, so focused on Lexi and what the night held.

Finally dinner ended and they headed back to the cabin.

"Time for charades!" Gemma bounced up and down as they entered the vacation home.

Dyson stifled a groan. Usually charades with his sisters was a rolling on the floor laughing kind of good time, but he didn't want to play games right now. Unless those games included Lexi and playing "find all her erogenous zones."

Sounded like the best game in the world to him.

But he didn't want to ruin family tradition—they always played charades the first night—or appear too eager to get his fake girlfriend alone, so he smiled and said, "I'll get the drinks."

He grabbed the six-pack of hard cider Macy placed in the fridge earlier and brought it to the living room. Gemma was already standing at the front of the room, eager and ready to go. Macy was sprawled across the recliner, her legs on one chair arm, head resting on the other. Lexi sat on the large couch. Glancing up, she smiled at him and patted the seat next to her.

Like he could turn down that invitation.

Handing each of his sisters a drink, he sat next to Lexi and passed hers over.

"Thank you." She smiled, placing a soft, but very hot kiss to his lips.

He wanted to deepen the kiss, but his sisters were a few feet away. Instead, he dipped his chin in acknowledgment and turned his attention to Gemma.

"Movie!" Macy yelled as Gemma started to pantomime her clue.

"Three words," Lexi chimed in.

Gemma started fake heaving; without any sound it was a hilarious thing to see, but he had no idea what kind of movie that could refer to.

"The Big Sick!" Lexi screamed.

"Yes!" Gemma hopped up and down with exuberance. "You're up, Lexi."

She handed him her drink and rose, high-fiving Gemma as his sister came to sit beside him.

"Winner on the first round," Gemma whispered to him. "She's a keeper, Dy."

She was, but not for him. He might be bending his rule with this whole adding benefits to their deal thing, but he wasn't breaking it. He didn't want to keep anyone. Not anymore. But he did like Lexi and he sure as hell was attracted to her. Luckiest of all, they were on the same page about what they wanted. Their expectations were clear and agreed upon.

He was just going to ignore that small pang of jealousy deep inside him at the thought of another man getting to be the one to spend forever with Lexi. That was just leftover sentiment from when he used to believe he could have that sort of thing.

The night dragged on far longer than he wanted it to. It was nice spending quality fun time with his sisters, but he really wanted to spend some quality naked time with Lexi.

Around eleven Macy gave a jaw-cracking yawn. "All right, I'm beat. I'm calling it. Goodnight all."

"I'm still good to go." Gemma smiled at Lexi. "Anyone up for a game of Risk?"

"Oh, I, um..."

Lexi frowned, glancing at him, desire burning in her eyes, but the worried expression on her face told him she didn't want to upset his sister.

"I'm kidding, Lex." Gemma laughed, heading for the stairs. "Risk takes hours to play, also I hate it. I know you want to get to...*bed*."

"Gemma," he warned, not wanting his sister to embarrass Lexi, but other than the small blush on her cheeks, she didn't seem upset by his outrageous little sister.

Everyone said their chorus of goodnights and headed off to their rooms. Then it was just him and Lexi. She rose from the couch, walking over to him with a sensual gait—or like a tiger stalking its prey. He would gladly let her eat him up any day.

As long as he could return the favor.

"Shall we?"

She ran her fingers across his chest, and he could have sworn the heat singed his shirt right off. He glanced down. Nope. Still there.

She moved past him toward their bedroom, and Dyson followed, enjoying the sway of her hips and the view of her fantastic ass as he trailed behind her. Once they were in the bedroom, he shut the door. The main lights were off, but the bathroom light had been left on and it cast a soft glow across the room. Lexi stood by the bed, a vision in shorts and a T-shirt. Honestly it was the sexiest thing he'd ever seen. Because it was her.

Neither of them spoke. The tension in the air was so thick, he was choking on it. Should he say something first? Wait for her to take the lead? Contrary to what Hollywood portrayed, men were not always confident and in control in the bedroom. He wanted to please Lexi. He didn't want her uncomfortable or unsure in any way. So he waited for her to make the first move.

Her gaze roamed over him, eyes eating him up with a hunger that he could feel deep inside. Still she said nothing, simply stared. That sexy gaze of hers was driving him wild. His control was hanging on by a frayed thread at this point.

Pushing away from the door, he took a few steps forward and asked, "What do you want?"

There. The ball was in her court now, and he would happily cater to her every request.

"Take your shirt off." Her eyes widened as if she shocked herself with the demand. A small smile curled her lips as she blushed. "Please."

Lifting one arm, he reached behind his back, grabbed a handful of his T-shirt, and yanked it off over his head, tossing it to the floor. Everyone knew you didn't have to use the laundry basket during vacation. Besides, he planned to have a pile of their clothing on the floor soon.

"Holy hell." The words whispered out of her.

His body burned as she licked her lips while staring at him. Oh yes, he planned to have them both naked, very, very soon.

• • •

Lexi sucked in a sharp breath at the glorious sight of Dyson's naked chest. She knew firefighters had to keep in shape for their job, but dang! Dyson didn't have a six-pack, oh no, there were eight of those delicious washboards on him and she couldn't wait to run her tongue over every single one of them.

"I want all of that between my thighs, right now," she whispered.

He chuckled and she looked up to see a wolfish grin on

his face.

"I meant to say that out loud," she stated, in case there was any doubt in his mind.

Dyson smiled, slowly and with just a hint of wickedness. "I know, and sweetheart, if that's what you want, I'm happy to oblige."

He gripped the bottom of her shirt, brow arching in question. She nodded, lifting her arms so he could pull it up and over her head.

"Damn." The word rushed out of him.

She was so happy she'd changed into the red lacy bra and panties set. The demi bra and thong were uncomfortable as all get out, but the expression on Dyson's face was worth it and he didn't even have her pants off yet.

"It is totally fine if they don't." He glanced up into her eyes. "But do the bottoms match?"

Curling her fingers into her palms to keep herself from reaching out and tossing him on the bed, she gave him a sly smile and said, "Why don't you find out?"

He growled, scooping her into his arms and gently placing her on the bed. He was so gentle, but not in a sexist way—as if she were glass that might break—but in a considerate way. Like she was precious, worthy of reverence.

"You are," he answered.

Oops, she better watch her mouth tonight or she might start calling the man a sex god and giving him a big head. Which was a laugh because if there was one thing Dyson was not, it was cocky.

His hands caressed her as he slid them down her sides, his thumbs gently rubbing against the underside of her breasts. Who knew that could be such an erogenous zone? But as Dyson rubbed back and forth she found her breath quickening, her thong dampening, and her patience running thin.

"Teasing again, Dyson?" she asked with a sassy smile. Her grin disappeared on a sharp breath as he leaned down to take one taut nipple in his mouth.

"Never. How about I take the edge off for you?"

Yes please!

His mouth left her breast—dang it—and traveled down her stomach, pausing to kiss right below her belly button and continuing onward. His thumbs followed suit, working the button and zipper on her shorts open and dragging them down and off. For a moment he was gone. She heard a soft swear, something about "holy shit, red, my favorite color."

She made a mental note of that.

"I gotta say, sweetheart. I feel pretty honored about the matching set."

He should. Matching underwear was a privilege. One reserved for super sexy, sweet, and kind firefighters who promised her a night of screaming orgasms. Thank all the white noise in the world his sisters were on the second floor and Gemma had a fan going. She would be mortified if they heard anything, even if they knew what she and Dyson were doing anyway.

All thought flew from her mind as she felt Dyson's knuckles softly rub against the fabric the fashion industry dared to call underwear. The combination of his light pressure with the silky sensation of the thong had her body tightening with need.

"Dyson!" she cried out, not sure what she wanted him to do, but wanting him to do it *now.*

Suddenly his knuckles were replaced with his mouth. She could feel his warm breath through the cloth as he kissed her between her legs. It was amazing, but not enough.

"I've just gotten started," he answered her.

He hooked a finger in the thin floss-like waistband and pulled the panties off, tossing them...somewhere—who the heck cared? Not her; she currently had the most delicious man ever between her thighs and she planned on concentrating on nothing but that for the rest of the night.

She cried out as Dyson placed his mouth over her again, this time flesh to flesh. Her knees clenched around his head. She supposed she should apologize, but he didn't seem to mind it. In fact, he was currently using that amazing tongue to render her completely and utterly speechless. She knew she must be making sounds, but none of them were actual words, because she couldn't remember what words were at the moment.

His hand slid up and over her hip, thumb finding just the right spot to send her flying into one of the best orgasms she'd ever had in her life. Even better than the one he gave her before dinner. How was that possible?

"Wow." She sighed, head fuzzier than when she drank an entire bottle of wine that one night at her twenty-fifth birthday party.

"You are so damn sexy."

She was sexy? This man had her reaching her peak in less than five minutes and he thought she was sexy?

She crooked a finger at him. "Lose the pants and get up here."

"Anything you say."

Ooooh, she liked that attitude.

Dyson shucked off his pants and boxers, reaching over to the nightstand and pulling open the drawer. He sat back on his heels and chuckled. Normally laughter during sex would make her think she'd said something embarrassing, but Dyson seemed amused by something else, and she knew he would never poke fun at her for her odd habit.

"What?"

He grinned, pulling out two boxes of condoms from the nightstand drawer. "Looks like we both had the same idea."

She smothered her laugh with a hand. How had she missed his box of condoms when she threw hers in there? Truthfully, she hadn't really been looking, she just opened the drawer and tossed them in, excited that he'd agreed. She'd brought the condoms up in hopes of this exact situation. The fact that he did, too, meant...well she didn't really know what it meant besides they were attracted to each other and prudent about safe sex.

She wouldn't read more into it than that.

"Mine are ribbed, but we can use yours if you'd rather."

"The lady gets what the lady likes. I prefer to cater to *her pleasure.*"

Damn, if he were her real boyfriend, she'd never give him up. As it was, she was going to enjoy the time she had.

Dyson opened the box, pulling a package off the strip and ripping it open.

"Let me," she pleaded, because it seemed he was the only one doing the touching tonight, and she really wanted a turn.

He held out his hand, and she took the condom from his fingers. Sitting up, she reached over and grasped his hard cock in her hand. He hissed out a breath as she pumped him, reveling in the velvety soft feel of his firmness.

"I think it's my turn now to say I don't like teasing."

"Desperate?"

"Only since the first moment I kissed you."

Seriously, he had to stop saying stuff like that.

Reminding herself his sweetness was just a part of who he was, and she shouldn't look deeper into it, she rolled the condom onto his length. Instead of lying back down, she rose to her knees. "Sit back and cross your legs."

Dyson obeyed her command, sitting back on the bed with a grin. She climbed into his lap, grasping his cock and positioning him perfectly. A gasp left her as she sank down. When she was fully seated, she wrapped her legs around him.

His large hands came out to grasp her hips, moving her slowly up and down. The position had her feeling every inch of him, and he angled her hips so she hit just right with each stroke.

"Fuck," he swore, forehead pressed against hers. "You feel amazing."

So did he. She tilted her face, capturing his lips, tasting herself on him as he quickened the pace. She leaned back, placing her arms against the mattress. Dyson's right hand left her hip, his thumb seeking out her clit and rubbing against it with delicious pressure.

"Yes," she cried out. "Don't stop."

He didn't. He kept up the tiny circle, using just the right amount of pressure that had her eyes crossing.

"You're so damn beautiful, Lexi."

Her eyes opened at his awe-filled words. She glanced into his eyes, seeing nothing but the truth in them. Guys had called her beautiful before, sure, but she'd never felt the words before. Not like she did now. Dyson's sharp hazel gaze focused completely on her. Not on her body, but her face. As he thrust into her, pressed his thumb against her, he was staring at her. Deep into her eyes. So deep she felt it in her very soul.

Worried at the intensity of the feeling she leaned forward, capturing his lips with her own, stroking her tongue against his. Her eyes closed, reveling in the sensation. She shouldn't be thinking right now, she should be feeling. Thinking and hoping would only lead her down a path she shouldn't even be considering.

His thrust increased, harder, faster. She moved along with him, pressing herself deeper until she wasn't sure where she ended and he began.

Soon she felt her body tightening again. She tried to hold off, but it was too much, too good, and soon she was screaming out with another orgasm. Dyson swallowed her screams, holding her to him as he lost himself inside her.

She collapsed against him, face pressed into his neck. He held her, their breathing rough and erratic. She'd never had sex as intense as that.

"Me either," Dyson said with a small laugh.

She kissed his shoulder, loving that her outbursts didn't bother him. "We should probably move a fire extinguisher near the bed."

"There's one under the bathroom sink," he said with complete sincerity.

She laughed, pulling back to look at him. "You are one of a kind, Dyson O'Neil."

He reached up and brushed some of the matted hair from her face. "I could say the same about you, Lexi Martin."

Her heart fluttered, but she attributed it to the two awesome orgasms and not getting all sentimental over her fake boyfriend. Maybe she should start repeating "cleaning in a clown costume" to herself after every kiss, just to remember what was at stake in case she started to get any silly ideas about all this.

"What do you say we go take a shower?" he asked.

Knowing she needed to keep all feelings out of this if she were going to get through it, she bit her lip and answered, "Only if we can bring the condoms."

"I think we can make that happen."

Good, because shower sex with someone was just fun, but showering with someone, without sex? That was intimate and Lexi intended to keep her promise to Dyson and herself. This was just fun. Not a relationship.

Even if it was the best, most connective sex she'd ever had in her life.

Chapter Nineteen

Dyson woke up to a strange sensation. A weight in his arms. One he wasn't used to—the weight of a woman. He tilted his chin down to see Lexi, sprawled across his chest, her silky blond hair spread across his shoulder. This close, he could see the multitude of color in the strands, from pale yellow to a dark tan. Lifting a hand, he curled a small section of the beautiful hair around his finger and twirled. So soft.

"Mmmmmm," she moaned, eyes still closed as the corner of her lips curled in a small, satisfied smile. "Is it morning?"

The sunlight streaming in under the bottom of the closed shades indicated so, but he had no idea what time it actually was. Must be early because he didn't smell any coffee, so his sisters weren't up. Gemma had coffee ready before she even brushed her teeth.

"It is." He placed a kiss to her forehead. "Good morning."

Her eyes cracked open, the dark brown irises still hazy with sleep. Lexi put her hand on his chest and pushed up, lifting one leg over him until she straddled him. Since neither of them put pajamas on after last night's…activities, it put all the good bits in full, bare contact. His morning wood was at attention and seeking out the warmth currently rubbing against it.

"It is a good morning, but how about we make it a great one?" she purred.

He was all for that. He reached up to pull her down for a scorching kiss when a knock on the bedroom door interrupted them.

"Fair warning, Gemma is making coffee and we have our zip-lining appointment in an hour, so y'all better put some pants on and get in gear."

Dyson groaned at the sound of Macy's voice through the door. Cockblocked by his sister. It was high school all over again.

Lexi giggled. "Oops, didn't know they were up."

"Me either." He groaned. "Guess we better get ready for the day."

She bit her lip, giving him a wicked grin and shifting her hips again, rubbing herself directly against his hard erection. He grasped her hips in his hands, holding her tight, wishing they had the time. But having sex while his sisters were awake and just down the hall, in hearing range, wasn't something he really wanted to do. Ever. He wanted Lexi, make no mistake, but he could wait until later tonight.

Honestly, he liked spending time with Lexi, in and out of bed. He didn't want to examine that too closely right now. The implication wasn't something he could deal with. Not with the memories of last night still swimming in his brain. The soft feel of her touch, the sweet, sexy little moans she'd make when he hit just the right spot.

Dyson had always enjoyed sex, but with Lexi...it felt more. He was usually in his head 24/7, but she managed to pull him out. Help him lose himself in the moment. Sensations had overtaken him. He hadn't planned his next move, he'd just seemed to be there. With her.

Truth be told it was a slightly terrifying realization and one he wasn't going to think about right now...or possibly ever.

She laughed again, slipping off him, her fantastic breasts bouncing slightly as she hopped off the bed. His dick twitched again.

Hell, today was going to be a long and torturous one.

Somehow, they managed to get dressed without taking each other against the wall. They headed out of the bedroom to the kitchen where Macy and Gemma sat on stools around the high counter, mugs of coffee in hand.

"Pot's ready," Gemma nodded to the half-full pot on the counter.

He got himself a cup and one for Lexi. She added cream and sugar while he downed his black. They headed into town, grabbing a light breakfast at a café, where Gemma ordered another cup of coffee because his caffeine addicted sister seemed to run on the stuff.

Once they all finished their breakfast sandwiches they piled back into Gemma's car and drove to the outskirts of town where one of the zipline parks was located. Dyson shifted in his seat the closer they got. His palms started to sweat.

"Hey, are you okay?"

He glanced over to see Lexi staring at him with concern. Trying his best for a smile, he nodded. "Never better."

She arched one brow, but just then the car came to a stop as Gemma parked, so she couldn't call him on his bullshit.

Everyone piled out of the car. Lexi gasped at the sight before them. Macy made an acceptable grunt. Gemma gave a soft "Wow." Meanwhile, he worried the bacon, egg, and cheese biscuit he'd just scarfed down was about to make a reappearance.

Dyson stared up at the high, thin wires, attached to large wooden poles, the harnesses dangling from them like tiny omens of death. One small mistake, one piece of equipment not checked and *bam!* You were falling toward your death. Or at least a broken leg.

Lexi's cool hand pressed against his hot cheek. "Dyson, you don't look okay, what is it?"

He opened his mouth to answer her, but nothing came out.

"He's afraid of heights," Macy answered.

He wasn't afraid of them. He was cautious about them. Nothing wrong with that. Most people were shocked when they found out. After all, firefighters were supposed to be adrenaline junkies, but he hadn't taken the job for the glory or the rush. He did it to help people and keep them safe. When he dealt with heights in the line of work it was all about the rescue. His mind worked through the fear by focusing on the end goal: saving someone's life.

But when it came to scaling the tallest towers for fun...

"Oh." Lexi took his hand and squeezed. "We don't have to do this if you don't want to."

He swallowed past the dryness in his throat. "Actually, I kind of do."

"Face-It time!" Gemma declared.

Lexi furrowed her brow. "Huh?"

He sighed, not realizing how much Lexi was going to learn about his family on this trip. She was supposed to be a fake girlfriend, but if things kept going this way, she would know more about him and his family than his last real girlfriend. Grace had never really enjoyed coming up to Estes for the family weekends.

Shoving thoughts of his ex aside, he explained. "After our parents passed, we all kind of became..."

"Giant chickenshits." Macy helpfully filled in.

"I was going to say overly cautious." He scowled at his sister. "Anyway, when we started coming up here, we made a pact that each year one of us would pick something that scares us, and we'd all do it. Face it together."

He grimaced up at the death trap people dared to call adventure. "I was up this year and ziplining was all I could think of."

She squeezed his hand again. "Fear of heights is actually very common. Lots of people struggle with it."

He glanced to the woman holding his hand, rubbing his back with gentle strokes. She worked so hard for the center and all those kids, her friends were great and clearly loved her, and his sisters did, too. She willingly helped him out by becoming his fake girlfriend, didn't push him for more than he could give, and literally was the best lover he'd ever had.

If he were to ever start dating again for real, it would be with a woman like Lexi.

So why not with Lexi?

The thought was a whisper in his brain. One he wasn't sure he was ready to deal with yet, especially since she had that whole agreement with her roommate about no dating. *That'll be over in just a few months, you can wait that long, right?* He ignored the whispered words in his head and took a deep breath, staring with determination at the zip line park in front of them.

"Let's do this thing." He nodded with determination. "Face-It time!"

"Face-It time!" yelled Gemma, with Macy joining in.

Fifteen minutes later, Dyson was thinking of changing Face-It time to Fuck-It time, because he was done with this.

"Are you okay?"

Lexi rubbed his arm as he clung for life to the pole attached to the platform they stood on. The tour guide said he started them on the beginner level. What the hell was beginner about this? They had to be at least fifty feet in the air. He glanced down and his stomach pitched, taking a nosedive right to his toes. His head spun. He shut his eyes and squeezed the pole tighter, sure he would be going down any minute.

"Hey, hey, Dyson. Look at me."

He felt the warm softness of her hands stroking his jaw, but he couldn't seem to pry his eyes open.

"Just breathe and listen to the sound of my voice. Everything is going to be okay. We've got safety lines on and Gemma and Macy already made it across the first line, so we know it's safe."

Logically he knew that, but fear was pushing logic right off a cliff…kind of like these zip lines.

Suddenly his mouth was covered with Lexi's sweet lips. Fear started to recede as desire took over. Now *this* was a perfect distraction. Kissing Lexi made everything better.

He inhaled, allowing the sweet smell of the lotion he'd seen her slather on this morning take over. The soft floral scent enveloped him, calming his racing heart, bringing him out of his panic and into the moment.

"We can take all this off and head back to the car right now," she said softly, pulling away to place her forehead against his. "Or, if you want, for every line you make it across, I'll let you make a special request in the bedroom tonight."

That had him cracking open his eyes. "Are you trying to tempt me out of my fear with sexual favors?"

She grinned. "Maybe. Is it working?"

He laughed.

"Seriously, Dyson. We can head back. Skip all this. I'm sure your sisters will understand, but I know you can do this. You're so strong, and not just physically. You've had to face things much scarier than this."

She was referring to his parents' death and she was right. Becoming a guardian to his sisters at nineteen had been terrifying, but he'd done it. And for better or worse, both his sisters were thriving, capable adults, so he supposed he didn't screw it up too bad.

"I believe in you, Dyson."

And there it was. The thing he needed to hear without even realizing. It was one thing to convince yourself you could do something, but when someone you cared about believed in you too it was like…a magic potion of strength.

And he did care about Lexi. Far more than he ever planned on.

Cupping the back of her neck, he tugged her to him for a brief but hot kiss. "For luck," he whispered against her lips before taking a deep breath and walking to the edge of the platform. He let the guide hook him up, then stepped off the edge with a loud scream. One that followed him all the way down the line to the next platform where his sisters were shouting and cheering him on.

His heart raced as his feet hit the platform, stomach returning from his throat to its proper position in his gut. Fear had his hands shaking, but the rush of adrenalin had his lips curling into a wide grin. There was something else, too. Something warm and bright burning in his chest…pride. He'd done it. Faced a fear. It wasn't even that bad.

Lies.

It was terrifying, but he did it and the smile on Lexi and his sisters' faces filled him with the strength to do it again. He wasn't about to make zip lining a regular thing, but people always said the first step was the hardest. Confidence filled him as he stared down at the rest of the high wires, each one—thankfully—lower than the one before.

"What are we waiting for?" he asked the group. "Let's do this!"

A chorus of cheers, and another scorching kiss from Lexi, and they moved on to the next one.

The rest of the excursion was much better. He wouldn't necessarily call it fun, but he faced his fears and came out victorious and with clean pants. He'd at least call it a win.

They grabbed some sandwiches in town and went up to Rocky Mountain National Park for a hike. After, they ate dinner in town at a delicious Mexican restaurant, then headed back to the cabin where everyone put on their swimsuits for a nice soak in the hot tub. After today's exertion, he sure as hell needed it.

One after the other, his sisters headed off to bed, leaving him and Lexi alone on the back porch, nothing but the bright light from the nearly full moon and the nightly sounds of nature around them. Crickets chirped, an owl hooted, it was nice. Relaxing.

"All alone," Lexi hummed, her hand resting on his thigh as she scooched closer in the warm, bubbling water. "And I do believe I owe you, what was it, eight requests."

All he had was one.

Her naked alone with him.

That was it.

Yeah, he might not be the most creative guy, but when it came to Lexi, he didn't need anything but her to be satisfied.

The water swirled around them as Lexi's palm slid up his thigh, under his trunks to grasp his hard cock. He bit back a groan, pretty sure everyone was already upstairs and in bed, but not wanting to risk it. Lexi stroked him up and down, driving him wild. He wanted her. Bad. But as sensual as the movies made it out to be, sex in water was nearly impossible.

"We need to head inside."

"Oh do we?" She chuckled.

He swore as she did some amazing twisty thing with her hands. "Yeah. If I don't want to embarrass myself and disappoint you, we do."

"You could never disappoint me, Dyson."

He stared into her eyes, seeing the truth of that statement in her gaze. And honestly, he felt the same about her.

He pushed the worry over what that meant to the back of his mind. Scooping her into his arms, he stood. The water sloshed around them, spilling over the side of the hot tub as he carried her out in a rush. He practically ran to the bedroom, tossing her onto the bed without care for how wet they were.

He planned to ger her much wetter in a moment.

Lexi tucked her thumbs into her suit bottoms and pulled them off with a sassy grin, tugging her top up and over her head next. He shoved his trunks down, kicking the soppy wet fabric off.

"Damn, your breasts are perfect," he said as he leaned over her and took them in his hands.

She sighed as he lavished them with attention. His mouth kissing every inch, tongue swirling around her perfectly peaked nipples. He could spend all night worshiping them.

"Dyson, you better hurry or I'm going to be the one embarrassing myself."

He moved one hand down her body, continuing to memorize her breasts with his mouth. She cried out when he cupped her sex, moaning his name. He roared inside, loving the sounds she made, the pleasure he could give her. He worked her, gently pressing two fingers inside while his thumb found her center, rubbing small circles that had her gasping out his name. He listened to her soft commands, ones he didn't even know if she realized she was giving. But he would gladly obey every single one.

"Dyson, please," she panted out. "I want to be with you when..."

He slowly removed his hand, reaching over to grab a condom from the nightstand. He quickly protected them, then positioned himself at her entrance. Slowly, torturously slowly, he entered her, reveling in the amazing rightness that was being with Lexi Martin.

"Yes! More."

Again, he was happy to oblige. He set a slow rhythm. Lexi tilted her hips so every thrust had them fitting together like a glove, crying out as each second felt better than the one before. A part of him wanted to stay like this all night, never leave the warm comfort of Lexi. While another part of him begged for release, but he would be damned if she didn't come right with him.

He reached between them, rubbing that spot he knew drove her wild. She bit back a scream and he felt her tighten around him. That was it. He couldn't hold back any longer. He shouted her name as he joined her in one of the best orgasms of his life.

Collapsing, he rolled to the side so he didn't crush her, dragging her onto his chest.

"Is it just me"—she spoke between heaving breaths—"or do we just get better and better at this?"

He laughed, tugging her closer and kissing her temple. Damn, he really liked her. In a way…he hadn't been sure he ever could again. Ward's warning about falling for his fake girlfriend whispered in the back of his mind. He swallowed back a shiver of apprehension.

"I'm going to go clean up." She leaned over, placing a kiss to his lips. "You coming?"

"In a minute." He smiled to hide the terrifying realization he just had about their fake relationship. "I need a minute to recover. Or a week."

Laughing, she rose out of bed and headed to the bathroom.

Dyson stared at the ceiling wondering how, of all people, Eli Ward might be right about his love life. At what point had he started to have real feelings for his fake girlfriend?

Chapter Twenty

"So how are we going to do this thing?" Lexi asked as Dyson came back from the bathroom. She was snuggled under the covers, her large sleep shirt on because, as much as she liked being naked with the man, they had to talk and if she did it naked, the only words would be her calling out his name as he brought her to completion again.

"Huh?"

"Our breakup." His smiled dimmed. Yeah, she knew it was a crappy thing to talk about after what they just did, but she was feeling herself falling a bit too much in this fake relationship and she needed to remind her inner romantic that it was indeed fake. Before she fell completely, lost her bet, and got her heart broken.

"Oh, right." He moved to his suitcase and pulled out a pair of cotton pajama bottoms, slipping them on before he joined her on the bed.

"I know you said your friends' bet was for a month. Do we end it there? Go longer? How long do you think we need to 'date' to convince your sisters you're over your phobia of dating?"

"It's not a phobia," he said softly. His eyes came up, gaze filled with anger and pain. "I was engaged once."

She started in surprise. That was the last thing she'd ever guess he'd been about to say.

"Grace. We met at a fundraiser the firehouse put on for the local school districts. She was a teacher from one of the schools and we just kind of hit it off. I thought everything was fine, we had our ups and downs like everyone else, but I never suspected anything was..." He took a deep breath, gaze falling to the quilted comforter on the bed. "She came on a few of these weekends with me, but she didn't really enjoy it. She wasn't much of an outdoors person. I was fine with that. Couples can't do everything together."

True, but spending time with your significant other's family was important. Especially if you were going to marry the person.

"On our trip three years ago she had a work thing so she didn't come. Then, Macy got food poisoning, so we came home early. I went to her place to surprise her, but I found her in bed. With my best friend."

"Dyson." Her heart shattered for him. "That's awful."

Anger and pain tightened her chest, a sick, heavy feeling twisting in her gut. How dare Grace do that to him! If you didn't want to be with someone, you broke up with them, you did not cheat. And with his best friend? Not much of a best friend if you asked her. What could drive two people to betray someone they supposedly loved in such a cruel way?

She wrapped her arms around him, trying her best to offer him comfort. Yes, it happened three years ago, but it obviously still affected him.

"They said they didn't mean for it to happen."

She snorted. "No one ever does. Doesn't excuse it."

He gave a low, rough chuckle. "No, it doesn't. But Grace

did write me a letter explaining things, apologizing. And Adam, my former best friend, he tried to apologize, but…I couldn't stand to be in the same room with him let alone talk to him."

Moisture gathered in her eyes, but she blinked it back. Dyson didn't need her tears. No matter how much her heart broke for him. He'd lost his parents, then in a way, his fiancée and best friend. No wonder the man didn't want to connect with others. How much loss could one person endure before it broke him?

"I don't hate either of them, but obviously I don't want them in my life anymore, either."

She could completely understand that. She would feel the same in his place.

"I've moved on, but the thought of dating again, trusting anyone that like again…" He sighed. "It's just not something I think I can do ever again. Which is why I…"

"Made the rule?"

He nodded. "For a long time, I wondered if it was me. If maybe there was something about me that made people… leave."

"Dyson, no." Her arms squeezed as she tried to pour all the love and comfort she could into him. How could he think something like that? An accident took his parents, no one was responsible for that and his ex…well, she made her choice. Her choice, her fault. Not his.

She felt his body tense and knew he was going to pull away, close himself off to her, but she couldn't let him do that. He needed someone to lean on; even if he didn't want it, he needed it. She might not be his real girlfriend but she could be here for him.

"You're an amazing man, Dyson O'Neil," she whispered. "Life just sucks sometimes and there's not much we can do about it, but you deserve all the happiness in the world."

He softened in her arms, body relaxing as he pressed closer.

"You do too, Lexi." A heavy sigh left him. "I hope one day you find someone who...who makes you smile every day."

Her heart broke even more. Not only for Dyson, but for herself as well. Because he made her smile, he made her happy. In all honesty...she hadn't started to fall. She'd already fallen. And hard. But she wouldn't push him, wouldn't ask for more than she knew he could give. He'd laid out his limits at the beginning of this thing and she wouldn't cross them.

No matter how much she wished she could be that person he finally learned to trust again. All she could do now was hold him in her arms. Offer some form of comfort, as small and late as it was, and listen to the sounds of crickets chirping as Dyson's breathing shallowed into a soft snore.

The next thing Lexi knew, she was opening her eyes as sunlight spilled in from underneath the curtains. They must have fallen asleep. She was still wrapped in Dyson's arms. They hadn't reached any decision about how or when to fake break up, but she wasn't going to bring it up again. She'd also be wise not to listen to the part of her that screamed she could be the one to help Dyson trust again, love again.

She rose from the bed, careful not to wake Dyson. After a quick shower, she dressed and headed out to the kitchen to make some coffee. Once the pot had finished brewing, she grabbed four mugs and placed them on the counter.

"Hey, I woke up and you were gone."

She turned at the deep voice. Dyson walked into the kitchen in jeans and a tight-fitting blue T-shirt that clung to every sculpted muscle on his chest. His hair was mussed from sleep and a small scruffy beard had started to develop on his square jaw. *Holy cow, the man looks beyond sexy in the mornings.*

"Thanks." He dipped his chin. "You look absolutely

stunning yourself."

Oops! She really needed to work harder about her unconscious blabbering or she might say something she regretted—like admitting her feelings or begging him to turn this fake relationship real.

"Coffee?"

He accepted a cup, his gaze turning serious. "Lexi, about what we discussed last night…"

Her heart squeezed, breath catching, closing off her throat. She wasn't sure if she wanted to hear his thoughts on the matter or not, but she was saved from her dilemma by his sisters trudging down the stairs.

"I smell coffee and I didn't make it," Gemma said with astonishment as she came into the kitchen.

"It's a Festivus miracle!" Macy exclaimed.

"It's not even fall yet, weirdo." Gemma lightly shoved her little sister.

The rest of the morning passed in a whirlwind of coffee and packing. Once the cars were packed and the house all cleaned, she gave Macy and Gemma big hugs. They gushed over how fun it had been to hang out with her and both promised to come by the center this week. Then she and Dyson hit the highway back to Denver.

"Thanks for letting me come on your weekend," Lexi told Dyson as he pulled up to her apartment. "It was so much fun."

"Thank you for coming. I hope my sisters didn't bug you too much."

"Are you kidding?" She grinned. "I love them. How else was I going to find out how you used to sing Backstreet Boys songs into your hairbrush?"

He groaned, leaning his head back against the headrest, that sweet blush rising on his cheeks as she brought up one of the childhood stories Macy and Gemma had laughed about over dinner one night.

His head rolled to the side; hazel eyes bright with humor as he stared at her.

"This is so unfair. I don't know any of your embarrassing childhood stories. Seems only fair I get to hang out with your siblings so I can get the goods on little Lexi."

She sucked in a sharp breath at his words, noting the exact moment he realized what they implied. The humor left his face. She knew he hadn't meant what he said. He didn't mean to imply they were heading anywhere real. That an actual relationship, one where he got to meet her family, could ever be a thing.

Still, she couldn't squash the tiny flame of hope inside. And she couldn't decipher Dyson's expression. There was fear there on his face. Very plain to see. But in his eyes…it might just be her optimism speaking, but she could swear she saw the same hopeful longing she felt deep within her.

The moment broke when he opened the car door and moved to grab her suitcase from the trunk. Stuffing down her disappointment, Lexi got out of the car, taking her bag from Dyson when he handed it over.

"My shift starts tonight, but I'll text you, and…maybe we can talk when I'm off?"

The light was back in his eyes. She couldn't stop the smile from curling her lips. Could she really have seen it? Did he want to talk about moving their relationship from fake to real? Trying her best not to sound too eager, she nodded with a slight shrug. "Okay."

He leaned down, kissing her softly before heading back to the car. She turned and made her way into her building, knowing Dyson would wait to make sure she got safely inside before driving away. He was so considerate, so sweet, so… already deep in her heart, it was scary.

She waved from the elevator as the doors closed. Her

tight smile and worried eyes shone back at her in the silver reflection of the closed doors. Oh no! What was she going to do? She'd fallen for her fake boyfriend. It was like some cheesy made-for-TV romcom, only she was pretty sure it wouldn't end with Dyson rushing across town in the rain to catch her as she got in a cab to go to the Bahamas to forget about the man who broke her heart.

Nope, she knew she'd never be able to afford the Bahamas and the likelihood of Dyson overcoming the damage his ex did to him to start something real with her was...nice to dream about, but she wouldn't hold her breath for that possibility.

The elevator dinged, indicating she'd reached her floor. Lexi trudged down the hallway, dragging her suitcase behind her. The sound of the television coming from her apartment could be heard all the way down the hall. Jordan must have Angel over.

She reached her apartment door and pushed it open.

"Hey, you're back!" Jordan waved from the couch where he sat snuggled next to Angel.

"Hey, Lex. How was your weekend?" Angel asked.

She closed and locked the door with a sigh. "Wonderful."

Jordan stared at her for a moment then his eyes got wide. "You slept with him."

Her face heated; not even one minute and her bestie could already tell. Did she have "I got laid" in big neon letters across her forehead? "Um...maybe."

Her friend stared harder, his eyes narrowing. Suddenly he gasped, jaw dropping.

"Oh my God!" Jordan reached for the remote and shut off the TV. "You not only slept with him, you fell for him!"

Dang it! Sometimes it sucked living with someone who knew you better than you knew yourself. Knowing she could never lie to Jordan and get away with it, she threw her hands up in the air, rushing into the living room.

"I totally did and now I don't know what to do."

Angel rose from the couch. "This sounds like a conversation that is going to need ice cream."

"And chocolate," she insisted.

Jordan shook his head. "Lex, do you really want to add a migraine on top of this?"

She pointed at her roommate. "I'm spinning out here, let me have my damn chocolate."

He held his hands up in surrender. "Okay, it's your head."

Angel smiled with understanding and nodded. "Ice cream and chocolate. I'll run over to the store and grab it, be back in a bit."

"Thanks, Angel."

"Of course." He gave her a hug, moving her to the couch to sit next to Jordan, whom he leaned down to kiss before he headed out of the apartment.

Once Angel left, Jordan raised a brow and leaned back against the arm of the couch, facing her. "Okay, spill."

She took a deep breath and launched into the events of the weekend, the drive up and how they got to know each other better, Dyson's agreement to be sex buddies, the fun activities with his sisters. She left out the story he shared about his ex because that wasn't hers to tell.

"So...the sex was good?"

"The sex was amazing!" She flopped back against the couch, sinking low into the soft, plushy cushions. "The things that man can do with his tongue."

Just thinking about it had her blushing and clenching her thighs.

"And you two never got around to discussing how long this would last or how the breakup would go?"

"No," she grimaced. "His sisters interrupted us."

"Hmmmm." Jordan rubbed his chin, the way he did when he was working out a puzzle in the escape rooms he and Angel liked to drag her to. "Do you think there's any chance he wants to continue the relationship? Maybe turn it into a real one?"

"Jordan!" She grabbed a throw pillow and smacked him with it. "You're supposed to tell me not to get in over my head. To stop dreaming things that are impossible. Not give me false hope. Besides what about the bet? Are you really ready to swallow *your* fear and move in with Angel?"

The corner of Jordan's mouth ticked up in a secret smile. She nearly jumped out of her seat with excitement, but her bestie held up his hand.

"Put the bet aside for a minute. This is about your happiness, Lex. Does Dyson make you happy?"

She snuggled deeper against the couch cushions, thinking about Dyson, about how he made her feel. He could be a bit of a stiff shirt with his rule following, but that was only because he wanted to keep everyone around him safe. He offered help to the center and Mateo. He loved his sisters. He was a great guy.

But to her…he was more. He made her laugh. Never made her feel bad for her accidental talking out loud quirk. He had been nothing but honest with her regarding their deal. But that wasn't all. He put her first. Something she wasn't used to in any relationship.

Dyson persuaded her to take time off and have fun. Sure, it was under the guise of playing girlfriend for his sisters, but he always checked in with her. Asked how she was doing, if she needed anything. He…recognized her needs, and that filled her with a sense of joy she'd never felt before.

"Yes," she whispered. "He makes me so happy. But we can't actually be together. It's impossible."

Jordan grabbed the pillow from her and tossed it to the floor. "Lex, nothing is impossible. Improbable, but not impossible. You should talk to him. Let him know how you feel, ask how he feels."

"I can't." She slumped down farther into the couch. "He's on shift for the next twenty-four hours and besides, I agreed to all this knowing he doesn't do relationships."

"Did he say why?"

Yes and honestly, she didn't blame him. What his ex and former best friend did was super crappy. Three years might be a bit long to still be keeping a lock on your heart, but different people took different amounts of time to heal. Who was she to tell Dyson to get over it? He clearly got enough of that from his sisters, who were pushing him back into dating.

"He did, and I get it. I understand."

"Doesn't mean you have to hide your desires because you made a promise to him."

She shifted, facing her roommate. "Meaning?"

"Look, Lex." Jordan took her hand in his. "You are an amazing person. You're sweet, you're smart, you're generous, but you tend to have a tiny problem with ignoring your own needs to see to everyone else's. I mean, that's what our 'no dating for six months' agreement was all about. It was supposed to give you insight. Allow you to realize that sometimes you need to put your wants first. Or hell, even voice them so people know you want something in the first place."

Her bestie's kind words and harsh truth hit her square in the chest. Emotions clogged her throat. She sniffed past the lump. "You forgot to say I'm pretty."

He rolled his eyes with a small laugh. "You're gorgeous, Lex, and he'd be a fool not to want something real with you, so just ask, okay? You might be surprised at what he says."

"But what if he says no?"

"Then we go dancing, get shit-faced, and talk about how small his dick is," Jordan said with a wink.

She laughed at her loving and supportive friend's

encouragement and the idea that anyone could think of what Dyson was packing as small.

But Jordan was right about one thing. She should talk to Dyson.

At the very least, they needed an exit plan for their breakup, but maybe, if luck and love were on her side, Dyson would be willing to take a chance and they wouldn't need one at all. He'd shared his painful past with her. That had to mean something, right?

He had to care just a little…

Or maybe that was just her hopeful mind turning normal conversations into wishful dreams. Whatever the case, this was a conversation to be had in person, which meant she would have to wait until Dyson was off shift.

Ugh! Why did she have to fall for a guy whose job took him away for a full twenty-four hours at a time?

"I'm back with the ice cream and the chocolate," Angel announced as he came in the apartment door. "I also got some OJ and champagne, because it's never too early or late for mimosas."

"You're going to do it, aren't you?" she whispered, slightly nudging her head in Angel's direction. "You're going to say yes."

Jordan's eyes widened. "Shhhh. I'm on the verge of possibly, maybe, finding the courage to discuss moving in with my boyfriend. If you can find your courage, then maybe I can find mine."

Moisture gathered in her eyes. She knew she'd never be brave enough to do this without Jordan, and it warmed her heart to know she provided the same support for him. Maybe this silly bet had been the best thing for the two of them.

Jordan held up a hand, peeking around her head to stare into the kitchen where Angel was dishing out the treats. "Don't say anything yet. I want it to be special when I tell him, but this means you have to talk to Dyson."

He held his hand up and stared at her. "Deal?"

"Deal." She lifted her own hand and shook.

She was going to do it anyway. She had to talk to him before she did something really embarrassing and spout out how she was falling in love with him. He hadn't minded her odd outbursts, but she had a feeling one like that would scare the poor man away.

"Here we are!" Angel came into the living room with a tray piled high with candy, chocolate, three bowls of ice cream, cups, and a pitcher of bubbly, champagne-filled OJ.

She gladly accepted the offerings and dug in while Jordan turned the movie back on, knowing she was going to regret the delicious chocolate bar she was currently consuming when tomorrow morning rolled around. But it didn't matter. She needed the sugar rush. She had twenty-four hours to figure out a way to tell her fake boyfriend and sex buddy that she liked the sex and liked him and wanted to continue the relationship. For real this time.

Time to put her big girl panties on and get what she wanted for a change.

Chapter Twenty-One

Big girl panties were overrated.

Lexi found herself standing outside Dyson's door a day later, hands shaking with nerves as she knocked. He'd texted this morning, asking if she'd like to come over after work. He was off shift for the next two days and wanted to cook her dinner as a thanks for the weekend.

As if she would ever say no to someone else making dinner for her.

Her promise to Jordan to talk to Dyson rolled around in her brain. She needed to ask Dyson about making this thing real. She could do this. She could be brave and ask for what she wanted. But the second the door opened her fear was squashed.

By lust.

Dyson stood before her, a towel wrapped around his waist, droplets of water running down his hard, bare pecs. His hair was damp and he had a sheepish grin on his face. She felt like the big bad wolf, all she wanted to do was eat him up.

"Hi, Lexi. I'm sorry I kind of…well dinner is…"

She stepped into his studio apartment as he stood back and motioned her in. His words barely registering over the rush of blood in her ears. Who cared about dinner? The only thing on her mind right now was seeing exactly how secure the knot on his towel was.

"I tried a new recipe, but the delivery didn't quite work out as expected." He grimaced, moving into the small kitchen area. "I kind of dropped it."

She took a look around, but nothing seemed out of place in his tiny studio. The kitchen looked spotless, in fact. When Dyson moved toward the trashcan in the corner, pushing back the lid she spied some kind of...

"Is that a casserole?"

"Was a casserole." He frowned. "It was supposed to be, anyway, but the damn dish slipped from my hands when I took it out of the oven. Spilled everywhere and when I was cleaning, I fell and it got all over me so I had to wash off and...shit, I'm sorry, Lexi. I really wanted to do something nice to thank you."

She slapped a hand over her mouth, stifling a giggle. What she wouldn't pay to have seen Dyson slipping and sliding in a mess of casserole all over his kitchen.

"It's okay."

"It's not." He shook his head. "Let me get dressed and I can order out. Anything you want."

What she wanted couldn't be delivered. Because it was right in front of her.

"Wait." She held up a hand, stopping him from disappearing into the bathroom. Stomach quivering with nerves, she dredged up all her courage. "Um I was thinking... you don't have to get dressed."

He stared for a moment before her meaning sunk in. His hazel eyes heated, muscles tightening as his hand went to grip the knot of his towel.

"But, we're not in Estes anymore."

Do it, Lexi. Ask for what you want. Ask for more.

"More?" His head tilted. "You want more?"

Damn her lack of mouth-brain filter!

"You want to continue our...sexual relationship until the end of the month?" he asked. "Until my friends' bet is over?"

Dammit, no! That wasn't exactly what she wanted. Her heart sank just a bit; the words she wanted to ask were stuck in her throat. But he had said relationship. Okay, technically he said *sexual relationship*, but the word was in there. Maybe if she started slowly with him. Kept it physical only, they could grow closer, he would see she was someone he could trust.

"Yes." She nodded, her logic allowing her to cheat a little on what she promised Jordan, but she'd deal with that later. "Why not still have fun for a while? No rule breaking, just more bending."

She winked, a sliver of relief filling her when his lips curled into a devilish grin.

"So then, you're not hungry?"

Her tongue came out to swipe her lower lips as her gaze raked over him, a husky whisper leaving her. "Not for food."

He was in front of her in a moment, his hands gripping her hips as he tugged her to him. She went willingly, throwing her arms around his neck and pulling him down so she could taste the sweet lips that tasted more delicious than any casserole ever could.

"Lexi," he growled between drugging kisses.

Her legs quivered, knees going weak, panties dampening at the sound of his rough, lust-filled voice. The things this man did to her.

As her knees started to give out, she followed them down. Sinking to the floor despite Dyson's protest.

"Lexi, what are you—"

His question cut off with a hiss as she flicked the knot

of the towel, letting the material fall to the floor, pooling at his feet. She stared at what she'd unwrapped. Dyson's thick, hard erection bobbed toward her. A present she had every intention of enjoying thoroughly.

Leaning forward, she pressed a soft kiss to the tip, reveling in the needy groan that sounded from above her. His large, warm fingers slipped into the strands of her hair, holding her, gently caressing her scalp as she parted her lips and took the head of his cock into her mouth.

"Fucking hell, that's amazing," he groaned.

She agreed. The taste of Dyson was unlike anything she'd ever known. Rich and spicy, addicting. She gripped the base, working him with her hands and mouth, swirling her tongue around the head as she sucked.

She'd never minded blow jobs in the past, but they'd also never been something she craved.

Until now.

Or maybe she simply craved this man and everything about him.

Her eyes closed as she enjoyed the sweet, guttural cries Dyson made, the encouraging words he praised upon her. His hips thrust forward, pushing his cock to the back of her throat. Eagerly, she widened her jaw, unable to stop the small gag from escaping her.

"Shit, I'm sorry," he panted.

She wasn't, she loved this. Loved Dyson losing some of the careful control he always wielded. Loved that she was the one to do it. Push him to the edge, make him bend his precious rules. A feeling of heady power enveloped her, making her feel unstoppable.

"Lexi, stop," he gently pulled her back.

She glanced up at him, pouting as he took away a treat she was very much enjoying.

"Why?"

"You said you weren't hungry,"

Yes, she had.

He gave her a wicked, promised-filled grin. "But I'm starving."

A shiver of need wracked her body. Before she knew what was happening Dyson bent down and scooped her up in his arms. His mouth crashed down onto hers. She felt them move and then suddenly the hard surface of the kitchen table was underneath her.

"The casserole might be a lost cause," he said with a soft chuckle. "But I'm in the mood for some sweet Lexi pie. What do you say?"

She said he better get her pants off right now before she exploded from anticipation.

Her unspoken wish was his command as Dyson quickly snapped open the button on her jeans and pulled them and her underwear down. The material snagged on her shoes, but he carefully removed them, one by one. Tossing everything to the floor.

Moving to her elbows she ripped her shirt up and over her head, flicking the clasp on her bra and tossing it away, leaving them both gloriously naked in his tiny kitchen.

"How do you get more beautiful every time I see you?" His head shook, eyes filled with wonder.

Her breath caught. Uh-oh, he better stop saying sweet things like that or she just might confess the real reason she wanted to continue doing this with him. And she was not about to ruin the chance of an amazing orgasm by scaring him off.

"I thought you were…hungry."

Feeling brazen and powerful, she grinned up at him, spreading her legs and beckoning him with a finger. Dyson grinned, his shoulders flexing as he moved down to his knees, pulling her to the edge of the table. With one more wicked smile he bent his head and press his tongue against her.

She cried out. The hot, wet feel of his mouth drove her wild. Her hips bucked, pressing against his face as he tormented her with mind-numbing pleasure. One hand reached up to caress her breast, cupping, squeezing, as the other traveled down. He slipped two fingers inside her, his mouth closing over her clit and sucking softly.

She cried out, body tensing as a wave crashed over her. She was so close. Words, commands might have left her lips. She had no idea. All she could do was feel. Within minutes Dyson was pushing her over the edge into one of the most amazing orgasms of her life.

She collapsed against the table, heaving out deep breaths as he continued to kiss her, bringing her down gently.

"Come on," he said, softly scooping her into his arms again.

She felt herself being carried across the room to the corner where his bed was. She supposed that was the great thing about a studio apartment. No pesky doors to get in your way.

Dyson laid her on the bed, reaching into the bedside table drawer. She watched as he donned protection and moved over her.

"Wait," she said.

He paused, not moving a single muscle. She saw the question in his eye, the fear that she might pull the plug on this. Yeah right, as if that was even a possibility. Rising up, she placed a soft kiss to his lips and turned, positioning herself on her hands and knees. She glanced over her shoulder at him.

"Is this okay?"

Fire burned in his gaze as he stared, his jaw tightened, chest heaving.

"Fuck yeah, it's okay."

And there it was again, that loss of control. She loved it,

craved it, wanted to do everything in her power to make it happen again and again.

All thoughts flew from her mind when Dyson gripped her hips and pulled her to him. The blunt head of his erection pressed against her. She sucked in a sharp breath as he plunged inside, letting out a throaty moan at the sensation of him filling her.

"Fuck, Lex you feel so good," he groaned.

"So do you."

She gripped the bedsheets as Dyson's fingers tightened on her hips. He set a furious pace. Thrusting into her with a wildness she craved. All the air left her lungs, her vision dimmed. She knew she was talking, crying out for more as he pounded into her. One hand reached around, the heel of his palm pressed against her. She cried out as the orgasm washed over her, pressing back against him. Dyson held her, pumping into her three more times before gripping her tightly and losing himself along with her.

They collapsed on the bed. His heavy breath tickling the hair on the nape of her neck.

"Wow," she sighed.

His arm came around her, tugging her closer as he nuzzled her ear. "Yeah, my thought exactly."

"Guess you'll need another shower now," she teased.

"Only if you join me."

How could she turn down an offer like that?

After they cleaned up and played some more, Dyson ordered from her favorite sushi place. Since it was so late by the time they finished dinner, when he asked her to stay over, she accepted.

In the dark of the night, Lexi snuggled deep into Dyson's arms, enjoying the comforting feel of being surrounded. She knew Jordan would give her crap later for this. Whatever. She was going to ask Dyson about turning their fake thing real.

Eventually.

But she was taking baby steps. There was nothing wrong with that. Besides, what she and Dyson had was working. For both of them. Why mess with a good thing?

Chapter Twenty-Two

Dyson headed out of Station 42, his body a vibrating mess of nerves. Not from his shift. It had been easy enough. Two false alarms and a teenager who got his head stuck in the safety bars of the playground equipment at the park. Nothing he hadn't dealt with before.

No, his nerves weren't job related. They were Lexi related.

These past few weeks had been amazing, but the month was almost up. The window on Ward and Díaz's bet was drawing closer and it looked like Díaz would win, which was great for him. And yet...

A small pang stuck in his chest like a splinter, barely felt until he examined it closer. He didn't want the time limit to come. He didn't want to stop hanging out with Lexi. Talking to her, laughing with her, smiling when she had dinner with his sisters and they all teased him. And he definitely didn't want to stop the amazing times they shared together in bed. And on the couch, kitchen table, his car, the shower. They'd found a lot of creative places to explore each other.

Tonight, she'd invited him over to her place for the first

time. Jordan was staying at his boyfriend's place so they had the whole apartment to themselves. He was excited to see her place, but also nervous because something had been bugging him more and more as their time together went on. Something he never thought he'd ever do.

Break a rule.

Dyson sucked in a sharp breath. The idea of breaking his no-dating rule for Lexi had been bouncing around in his head for a while now. He rubbed at his chest, hands trembling slightly as fear still held him back. Logically he knew Lexi wasn't Grace. He could trust her, she wouldn't abandon him for someone else. But logic and emotions were two different things and some scars ran deep.

Too deep to be healed?

He had no idea, but he wasn't sure he could push away these feelings much longer.

He still couldn't believe he shared with Lexi the history about Grace and Adam that weekend in Estes. He never told anyone about his ex. The only reason the men and women at the firehouse knew is because they'd all been invited to the wedding so when it broke off, he had to tell them why. And even then, all he said was they broke up and she's with Adam now. His friends were smart enough to put two and two together.

He could blame his confession on the darkness of night or his brain turning to mush after the amazing sex, but truthfully, it was Lexi. She made him feel...safe. Like he could tell her anything and she wouldn't judge, wouldn't pity him. She just accepted it and offered comfort.

She cared.

And damned if he wasn't finding himself caring a lot more than he ever intended to. She was a good person, and he felt good when he was around her. This whole thing had started in order to convince his sisters, but somehow, at some point, he'd started convincing himself, too. Believing that maybe, just maybe this thing could turn into something real.

Could he trust that feeling? Trust himself? He'd fooled himself into thinking he was in love once before and look how that turned out. Obviously, what he and Grace shared wasn't love or she wouldn't have cheated on him. How did he know what he felt for Lexi was real? It could just be his mind confusing things. Adding feelings they'd been faking for the sake of his sisters.

Then again, there was nothing fake about the way he felt when she touched him, how his heart pounded when he held her in his arms. The rush of euphoria bursting from him when he brought her to the peak of pleasure. Nothing fake about that.

But sex was sex. It didn't necessarily mean love.

And in his experience, love often came with loss. Did he really want to risk going through all that again?

"Hey, man. You okay?"

Dyson glanced up to see Finn Jamison walking down the sidewalk toward the station. "Huh? Oh yeah, just...thinking."

"Seems like pretty heavy thoughts. Need an ear?"

He shook his head. "I'm good. Besides, you have next shift, right?"

Jamison glanced over Dyson's shoulder and shrugged. "I got a minute."

Dyson shifted on his feet, wondering how to put into words the jumbled mess that was his brain right now. If there was anyone to ask about relationships, Jamison would be the one to go to. The man had accidentally gotten his best friend pregnant, but it ended up working out, because they realized they loved each other and were now happily married with the most adorable twins Dyson had ever seen.

"Um, how did you know...I mean when did you know... when you and Pru, um..."

Jamison smiled. "When did I realize I was in love with Pru?"

"Yeah." At least someone knew what his brain was trying to say. Dyson felt like his head was filled with glue and the words he wanted kept sinking into the sticky mess. "How did you know it was real, what you felt, and not just due to the... circumstances?"

Jamison rubbed his chin, staring into the distance. "I think it was always there, in the back of my mind. But I ignored it for years out of...fear, I guess."

"But how did you get over that fear?"

"Do we ever get over fear?" Jamison lifted one shoulder in a small shrug. "I think I eventually saw that the thought of not being with Pru was more terrifying than the thought of going for it and losing her. Losing her I could live with because at least I tried, but never trying? Always wondering? Man, that felt like torture."

Dyson felt like he was being tortured at the moment. Torn between the risk and the reward. The what-if. That tiny jump off the cliff of possibility landing you on a cloud of happiness or smashing into the ground, a broken pile of pain. Would the wondering drive him mad if he never took that leap? Did he dare risk it?

All good questions, but he was forgetting one thing.

Lexi.

He was so concerned with what he wanted, what he felt, he hadn't even thought that she might not feel these same things. She might be just fine with what they had. She hadn't indicated anything to suggest otherwise.

He was getting ahead of himself. First, he had to go talk to Lexi before he made any decisions.

He glanced up with a smile. "Thanks, man."

"Glad to help." Jamison slapped a hand to Dyson's shoulder and gave him a firm pat. "Follow your heart, O'Neil.

You might not get the outcome you want, but it'll never lead you astray."

With that, his buddy headed into the station and Dyson got in his car and drove over to Lexi's. She'd promised to cook him dinner. His body was anxious for the possibilities that brought up, but his mind was terrified. Because he decided Jamison was right, he needed to follow his heart and as scared shitless as it made him to realize it…

His heart wanted Lexi.

He arrived at her complex, taking the empty parking spot on the street right in front of the building as a good sign. Locking his car, he headed up to her apartment, picking the stairs over the elevator. Yes, he just got off shift, which usually exhausted him, but his nerves were strung so tight, a little calisthenics might just do him some good. Work off a bit of this anxious energy.

He lifted his hand to knock and the door swung open.

"Hi, ten minutes early." Lexi smiled. "Right on time."

He chuckled, stepping into the apartment when she opened the door. It was a nice place. Bigger than his.

"Dinner is just about ready. I made lasagna, hope that's okay."

"Smells delicious."

Lexi headed off to the kitchen to check the oven. "Make yourself at home. I opened a bottle of wine. It's on the coffee table."

Dyson headed in that direction; with the open floor plan, the kitchen was visible from the living room area. He sat on the plush brown couch, grabbing the open bottle of cabernet and pouring it into the two glasses sitting next to it. His hand shook slightly, almost causing him to spill the deep red liquid, but he took a steadying breath, managing to keep all the wine in the glasses.

Should he bring up his question now or after dinner? Was

this an after-sex kind of talk or before? And why the hell was he so nervous about it?

He wiped his sweaty palm on his jeans and took a healthy swig of the wine. The rich, berry flavor followed by crisp oak hit his tongue, soothing his jagged nerves slightly. He needed to calm down. This wasn't a big deal.

Yes it is.

He was on the cusp of admitting he was ready to start a real relationship again. That was a big freaking deal. And if Lexi didn't feel the same way... The thought alone crushed him.

Dyson went to take another sip when something warm and heavy landed in his lap. He started, almost dropping his wine. A tiny red droplet plopped out of the glass and slid along the side. He looked down to see a black cat with one blue eye and one green, staring up at him.

"Meow!" The cat screeched at him as if Dyson had offended him in some way.

"Oh, hi there...cat."

"Lucifer!" Lexi called as she pulled the lasagna out of the oven. "Don't bother my guest."

"Meow!" the cat said again.

Dyson wasn't that great with animals. He'd never been around them much. His mother had been allergic to pet dander so they never had one growing up and after...well, pets were another mouth to feed and he had enough on his plate taking care of his sisters.

"Be careful, he likes to nip, but it never breaks the skin, I promise."

Lucifer stared up at him with bright eyes. The cat licked his nose, pawed Dyson's lap, then lay down, placing his head on his paws.

"Seems nice enough to me."

Lexi came over with a puzzled expression on her face.

"Well that's weird. Lucifer doesn't like...anyone. You must be something special."

She was something special.

"It's a good thing Lucifer likes you, because any guy I date has to pass the kitty test." She sat down on the couch, grabbing her glass of wine. "And most of them don't. Lucifer is like my own personal douchebag meter."

His eyes widened at her words and she laughed, her cheeks pinkening as she clarified, "Not that we're really dating, I just mean—"

"I know what you mean." The vise around his chest eased slightly. Maybe she did want the same thing as him, maybe this could all work out, maybe everyone was right and it was time for him to take a chance on love again. "Lexi, about our deal."

"Yes?" Her fingers tapped lightly against her wineglass.

His nerves started to ramp up again. He had to do something with all this energy but, since there was currently a sleeping cat on his lap, he couldn't move. He placed his wineglass on the coffee table and stroked the cat's fur. It was soft and soothing. Lucifer made a rumbling approval type of sound.

He opened his mouth, but his throat was tight. Damn nerves. He cleared his throat, blinking as his eyes started to water. What the hell? Was he getting emotional already? He hadn't even started to speak yet.

"Dyson?" Lexi's smile dipped, her brow furrowing as she stared at him. "Is everything okay?"

Yes. No. Maybe?

If he could just get the words out, ask her how she felt... but something was stopping him. He couldn't be this nervous, could he? Damn, he was actually starting to itch now. What was going on?

"I—" He rubbed his throat with his free hand—shit, the

thing was tight. His chest was starting to hurt, too. Lucifer purred in his lap, the cat blissfully uncaring that he was having a panic attack trying to talk to his human. "Lex—"

Lexi gasped. "Dyson, your face is swelling!" She glanced down to his lap. "Oh no, are you allergic to cats?"

He had no idea. He'd never really been around cats. Passed a few on the street a time or two, but he'd never spent any amount of time with the animals.

He shrugged, or tried to—honestly, everything was starting to get bleary as his eyes watered to the point where he felt a warm tear slide down his cheek.

"Shit!" Lexi swore, grabbing her cat from his lap and rushing the animal to her room as he hissed in protest. "Hold on, I think I have some antihistamine."

Yeah, it was too late for that. He'd been called to allergy emergencies before. They needed to get to the ER now.

He stood, stumbling a little as the breath wheezed in and out of his rapidly tightening airway. His chest felt like it had crushed in on itself.

Lexi's eyes widened, and she rushed to his side, holding a bottle of pink medicine in her hand.

"Take this. I'll drive you to the hospital."

He took a swig of the liquid antihistamine, grateful she didn't offer him any pills. He didn't think he could get those past his throat. It felt like it had almost completely closed off. *Shit!* He had no idea he'd inherited his mother's allergy. He should have gotten tested or something.

With the help of Lexi, he made it to her car, where she drove far above the speed limit, almost clipping a truck as she hurried to get them to the ER. Lucky for them, they didn't get pulled over. Dyson's entire body felt tingly, and not in the fun "I'm about to get laid" way. In the "oh shit I think I might die" way.

She stopped the car right at the ambulance entrance,

rolling down the window and screaming at the security guard for help. A nurse came out with a wheelchair and he was whisked away, only managing to gasp out a futile shout for Lexi as he passed through the emergency room doors.

The next ten minutes were a whirlwind of activity as the nurses and doctor asked him questions that he couldn't answer because his damn throat has closed up. Luckily Lexi rushed inside, telling them about the cat and his possible allergy. Next thing he knew, the doctor had a giant ass needle. Dyson hated needles. Freaked him the hell out and no, he was never making his needle phobia a Face-It challenge. Heights he could do, but needles, fuck off with that shit. He even got his flu vaccine with the nose mist stuff every year.

But, since he was in no condition to argue, the doctor stuck him with the sharp instrument of pain. He groaned, tears leaking from his eyes. Due to the needle or the allergic reaction, he wasn't sure, but soon he felt the pressure on his chest easing. His throat loosened. The tingles abated and his eyes stopped watering. Within ten minutes he could take deep, steady breaths again.

"Mr. O'Neil, have you ever had a reaction like this before?" The doctor asked, once Dyson could speak again and they'd used another giant ass needle to take some blood.

"I don't know. I haven't really been around cats much. My mom was allergic. We never had any pets growing up."

The doctor nodded, making some notes on her clipboard. "Okay, then we'll let you rest while we do a few tests."

He nodded, but the doctor was already moving away. Dyson closed his eyes, enjoying the feel of air filling his lungs as he took deep breaths, in and out.

"Dyson." Lexi's wavering voice hit his ears. "I am so, so sorry. I had no idea you were allergic. I would never have suggested you come over if—"

"Lexi." His eyes popped open, falling on the terrified

woman who probably saved his life tonight. He grabbed her hand, pulling her closer to the hospital bed. "It's okay. How could you know? I didn't even know."

"I know his name is Lucifer, but I swear my cat wasn't trying to kill you." She grimaced. "At least I don't think he was. I love him, but he is kind of a jerk. But cats don't know when humans are allergic to them, or maybe they do, but he's not evil—"

"Lexi," he said again with a small chuckle. "It's fine. You got me some antihistamine, you got me here faster than I ever thought was humanly possible. I mean, I'm pretty sure you found a secret wormhole or something. Even the rigs never make it to the ER that fast."

Laughter left her lips, a tiny sob choking the end of it. She blinked, a lone tear falling from the corner of her eye to trail down her cheek as she admitted in a hushed voice, "I was so scared."

He had been, too, but he was here and breathing. It was over now. Tugging her closer, he reached up to cup her face, bringing it down to his so he could kiss her. It was sweet, with a bite of salt from her tears.

"Thank you."

She snorted. "For what? Having my cat almost kill you? Oh God, this is even worse than the time I thought you were a strip-o-gram."

He laughed, kissing her again, deeper this time. The tingle on his lips had nothing to do with any allergy and everything to do with the woman before him.

"For saving my life. And like the strip-o-gram incident, we probably shouldn't tell my sisters about this. They'll just freak out and—"

"Ooooooh." Lexi winced.

Crap, that wasn't a good sound.

"What?"

She bit her lip, scrunching her nose slightly as she admitted, "I kind of already texted them as I was running inside after I parked the car. I'm sorry. I didn't know you—"

"Dyson!"

"Dy!"

Double crap.

The vultures were already here. Seconds later, the curtain partition was pulled back and both of his sisters stood there, the same worried expression on their faces.

"I'm okay, I just—*oof!*" He grunted as four arms were suddenly flung around him.

His vision was covered by hair, so much hair, as his sisters tried to love the life out of him with their hugs.

"A little air here. Just had an allergic reaction that closed my throat."

Immediately they released him.

"What happened?" Gemma asked.

"Since when do you have allergies?" Macy added.

Lexi gave them the quick rundown of Lucifer curling up in his lap and the quickness of his attack.

"Our mother was allergic to cats, too." Macy nodded. "All animal dander, actually. We never had any pets."

"I knew we all should have gotten allergy tests." Gemma sniffed, a few tears escaping the corners of her eyes to roll down her cheeks. "Dyson, I know you have a massive fear of needles, but if you'd had a test, then this wouldn't have happened!"

His baby sister had a point, but he knew her scolding him was simply cover for the terrifying scare he'd just put his sisters through. He reached out, snagging her behind the neck to pull her in for a hug and a hair ruffle.

"I'm okay, kid."

"I'm twenty-seven, not a kid," she complained, but squeezed him tight.

The doctor came back in then and explained the results of Dyson's tests. He had a severe cat allergy. Not the kind you could take an OTC antihistamine for or even the kind that would be controlled with a prescription pill. Oh no. He had the kind requiring a shot, and not just one shot.

"You'll need to get the shot on a regular schedule if you choose to address your allergy," the doctor said, handing him some paperwork. "Some people do see improvement and can decrease their shots over time, but not everyone. I would check to make sure your insurance covers it. Not all do, and it can be pricey. I also recommend staying away from all felines until you do decided to get the shots, so if you can let someone else watch your cat while—"

"It's my cat," Lexi's soft voice said from the corner. "I… uh, we don't live together."

The doctor nodded. "Then I recommend not visiting your friend's house until you've received your shot and know there are no adverse side effects. Then make sure you keep up a regular schedule of doses."

"I…" He swallowed hard, heart pounding louder each time the doctor said the word "shot." "I don't think I can get the shot, doctor. Is there any other treatment for a cat allergy?"

The doctor shook her head. "Not for one as severe as yours, Mr. O'Neil. If you don't wish to receive the shots, I suggest you keep your distance from all cats and any areas where cat hair might be shed heavily."

He glanced over to Lexi, her face pale, worry and sadness heavy in her eyes.

The doctor left, and the room was silent. It was Lexi who finally broke the tension.

"You should probably drive him home. I don't want to chance any… There might be cat hair in my car."

Both of his sisters passed a worried look between him

and Lexi. Gemma nodded, grabbing Macy's arm and pulling her away.

"We'll just go make sure the front desk has all your information, Dyson. Okay?"

"Well," Lexi sighed when his sisters were gone. "Now we have the perfect excuse for our breakup."

His heart slammed in his chest, breath stopping again, but this time it wasn't a physical reaction. Her words bounced around in his head. *The perfect excuse for our breakup. Breakup. Breakup.*

Hell, they did. But he didn't want that anymore. He wanted Lexi. He never planned on this happening—hell, he was all against it. But somewhere along the way, he'd forgotten his no-dating rule and fell for her. Hard. He couldn't explain it, but that panicked feeling he'd been getting for years whenever he started to get too close to someone just wasn't there with Lexi. Instead, he felt happy.

Warm.

Safe.

He didn't want to give that up. He didn't want to give *her* up. He knew that was always the plan, but plans could change. Life had proved that to him time and time again.

"You still want to break up?"

She stared at him, confusion turning down her lips. "That was the plan, right?"

"Yeah, but..." He cleared his throat, having no idea if it was still tight from the cat or the fear of the words he was about to utter. "I...want to change the plan."

"You want to change the plan?" she repeated, as if she hadn't heard him properly.

"Yes. I don't want to break up. I want to break my rule. I want to date you, Lexi. For real."

A smile started to brighten her face. "Really?"

His heart beat a furious tempo in his chest. Her joy made

him hope, hope he was doing the right thing, hope this time it would work. He could do this. They could do this. If they cared about each other, nothing could stand in their way. Warmth filled him as he stared into her eyes, so bright and full of happiness—the same happiness coursing through him. Excitement at the prospect of what the future held for them had him sitting up in the bed, reaching for her.

"Really."

"Oh Dyson." She stepped forward, but her footsteps faltered as she paused before reaching his bedside. "But what about Lucifer? Will you get the shots?"

"Fuck no." He shuddered as the memory of the needle the doctor had used on him when he first arrived caused his palms to sweat. They could find another way to—

"Fuck no?" Lexi's voice came out as a strangled whisper.

Shit, that hadn't been the right way to say it. His heart skipped a beat. A quick glance to her face let him know his terror-induced reaction to her question had been received wrong. He should have been gentler with his refusal. Fear started to claw its way up his throat, but he pushed it down. This wasn't a big deal. She had to know how utterly terrifying the thought of getting a shot on the regular was to him.

She'd understand. Lexi always understood. They would just have to find another solution. Softening his voice, he tried again.

"I can't get the shots."

"Then how can we be together?" She shook her head, smile gone, replaced with a pain-filled frown.

"We can figure it out." He scrambled, frantically searching his brain for some way to fix this. It wasn't a deal breaker, just a small stumbling block. "I never had a reaction before going to your place."

She took a small step back. "Yes, because I'm meticulous about cleaning the cat hair from my person before leaving the house."

That would explain why being near her never stirred up his allergy before. A small sigh of relief filled him. See, they could work this out. He knew there was a solution if they just talked about it.

"So I just don't go to your place then. Problem solved."

She took another step back and his gut tightened, hope fading as the cold sinking dread of fear started to seep into his body.

"Problem solved?" she scoffed. "So we can still be together as long as you never come over."

Yes, for safety's sake, that would be best. He didn't understand the angry glint in her eyes. Lexi had never looked at him like that before. He'd never seen Lexi angry at *anyone* before. The dark emotions crossing her face worried him, the painful twisting in his gut getting worse with each second. He opened his mouth to speak, but she plowed on.

"But what about down the road?" She shook her head, stepping back again. "What happens if things get more serious? If we want to move in together or get married? What then, Dyson? Am I supposed to give up Lucifer because you're afraid of needles? I can't, he's not just a pet, he's family!"

Shit, this was all going sideways and he had no idea how to stop it. "I would never ask you to give up Lucifer, Lexi."

"Then what do you propose? Huh? What's your solution?" Her voice waivered as she demanded he answer.

He lay there in the bed, unable to think, unable to move, unable to do anything to erase the pain and anger coming off her in waves. All of it directed at him. It wasn't fair of her to put this all on him. Besides she was thinking way too far in the future. They didn't need to figure out a solution right away. It could wait. They could just keep going as they were for the time being.

"I don't know, but we don't have to deal with any of that right now." He gave her a hopeful smile. "Why don't we just keep things as they are? Worry about the allergy stuff if it comes up later."

She blinked, tears drying up as her jaw dropped. "If? If it comes up?"

Shit, that hadn't been the right thing to say, either. He was screwing this all up. All the hope and joy that had been inside him just moments ago was snuffed out, like a single candle left out in a raging hurricane.

"I can't." She shook her head, stepping back once more until her feet were at the edge of the doorway. "I've given up so much, but I can't—I won't. I won't risk it. This won't work. We can't work. I have to do what Jordan said, focus on what I want. Lucifer and I are a package deal. If you can't grow up and get some damn shots, then you're not worth my time."

He sucked in a sharp breath as her barb hit him like a slap in the face.

Not worth my time.

He was such a fool. How could he have thought this time would be different? Hadn't he learned by now, no one stayed with him. Cold resolve settled over him as he clenched his jaw so tight his back molars ached. He should have known better than to dream, to hope. No one stayed with him.

Lexi made her choice, and it wasn't him. Fine. Whatever. And yet he still couldn't squash that tiny flame burning deep down inside. The one that whispered all wasn't lost, it could still work out. Staring into her eyes he clutched the hospital bedsheet in a tight grip.

"Guess you better leave then." He stared at her, eyes blurry, throat raw like he'd swallowed a fistful of glass. "Our deal is over. You don't need anything from me and I—I don't need anything from you anymore."

A few tears fell from her eyes, rolling down her cheeks as

she stared back, head shaking. "Goodbye, Dyson."

With that, she turned and ran from the room.

He lay in the bed, staring after her. Wondering why his heart—which should be cracked in two right now—felt nothing. There was nothing in his chest but a hollow, empty shell. He didn't feel anything. There was a deep yawing void where his emotions should be. Was this what it felt like to finally give up? Finally admit love wasn't for him and never would be? Had Lexi been the final straw?

Yet another person in his life who left him. Another person he imagined opening himself up to, possibly sharing something special with. Life made sure it wouldn't happen. He'd been right. Ward had been right. Dyson wasn't meant for long-term. People didn't stay with him. And he never should have entertained a damn fantasy about it working out with Lexi.

Fuck. He knew he should never have broken his rule. It was there to protect him and look what happened. A giant fucking needle and a broken heart all in one night.

Message received, universe. Love wasn't for him.

And it never would be.

Chapter Twenty-Three

Lexi trudged to the coffee maker, wishing she'd had the foresight to set the timer last night. She had zero energy this morning. Even the thought of making coffee exhausted her. She'd spent all last night crying into her pillow, guilt and sorrow mixing into a heavy brick that weighed down on her shoulders, cracking her heart with the pressure. Lucifer had crawled into her lap and stayed all night. Very unlike him. She wondered if the kitty felt bad for nearly killing Dyson.

Probably not.

She felt bad, terrible. For numerous reasons, the obvious one being her beloved pet causing the man she cared so much for to have an allergic reaction. She'd never seen one that bad. Over the years she'd had a date or two who was allergic to cats. One took an OTC antihistamine and was fine, the other claimed he couldn't take any medicine and bailed.

When she'd seen Dyson lying there in the hospital bed, gasping for breath...it terrified her. Much like the terror she witnessed in his eyes when the doctor stuck him with the needle. He might not have realized it, but his body was literally shaking with fear.

She understood his fear, but what she couldn't understand is how he thought they could work when he refused to even discuss the possibility of getting the shots. His refusal had been so quick, so adamant. As much as she wanted to do as he suggested and keep going as they were, see where things led and address the issue later, she couldn't.

That was old Lexi.

No way could she risk the possibility of spending more time with Dyson, falling even deeper only to one day face an ultimatum. Him or the cat.

Why the hell couldn't he just be a grown-up and get the shots? It was just a tiny prick of a needle.

Another tear leaked out. She brushed it away with the back of her hand. She really had to pull herself together. How was she going to get through the workday if she was a blubbering mess?

The apartment door swung open. Lexi quickly busied herself with filling the coffee maker and pressing the brew button.

"Hey Lex, how was the big night?" Jordon's cheerful voice filled the air. "Did Mr. Sexy Firefighter stay over?" He laughed, shouting toward her bedroom, "Yo, Dyson, you decent?"

She tried her best to cover the waver in her voice as she replied, "Nope, just me this morning."

"Lexi." His jovial tone dropped, concern replacing it. "What happened?"

She turned, not at all surprised to see her best friend suddenly by her side. She was crap at hiding her emotions. She glanced up. Jordan's concerned face stared down at her.

"Lucifer tried to kill Dyson." She glared at her beloved pet who sat on the kitchen table, licking his paw without a care in the world.

"Sit down." Jordan placed a gentle hand on her shoulder

and nudged her toward the table. "I'll get us coffee and you can tell me everything."

Oh goody, a rehashing of her horrible night. The very last thing she wanted to do. But, since she knew Jordan wouldn't let her leave the house until he knew she was okay, she sat. Lucifer reached out his furry paw and tapped her fingers. His way of apologizing?

"I'm sorry, sweetie." She reached up to scratch behind his ears. "I didn't mean to blame you, it wasn't your fault."

Satisfied the person who provided his food would continue to do so, Lucifer stood and leaped off the table, making his way to the well-worn cat bed in the corner of the living room.

"It wasn't done brewing yet," Jordan said as he placed a cup of coffee in front of her. "I might have spilled a bit on the burner filling the cups when I moved the pot."

He took a seat next to her at the table, his own cup of steaming coffee in front of him.

"So, what happened?"

Lexi blew on her drink, the rich scent of the caffeinated brew perking up her sleep-deprived brain a bit. She took a tentative sip, but it was still too hot so she set it back down. Her chest ached as she took a deep breath and launched into the events of last night. Dyson coming over, her slipup about calling him her boyfriend, Lucifer causing him to have an allergic reaction, the trip to the ER, and their subsequent breakup and Dyson's insistence that they could work things out but his refusal to get the shots.

"It wasn't even real," she sniffed. "How silly am I getting this upset over something I knew was coming?"

She tried for a laugh, but it came out as more of a watery sob.

"Because you wanted it to be real," Jordan said softly. "And it sounds like he did, too."

Her head snapped up, mouth opening in shock as she glared at her bestie. "He refused to get the shots, Jordan. I'm not giving up Luci for a guy."

"Did he ask you to?"

No," she grumbled, staring back down into her coffee. "But he said he would never take the shots, so what other option did I have?"

"The guy had a massive allergic reaction, Lex. Probably not the best time to discuss facing his greatest fear."

"You're supposed to be on my side!"

"I am on your side." He put down his coffee, reaching across the table to place a hand on her arm. "Lex, do you remember why we made the bet in the first place?"

'Cause she had crap taste in men and her bestie needed to be kicked into the next stage of his relationship. They were both chickens. But at least they were chickens together.

She took a sip of her coffee, cooled enough to drink without burning her tongue now. Jordan remained silent, waiting her out. He was so good at that. Got her to talk every time.

"We made the bet so I could focus on me."

"Yeah, but also so you would learn to ask for the things you want from the people around you."

She frowned. "I ask for stuff."

"You don't, Lex." He shook his head. "Unless it's for work. You never put yourself first or hell, even second. You're always tending to the needs of others while ignoring your own."

She shifted in her seat. This conversation was making her uncomfortable.

"What in the world does this have to do with Dyson and me?"

"You care about him," Jordan stated plainly. "Maybe even love him."

Her heart thumped in her chest at the word. Throat

tightening as a fresh wave of tears threatened to appear. Choking them down she shook her head. "It was fake."

"It wasn't, Lex." Jordan insisted. "Not for you, and not for him, either. Otherwise he wouldn't have asked to keep going. But before you two could figure things out you had this pretty traumatic event happen and it threw a wrench into everything."

"A sign from the universe," she sniffed, doing her best to staunch the tears threatening to fall.

"No, it was just crappy timing. As was your ultimatum to him."

"Hey!" Plunking her coffee down on the table, she glared at her roommate. "That's not fair. First I'm too soft, now I'm too hard. Which is it, Jordan?"

"You're scared."

Her heartbeat raced, nearly exploding as the truth of her roommate's words hit her full force.

"You're afraid and I bet he is, too." Jordan stood, scooting his chair until he was next to her. He wrapped a large arm around her shoulders and tugged her into his side. "Give him a few days. Let you both cool down. Then go, talk to him. Tell him what you want. Ask if you can help him work through his fear of needles. The guy has fears. So what? We all do, Ms. Coulrophobia. But the point is, we can face our fears, especially if we have the people we love by our side. Who knows? He might say yes."

"He might say no," she sniffed, rubbing her leaky eyes on her bestie's shirt.

"Maybe," he agreed. "But at least you would have asked for what you wanted. You want this guy, Lex?"

She nodded against him.

"Then go for it. Be direct, but kind. Ask for what you want."

Taking another sip, she stared into her coffee, admitting

in her mind that yes, Jordan had a point about her clown phobia, and thinking of Dyson and his sisters' Face-It challenge. How they worked every year on helping one another overcome a fear. Maybe she had been too harsh at the hospital, demanding he get the shots. Looking back, shame filled her.

Dyson had just suffered through something terrifying and there she'd been insisting he face his biggest fear. What was wrong with her? Why had she panicked like that?

"Because you freaked out," Jordan said, answering her unintended question. "We all do from time to time, but the real question is, what are you going to do about it now?"

She had no idea. Her head ached and the real crappy part was she couldn't even blame it on any delicious chocolate. Now the pounding in her skull was all due to this crap sundae of a situation. Dyson admitted he wanted to be with her, then turned around and refused to do the one task that would allow that to happen. Based on her past experiences, that should be a glaring red flag.

But then she remembered all the help he gave to the center. How he was working with Mateo on the junior firefighter program. How much his sisters loved him and how he looked after them. All the times he made her laugh, insisted she take a break, sent her body into the stratosphere with pleasure.

Those weren't the actions of a red flag.

Dyson was a person, just like her. With fears, just like her. And maybe, she could find a way for them to be together. Maybe they could face their fears.

Together.

"Ask, Lex," Jordan insisted. "Ask for what you want."

She took a deep breath, blowing it out as nerves tingled along her skin.

Ask. As easy and as difficult as that.

Chapter Twenty-Four

"Hey, O'Neil, you sure you're up for this?" Díaz asked. "Heard you had a rough one the other day."

Dyson hopped onto the rig, finding his jump seat in the back across from Díaz.

"Yeah, dude. We can handle the kiddie trip if you wanna hang back at the station," Ward said from his seat next to Díaz.

"I'm good. Besides, what if we get a call while you're out?"

They were headed to a local elementary school for a fire safety training presentation. They were always a lot of fun. Dyson got a kick out of the wide-eyed excitement of the kids when they came in wearing full gear. The shouts and declarations of the children who said they wanted to be firefighters, too. Of course, there was always one kid who wanted to start a fire to see them put it out. That kid always worried him.

He could use some good right now. Ever since Lexi left the hospital after literally running out on him, breaking up, and accusing him of being a coward, he'd felt like shit. *Fake* breaking up. Because they hadn't gotten a chance to make it real. She'd turned that idea down the second he refused to discuss getting the shots. It was for the best anyway. Stupid of him to think he could actually find happiness again. Hadn't he learned yet that life liked to rip the rug out from under him right when it would hurt the most?

He didn't know what sucked more, the allergic reaction to Lexi's cat or knowing they were over before they even had a chance to see if they could be something real.

"He's got a point," Kincaid said from up front. "We can't leave him behind, but seriously, man. You okay? I heard you had some kind of animal attack or something?"

"Okay, one, which of my sisters have you all been talking to? And two, it was an allergic reaction, *not* an animal attack."

Lexi might call her cat Lucifer, but he'd been sweet as an angel to Dyson. Except for the whole almost-killing-him thing, but that hadn't been the cat's fault.

"I didn't know you were allergic to cats, dude."

"Me either." He sighed as Kincaid pulled the rig out of the station and onto the streets of Denver. "It's really bad, too. I'd have to get regular shots."

"Shit man, that sucks." Kincaid swore.

Díaz pulled her dark, curly hair into a high ponytail, staring at Dyson. "No one talked to your sisters. Chief just said something about not letting any cats into the station or you might die."

Right, the Chief. He told his boss about his allergy because it could affect his job if they ever had a rescue with felines. One touch of a cat and Dyson would soon become the emergency.

And unless he got the shots, he always would.

Chills wracked his body just thinking about it. He couldn't. But remembering the pain in Lexi's eyes as he denied even the possibility made his stomach churn with guilt. A part of him wished so badly he could just suck it up and do it. Get the shots. But something kept holding him back. And it wasn't just his fear of needles. There was something deeper, a sinister voice whispering that it would change nothing. He'd never deserve love so why even try.

"What were you doing with a cat?" Ward asked. "I didn't think you had any pets."

"I don't." His jaw clenched. "It's Lexi's cat."

Ward sucked in a sharp breath. "Ooooh, that sucks dude."

"You gonna get the shots?" Díaz asked.

"I don't need to get the shots," he insisted.

Ward and Díaz exchanged a glance. Díaz raised an eyebrow, but it was Ward who asked, "Dude, how you gonna hang with Lexi if you're allergic to her cat? You're not making her give up her pet, are you?"

"Of course not!" He scowled at his crewmate. How could the guy ever think Dyson would pull such a dick move? "Our hanging days are o-over." He stumbled on the word, ignoring the sharp pain it caused in his chest.

"You two are done? Just like that?" Díaz asked, the second brow rising to join her first.

He nodded. "This gives us the perfect excuse for a breakup. Hell, Lexi even suggested it herself."

"Wait." Kincaid glanced quickly in the rearview mirror before turning his attention back to the road. "I'm missing something here. You and Lexi broke up? And it was planned?"

Dyson slumped back against his seat as Ward and Díaz filled him in on the whole fake dating Lexi to appease his sisters thing. When they finished, Kincaid shook his head and whistled.

"What?"

"Nothing, I didn't say a thing."

Yeah, but that head shake spoke volumes. He had

something to say, Dyson knew it. Everyone did. All a bunch of Nosy Nellys at Station 42.

"So that's it then?" Ward glared at him. "You two are over?"

Why was everyone suddenly so invested in his fake relationship?

"Yeah, Ward, we were always going to break up eventually, and why the hell are you so interested in my love life? I thought you'd be happy, we didn't make it a month so this means you win your bet with Díaz."

"You guys bet on his love life?" Kincaid asked, eyebrows climbing his forehead. "That's kind of messed up."

"It was his fake love life," Díaz countered. "And this doesn't mean Ward won shit."

Ward chuckled. "What do you prefer, Díaz? Lasagna or stuffed chicken?"

"I'm going to stuff my foot up your ass if you don't knock it off, Ward." She glared. "Our friend is hurting."

"I'm fine."

"Bullshit, dude." Ward shook his head. "As much as I'd love to watch Díaz choke down a Ward dinner special, she's right."

"If you all have something to say, stop tiptoeing around it and spit it out." Because he was tired of trying to guess what people were feeling. He never got it right anyway. Sure as hell hadn't with Lexi, considering how fast she ran out of the hospital the second she had the chance.

"Fine." Díaz leaned toward him. "You want the truth? The bet was just a way to help you get your head out of your ass and start letting yourself open up to people again."

"You're just saying that because you lost," Ward snickered.

"Shut up, Ward."

The man mimed zipping his lips.

Díaz rolled her eyes and continued. "You've been a hell of a lot happier since Lexi came into your life. We all noticed."

"I don't really know much about Lexi," Kincaid said. "But I have noticed you smiling more the past few weeks."

Díaz nodded. "You're a great guy, O'Neil, but ever since Grace broke your heart and Adam betrayed you, you kind of crawled into yourself. Shut a part of you away. And since Lexi, that part has come to life brighter than we've ever seen before."

"Why the hell am I even a topic of conversation?"

"Because we love you, dude, and Díaz refuses to talk about her feelings because she doesn't have any on account of being a robot, so she has to decipher others' human emotions to replicate them."

"I swear to God, Ward, I will put itching powder in your boxers again, do not test me. Just shut up before I decide the kids need a real-life stop drop and roll demonstration and light your ass on fire."

Ward saluted her with his middle finger.

Díaz returned the gesture, but her lips curled in a small smile before she turned back to Dyson. "As I was saying, you seemed a lot happier since you started hanging out with Lexi. Even if it was all fake to begin with, then I think—we all think—if there's any chance it could turn into something real, you should probably go for it. Get the damn shots and go for it."

Easier said than done. None of them broke out into a cold sweat when they saw a sharp object about to pierce their skin.

"I know no one asked my opinion," Kincaid lifted one hand from the wheel to give a tiny wave before replacing it. "But I am the only one here with recent experience in this area."

Considering the guy was getting married to the love of his life in just a few months, Dyson figured he would be the one to take relationship advice from. He knew Kincaid and Tamsen had a bit of a falling out that almost ended their relationship. Somehow Kincaid managed to pull his head out of his ass to win over the woman he loved.

"I'm listening." Dyson dipped his chin.

"Relationships are terrifying."

Oh good, off to a bad start already. He couldn't wait for the rest of Kincaid's sage advice.

"But"—the man held up a finger—"if they're right, they can be the most wonderful, rewarding, and safest thing in your life. The key is communication. You have to talk to your partner, make sure you're both on the same page. Even when it's right, it's not easy. Love isn't magic. You have to work hard, learn to compromise, face your fears. But when it's real, you do those things together and it makes it so much easier."

Was he serious? There was nothing simple about exposing your vulnerabilities to someone you cared about. It basically made you the deer standing in front of the hunter, hoping he just wanted a shot with a camera and not a bullet that dug so deep into your heart, it killed you.

"We're here," Kincaid announced.

The rig pulled into a large bus turnaround at the end of the elementary school. Dyson looked out the window, mustering up a smile to wave at the forty or so kids lined up on the sidewalk, all jumping and shouting with more enthusiasm than should be humanly possible.

Once the rig was parked, they all filed out. A tall woman in a bright yellow dress did one of those rhythmic clapping things that got all the kids to stop shouting and jumping as they mimicked her. After two different patterns, the woman spoke loudly while a shorter man dressed in all black beside her interpreted with ASL.

"Okay, children, I know you're all very excited to see the firefighters of Station 42. They're going to share with us what it's like to be a firefighter and how to stay safe around fire, so I want you to pay attention and give a big Cougar Springs welcome to Station 42."

The kids all lifted their hands in imitations of cat paws and let out loud roars.

"Wonderful! Now, everyone come sit crisscross applesauce. Mr. Agate's class, good, good. Mx. Gray's class, Ms. Peterson's class."

Dyson's head snapped up, eyes scanning the crowd of children being shuffled around by their teachers. Peterson was a fairly common last name. It didn't mean anything. She hadn't had a full-time teaching assignment when they'd ended things. She and Adam could have moved out of state for all he knew. Hell, he had no idea if they were even still together. But then his eyes snagged on a familiar head of red hair, pulled back into a no-nonsense ponytail that he remembered well.

Grace.

What the hell were the odds that today of all days he'd run into his ex? Fucking hell, fate really wanted to give him the business lately. There was no chance for him to hide or pretend he didn't see her. She was staring straight at him. She offered him a small wave and his hand went on autopilot, waving back.

Thankfully he had a job to do to distract him. For the next forty-five minutes, he worked with his crew on the teaching material they'd done a million times before. The school programs were fairly easy and pretty fun. The children were always excited to learn about fire safety, but of course the best part was at the end when they let the kids check out the rig.

As they all formed a line to wait their turn, he felt a small tap on his shoulder. Turning, he came face-to-face with the woman he once thought was his forever.

"Hi, Dyson."

"Grace." He waited for the anger to burn his gut, the pain of betrayal to sting, but it never came. Instead, as he looked into the face of his ex, Dyson felt...nothing. A strange sense of relief washed over him at the realization.

"Can...can we talk? Just for a minute?"

He glanced over to his crewmates, who nodded.

Kincaid gave him a thumbs-up. "Go ahead, we got this."

He motioned with his chin to the far side of the rig. Once he and Grace were far enough away from the prying ears of the kids and his crewmates, he turned to her.

"I didn't know you'd gotten a full-time position."

"Yeah, two years ago. Adam's boss's husband is on the school board and he told me a teacher was retiring and..." She trailed off, clearing her throat. "But that's not important. What I wanted to say was, I'm sorry."

He nodded, accepting her apology.

"Adam and I never meant for any of this to happen, and I understand why you cut us out of your life. Honestly if the situation were reversed, I would have done the same. But over the years, I've come to realize I didn't apologize for the right thing."

His head tilted, wondering if it wasn't the cheating, what else she could be apologizing for. "I'm listening."

She took a deep breath, and he noticed that while she was still Grace, still attractive and smart and everything he remembered about her, she didn't make his heart beat faster. He didn't feel that attraction he used to. No love, no anger. Perhaps a touch of nostalgia, the way one did when running into an old friend at a high school reunion. Curious, but not overly moved in any direction.

"I never should have cheated on you. That was wrong, but what I *also* should have apologized for was not talking to you." She shook her head. "I know you think everything in our relationship was going fine, but for me, it wasn't. I was feeling...off and having doubts. I should have shared them with you. That was my fault. But I thought they were just normal pre-wedding jitters that all brides-to-be get."

She had doubts? He had no idea. Though if he was honest with himself, he'd had them too. Tiny whispers in the middle of the night that something wasn't quite right. Like her, he chalked them up to cold feet. Everyone had them. Or so he thought.

"That night with Adam...when you came home...it was the first time, I swear. We didn't mean to hurt you like that, but"—she covered her face with her hands—"Oh, this still sounds awful, but it's true."

Dropping her hands, she stared straight at him, regret and truth shining from her eyes. "That tiny bit of doubt I felt with you, I never felt around Adam. I knew doing anything with him while I was still with you was wrong, but I've never felt wrong with him. I've always felt..."

"Safe," he finished.

"Yes," she smiled. "I've never doubted my feelings for him."

He couldn't believe he was about to do this, but he opened his mouth and asked his ex-fiancée, "Do you ever doubt his feelings for you?"

She chuckled. "I wouldn't be human if I didn't doubt every now and then, I think, but I've learned to be better about voicing my concerns. We talk about things, everything. He shows me how much he cares every day and tells me, too, just to be sure. It's easy to know how you feel, but people aren't mind readers. You have to talk things out to be on the same page and that's where I failed you, failed us. For that I will always be sorry. Because maybe if I had spoken up...it wouldn't have ended the way it did."

"But it would have ended," he stated, because it was the truth. He knew that now. He and Grace were never meant to be forever. But he'd been so hurt, so triggered by the loss of yet another person in his life, he hadn't faced the truth that they never would have made it because they didn't love each other. Not in a forever kind of way.

"Yes, it would have," she agreed. "Anyway, I just wanted to tell you that and also…Adam says if you ever want to punch him in the face, he deserves it."

He chuckled. Yeah right, his ex-best friend knew Dyson didn't get violent. Cut people out of his life, sure, but physical violence? Wasn't in his nature.

"Thanks, but I'll pass." Though maybe it was time to move on, heal old wounds and all that.

"He really misses you, Dyson."

Shit. If he was being honest with himself, he missed his best friend, too. Adam's betrayal hurt, but cutting the other man from his life felt like severing a limb. Both realities were painful in their own way. Maybe it was time to sit down with his former best friend and see if things could be mended. They'd definitely never get to where they had been in their friendship, but maybe they could be something new.

Maybe he didn't have to always lose the people he loved.

Grace started to head back to the kids.

"Hey, Grace?"

She turned her head.

"Maybe…someday we can all grab a cup of coffee and… catch up."

She smiled, a shuddering breath leaving her as tears welled in her eyes. "I'd like that, and I know Adam would, too."

He never thought he'd say this but, "All right then, I'll shoot you both a text sometime."

With a nod, Grace walked back to the slowly dwindling line of kids waiting their turn for a tour of the rig.

Dyson tried to get ahold of all the feelings swirling inside him. The truths that had just been revealed. The ones that he finally acknowledged for himself. And one that he had been ignoring for days now. He didn't just care for Lexi.

He loved her. Even though he doubted her feelings for him, he realized he'd never doubted his feelings for her, and never would.

But there were a few obstacles in his way. One being the bet. That was fine. He could wait a few months to officially start dating her, if she wanted. And according to everyone in his life, he needed to put his grown-up pants on and work up the courage to talk to her. *Communication is key.*

Yeah, but it was also scary as hell. He'd put himself out there with her once, and she'd turned him down.

Because I was too chicken to get a shot. Come on man, even babies get shots.

Right. He could do this. He could face his fears. Lexi didn't need maybes or empty promises. She had enough of those from her jerk exes. He needed to show her he cared. Prove to her she was worth it.

And she was worth it.

Lexi was worth everything.

This was his own personal Face-It challenge.

A grin tilted the corner of his lips. Looked like he had a call to make. Slipping his phone out of his pocket, he texted his sisters.

Dyson: *I need you two to hold me down.*

Gemma: *For what?*

Macy: *I got some old furniture straps somewhere.*

He smiled and texted them his plan, laughing when they texted back varying emojis and gifs both insulting him and congratulating him.

Gemma: *We're there!*

Macy: *Name the time, Dy.*

He laughed, slipping his phone back into his pocket and heading to the rig to help finish the work he was supposed to be doing. When he got back to the station, he'd work on the next part of his plan.

"Dude, was that Grace?"

He nodded to Ward. "Yup."

"Fuck, man, I'm sorry."

He shook his head. "Don't be. Talking to my ex might just have been the best thing in the world."

Ward raised a brow, looking at him like he'd lost his mind. Maybe he had a little, but what he knew for sure was he lost his heart, and hopefully the woman he lost it to felt the same.

Chapter Twenty-Five

"Okay, Mr. O'Neil, are you ready?"

No, no, hell no, he wasn't ready.

This had seemed like such a good idea when he made the appointment yesterday.

Dyson stared at the giant fucking needle in the nurse's hand. Why was the damn thing so big?

"It isn't big," Macy stated. "It's a normal sized needle, your fear is just exacerbating it and now you're talking with your outside voice like your girlfriend."

"She's not my girlfriend," he answered, unable to take his eyes off the pointy instrument of pain. "Not yet."

Hopefully all that would change tonight. Right after he passed out from fear.

His vision dimmed as the needle got closer, breath shallow. Sweat started to bead on his forehead, rolling down the side of his face.

"Hey, Dy." Gemma snapped her fingers in his face, grabbing his chin and turning it so he was staring at her instead of the shot. "Don't focus on it—think of Lexi. You're doing this for Lexi."

No, he was doing it for them. For him and for Lexi. Because he wasn't afraid anymore.

No, that was bull. He was still petrified. Of needles and of opening himself up again, losing someone else he loved. But he'd rather be terrified with Lexi than without her. Better to face his fears with someone by his side than ignore them and try to push them deep down inside. All that did was let them fester and grow until they consumed him, convincing him he was happy and fine when in reality he'd been slowly dying. Becoming a husk of his former self.

"Are you sure you can't give him something to sedate him?" Gemma asked the nurse, gripping his hand tightly.

The nurse shook her head. "I'm afraid not. We need him fully coherent and alert so he can be aware of any side effects."

"You got this, Dy." Macy nodded to him.

"We're right here for you," Gemma added.

He smiled at his sisters. Opening his mouth to thank them right before a sharp, stabbing pain lanced into his upper arm. His thanks turned into a sharp and very loud curse.

"Holy fucking shitty fuck balls!" His chest heaved as he sucked in deep, heaving breaths of air, the burning pain dimming but not disappearing. A light sting hit his other arm. He glanced up to see Gemma scowling at him.

"Did you just smack me? Right after I got a shot?"

"Yes, but at least I smacked the arm you didn't get a shot in."

"Why?"

"Even if it hurt that's no excuse to swear like that." She motioned to the nurse with a roll of her eyes.

He winced when the nurse placed a bandage over the spot where the needle had been inserted. His face burned worse than his arm. Chastised and embarrassed, he offered an apology to the nurse who was only doing her job. "Sorry. I didn't mean to yell like that."

"You're fine, Mr. O'Neil. I've had worse. Once a poor kid accidentally kicked me in the stomach during a flu vaccine. Sweet kid didn't mean it, but it sure did hurt."

That sucked. He'd had to dodge a swing a time or two from rescue victims. People panicked when they were in pain or afraid. Sometimes when they rescued people from burning buildings the people were so terrified, they didn't recognize the rescue and tried to fight to get free. He understood. Still sucked to get battered and bruised just for doing your job trying to help.

"I should have tempered my reaction, I'm sorry."

The nurse smiled, tossing the trash from the bandage and the gauze in the garbage and putting the needle in the red and white disposal bin attached to the wall.

"You're all set, Mr. O'Neil. Here's the paperwork with all the listed side effects—please call the office immediately if you experience any of them."

He took the paper, glancing over the list of things that could ruin his grand plan.

"How long before we know if the medication works?" He was normally a pretty patient person, but this, with Lexi, he couldn't wait. Not one minute more. "When can I be around a cat?"

One cat in particular and his beautiful, wonderful human.

The nurse noted something in her chart before glancing up with a smile. "You can test it out within the hour, but be cautious. If you notice any sign of an allergic reaction, go to the ER immediately."

He would, but he really hoped he didn't have to. This had to work. He was facing his fears and he'd be damned if a five-pound ball of danger fur kept him from the woman he loved. He'd buy a duplex and let Lucifer have the entire second side all to himself if that's what it took to keep Lexi in his life.

"Remember, you'll have to schedule regular doses, you can do that on your way out," the nurse said before leaving the room.

Anxious to get to Lexi he started to slip off the table, but his phone pinged with an incoming message. Pulling it out of his pocket, he glanced at the message and swore.

"What?" Macy asked, glancing over his shoulder at the phone.

"Work," he muttered, cursing fate who was still being quite the bitch to him. "Turner got the flu. Chief needs me to come in."

Dammit, he wanted to go to Lexi. His body was vibrating with anxious nerves. Now he'd have to work an entire twenty-four-hour shift before he could see her, show her what he did. Tell her how much she meant to him.

"Damn," Gemma swore. "Want us to tell her to meet you at the station?"

"No." He shook his head. This just gave him more time to plan a perfect sweep-her-off-her-feet moment anyway. "I can wait."

Life made him wait for her this long. What was a few more hours? He loved her, and if she loved him, too, there was nothing in this world that would keep them apart.

Not even the risk of death by kitty.

• • •

"Did I really use the word 'feel' twenty-seven times in this letter?" Lexi stared at the paper scrawled with her sloppy handwriting. No matter how much her fifth grade teacher Mr. Critchlow made her practice, she never managed to perfect the pretty swoops and neat lines of penmanship. Not that it mattered much, since almost all forms of communication came from a computer these days.

But not this one.

This was special, important. This letter had the potential to create happiness or devastation. That is, if she could make it sound like a coherent adult wrote it instead of a toddler whose entire vocabulary consisted of five words. Seriously, how many times did she say "think?" Was it fifty? It felt like fifty.

"Come on, Lexi. You write grant proposals all the time. If you can ask rich tightwads to part with thousands of dollars, you can do this. It's easy."

It wasn't. Asking for money was one thing. If she got a no from a grant, there was always another to apply to. But this, this was asking for someone's heart. Someone's love. There was only one Dyson. If she was rejected…

She knew there were plenty of fish in the sea and all that, but she loved *this* fish.

"You love what fish?"

Lexi jumped, quickly shoving the letter under a pile of paperwork on her desk. She glanced up to see Zoe leaning against the open doorframe.

"Fish are gross. They swim in their own poop."

Zoe nodded, walking into the office and sitting down in one of the chairs across from Lexi's desk. "Agreed, it's why I don't eat it. Well, that and I'm a vegetarian, but you were the one who said you loved a fish."

Lexi shifted in her seat. "I was speaking metaphorically."

Zoe's lips spread in a knowing grin. "Let me guess, is it a firefighting fish who's super sweet, donates his time to fix up the center, is sexy as hell, and goes by the name Dyson?"

Thunking her head down on the desk, she groaned, "Yes."

"And this is a problem because?"

Lexi took a deep breath. She launched into the

explanation. Offering to be Dyson's fake girlfriend, getting closer to him, sleeping with him, falling for him, her cat trying to kill him and their subsequent "not a real breakup" breakup, his refusal to get the shots. Ending with her talk with Jordan and the realization that she hadn't been quite fair and she needed to start asking for what she wanted.

Namely a real relationship with Dyson.

After she was done, she slumped back in her chair, watching Zoe's face as her friend processed all the information she'd been given.

"Wow," Zoe finally said. "That's...that's a lot."

"I know! And so now I'm trying to write him a heartfelt letter explaining how I feel, but it reads like a two a.m. rambling drunk text. It's redundant and repetitive and I keep saying the same thing so it sounds silly and how is this going to convince him I love him, can be patient with his needle phobia, and we should take a chance?"

Zoe laughed, smothering her mouth with a hand when Lexi glared.

"I'm sorry, Lex, as cool and calm as you are when dealing with center emergencies, you're the exact opposite with personal ones."

"Exactly! That's why I need help." She grabbed the letter out from under the pile and shoved it toward Zoe. "Here, you write it."

"Oh no." Zoe held up her hands. "I am not going to be your Cyrano. Whatever you write will be perfect because it's coming from you—it's the truth, your truth. And if the guy is as smart as he is sexy, he'll get the shots."

She chewed on her lip as the memory of Dyson in the hospital bed filled her mind, his forehead damp as the doctor talked about the allergy shots.

"I don't know, Zoe. He's really freaked out by them."

"We all freak out about something, Lex, but I know one

thing for sure: love is stronger than fear."

She hoped her friend was right.

Her office phone rang. Lexi glanced at the ID and saw it was the front. One of the college volunteers was manning the front desk today. She answered as cheerily as she could, "Hello?"

"Hi Ms. Martin. There's a person from the fire department here to do the re-inspection."

"Send them on back."

She hung up the phone. Her heart jumped into her throat. Butterflies swarmed in her stomach. Dyson was here! No, she wasn't ready yet. The letter needed at least two more passes and a spell check. She hadn't realized he'd be coming in today for the final inspection. Why didn't he text her?

Because you basically called him a coward and ran out on him after he nearly died from your cat.

She winced. Oh right. Oh no, what if she was all wrong about this? What if Dyson was so angry with her, he refused to listen?

Didn't matter, he was here now. This was her chance. She had to talk to him, lay it all out on the line. Here went—

A figure filled the open doorway. A much smaller, curvier, decidedly *female* figure.

Nothing. Here went nothing because the person standing there in a Denver FD T-shirt, clipboard in hand, was not Dyson. She looked familiar, though. Lexi searched her memory. Oh right, trivia night. She was the woman on Dyson's team.

"Díaz, right?"

The woman nodded. "Good memory, Lexi. Is it okay if I call you Lexi?"

She nodded, even though what she really wanted to do right now was curl up into a ball and cry. Her heart sank from her throat to the pit of her stomach that no longer had fluttering butterflies but churned with gut-wrenching disappointment.

Where was Dyson? Why did he send someone else to do the inspection? What did it mean? Was it because she broke up with him?

"I'm here to complete the inspection. Since Dyson did the work, he can't sign off on the final paperwork. It doesn't have anything to do with your...thing." Díaz smiled warmly.

One of these days she was going to get a muzzle for her annoying brain. Maybe she could enter some kind of scientific trial. A pill for people whose mouths didn't know when to shut up.

"Sorry, I kind of—"

"Talk out loud when you don't mean to?" Díaz chuckled. "Yeah, Dyson told us."

She wondered what else Dyson told them.

"Are you ready?" Díaz held up the clipboard.

Coming around her desk, she nodded. "As we'll ever be."

After handing off some more grant proposal papers to Zoe, Lexi took Díaz around the center while the woman inspected things and made marks on her clipboard. Lexi wanted to ask so many questions, but not about the inspection. She had full and complete faith that Dyson had done excellent work. It was the man himself she wanted to know about.

How was he? Where was he? Had he talked about her? Did he want to see her? Did he care for her?

But that wasn't why Díaz was here, and Lexi didn't want to be unprofessional.

Twenty minutes later, they were back in her office and Díaz was handing over a yellow copy of the report with a smile.

"You passed with flying colors. Dyson sure did a great job here."

Naturally. The man was amazing and sweet and sexy

and, oh sweet chocolate hell she really missed him.

Díaz started to leave but stopped. The other woman turned to face Lexi, her jaw working back and forth as if she wasn't sure she should speak or not.

"Listen, Lexi, we don't know each other that well, but Dyson is my friend and I just want to know if you care about him? Like for-real care?"

Right, Díaz was one of the crew members who was in on the bet, if Lexi remembered correctly. The woman had to know their entire relationship was fake. So then why was she asking if Lexi cared for real?

"Yes," Lexi said, unable to lie about it anymore. "I care very deeply for Dyson."

The corner of Díaz's lips curled. "Good to hear."

She turned and Lexi touched her arm, pulling Díaz back around to face her.

"Wait, that's it? That's all you wanted to know?"

"Yup."

"Why?"

Again, the woman appeared as if she didn't know if she should speak or not. She chewed on her bottom lip before saying with a secret grin, "Let's just say if your answer had been no, things would be really awkward for you tomorrow."

"Tomorrow?" She shook her head, not following the woman's cryptic statement. "What's happening tomorrow?"

Díaz zipped her lips. "I can't say, but Dyson is off tomorrow."

Meaning he was working today? Dyson was at the station right now?

Díaz winked. "See ya round, Lexi."

What? What did that mean? But Díaz was gone, leaving Lexi holding their passing inspection papers in one hand and a million questions in the other.

Chapter Twenty-Six

"Mateo, what are you still doing here?" Lexi locked her office and turned to face the teen standing in the hallway. "Is your mom coming to pick you up or do you need a ride home?"

"Oh no, Ms. Martin. My mom's here, but she wanted me to give you this."

He handed over a covered dish that smelled so delicious, Lexi wanted to rip off the foil and eat it right there. A rich meaty scent wrapped itself around her, tempting her as her empty stomach growled in anticipation. That's what she got for skipping lunch.

"Is this your mother's carne guisada?" Please, oh please let it be her carne guisada. The last time Lexi tasted it she'd thought she'd died and gone to foodie heaven.

Mateo nodded. "My mom made it for your boyfriend, Dyson."

Her mouth stopped salivating. Heart dipping at the sound of Dyson's name. Pain and hope warred within her. Díaz's secret smile had been tormenting her brain all day. What did the woman know? What was happening tomorrow?

It had sounded like Dyson might have a plan to see her. Her heart raced with the thought. Did he want to talk? Had he forgiven her for what she said at the hospital? Was he willing to give them another shot...maybe talk about eventually getting the shots?

So many questions and none she could get answers to until tomorrow.

Unless...

"She wanted to thank him for helping me get into the Junior Firefighter Program."

Pushing her own issues to the side, she focused on Mateo and his excellent news. "You got in? That's wonderful, Mateo."

He smiled, so pure and full of hope, it warmed her heart.

"Yeah, Dyson even helped me fill out the paperwork so I got a scholarship. He's a badass— I mean he's pretty cool, Ms. Martin."

She agreed. He was badass. She understood why Díaz had to do the inspection today, but that didn't mean her heart wasn't breaking at not being able to see him. The fact that he didn't even text to let her know. Still, he kept his word to Mateo, helped the kid while most people would have just tossed out the program name and let him figure it out himself. Dyson actually spent time with the boy, guiding him, offering any help he could because that's the kind of person he was.

A good one. The best, actually.

"Well congratulations, Mateo. I can't wait to see you succeed in the program. Tell your mother thank you and I'll be sure to get this to Dyson."

Mateo nodded, hiking his backpack up on his shoulder and offering her a little wave as he headed down the hall and out of the center.

Lexi stared after him, the warm dish heavy in her hands. Weighted by much more than the nourishing meal it held.

She supposed she had to give this to Dyson. And why not give it to him now? The station could always use a tasty meal, right? Why shouldn't she go deliver this and if she got the chance to talk to Dyson that was just a bonus.

Her hands trembled and she tightened her grip. Tomorrow was too long to wait. She'd be an absolute wreck. No, going tonight, now was better. But first she had a stop to make.

Pulling out her phone she hit her speed dial. After two rings Jordan picked up.

"Hey, Lex. You on your way home?"

"No. I need a favor."

"Anything. What's up?"

Wondering if she was losing her mind, she sucked in a deep breath and spoke, "I need you to meet me at the costume store on Broadway and help me pick out a clown costume."

Silence filled the other end of the line.

"Jordan? Hello?"

"Yeah, yes, I'm here I just can't believe you asked me that."

Her either. But she asked Dyson to face his fear of needles. What kind of hypocrite would she be if she didn't face her own? Terror made her throat dry and her hands clammy, but she pushed it aside. She had to do this, had to show him how serious she was.

"Will you come or not?"

"Already out the door, Lex."

A pinch of calm settled over her. She loved her bestie.

Twenty terrifying minutes later she was dressed in a red and white polka dot oversized jumpsuit. A curly rainbow wig sat on her head, squeaky oversized shoes lay in the passenger seat beside her, and the red rubber nose covered her real one smelling like rotten plastic.

"I can do this, I can do this, I can do this." She whispered the mantra over and over as she drove toward the station.

She could do this. As long as she didn't look at herself in the mirror. The letter for Dyson was tucked away in the pocket of the ridiculous outfit. She'd gone over and over it all afternoon, making sure every word was perfect, every meaning clear. All she could do now was read it to him and hope it conveyed how sorry she was and how much he meant to her. As she parked in front of the station she reached a hand in and grasped it, feeling the weight of possibilities it carried on its pale, lead scribbled page.

Funny how a few ounces of paper felt so heavy.

Taking a few deep breaths, she released her death grip on the steering wheel.

"I can do this. I can do thi—"

"You can do it a lot better if you get out of the car, Chuckles." Jordan's smiling voice sounded from outside her closed window.

She turned her head, glaring at her best friend. "Give me a second, and don't call me Chuckles."

"You gotta pick a name for the video, Lex." He held up his phone, giving her a teasing grin.

She flipped him the bird, opening the car door. "No videos and I'm not wearing this to clean the apartment. I'll clean, but this outfit is a one-time thing."

Jordan shrugged. "Okay, fine. I'll let you get away with it, but only because I love you."

"I love you too." Her legs shook as she slipped off her shoes and reached for the oversized clown ones, placing them on her feet with a grimace. "Thanks for helping me with this but..."

Fear clogged her throat, making her question everything. She stared down at the obnoxious red and yellow boats disguised as footwear currently enveloping her feet. While the sight alone terrified her, the thought of doing this, putting herself out there, asking for what she wanted and having

Dyson reject her...

That was scarier than anything she'd ever faced in her life.

"Lex," Jordan said softly, crouching down and staring into her face. "You got this. Go in there and tell that man how you feel, tell him what you want."

"But what if it's too late?" She'd been awful at the hospital. The things she said, the way she ran. What if he didn't forgive her?

"It's never too late to tell someone how you feel. In fact..." He smiled, pure happiness radiating out of his dark brown eyes. "Just this morning I took Angel out for breakfast and told him I'm ready to move in together."

"What?!" A squeal of delight left her, nerves replaced with joy as she threw her arms around her best friend's neck, which was very awkward with her current position. "Jordan! Why didn't you tell me? I'm so happy for you guys!"

"I was going to tell you tonight, but then..." He trailed off, nodding toward the station.

The nerves were back, twisting and turning her stomach into knots.

"It's going to be fine." Jordan gave her an encouraging nod. "Besides, who could resist you in that sexy outfit?"

"Ha-ha." A shiver of discomfort ran along her spine as she caught a quick glance of herself in the side view mirror.

"Okay." She nodded, standing and shutting the car door. "Let's do this!"

Jordan grabbed the dish from Mateo's mother from the back of her car and they headed inside Station 42. Ward greeted them at the front door, his eyes going wide.

"Hey, Lexi. Jordan. What's, um...did you have some kid event at the center or something?"

Swallowing past the lump of nerves in her throat, Lexi shook her head. "No. I'm here to see Dyson, actually."

Ward's lips turned up in a wide smile. "Dude, please tell me O'Neil has some weird clown fetish I can tease him about until the end of time. I have so many jokes. The big shoes alone, I mean—"

"It's not a sex thing," Lexi interrupted, face heating. At least it better not be. Putting on this horrifying outfit for a confession was one thing, but she planned on burning it after this and never looking at another one again. Okay so she'd probably donate it, not burn it, but the principal remained.

"We also brought food," Jordan said, holding up the carne guisada.

"Sweet, dude." Ward motioned them forward with a hand, leading them into the common area of the station. "We always welcome food."

"Especially when Ward hasn't cooked it," Díaz's voice teased as she came into their sight.

"Shove it, Díaz," Ward grumbled.

She laughed, glancing at Lexi with raised brows. "Nice… outfit."

Embarrassment tried to sneak into her, but there were so many other emotions overwhelming her, Lexi didn't have time to think about what Dyson's crewmates thought of her right now.

"Thanks, is, um, Dyson here?"

"Yo, Dyson!" Ward called out over his shoulder. "There's a clown here looking for you."

A groan left her. This was not at all going how she planned. Not that she planned it all that well, she just kind of went with her gut on this one and now—

"Lexi?"

She turned at the warm, wonderful voice she'd missed so much the past few days. Heart skipping two beats as she spotted the man who had taken up every space available in her brain lately. The man who made her laugh, who made her take time for herself, the man who challenged her and comforted her.

The man I love.

"You love me?" Dyson asked, eyes wide.

Shoot! Damn her wayward mouth. Covering her face with her hands she let out a small groan.

"Dang it! I didn't mean to just blurt it out like that. I have a whole letter and everything." She reached into her pocket and pulled out the folded square of paper, opening it and glancing over what she wrote. "I was going to start off by telling you how sorry I was for what I said at the hospital. It wasn't fair of me to demand that of you. And I talk about how much you mean to me and how much fun I have around you. How I feel like I can be myself without any judgement. How much I love it when you…"

Her face heated as she spied the racier bits of what she liked about Dyson that she'd included.

"Um, never mind."

She crumpled the paper and shoved it back into her pocket.

"The point is…" She took a deep breath. "Yes. I love you, Dyson. And I'm sorry I reacted the way I did before. I guess I was scared, but I want to face my fears. As you can see."

She waved a hand over her outfit. Dyson's lips twitched, but he was smart enough not to laugh out loud.

"So, this is me, standing here before you in an outfit that I'm sure will bring me nightmares for years to come, asking if we can give it a real go. Be together for real. Not for your sisters' or your friends' bet, but for us. Because I love you, Dyson, and if we're together I know we can work through both our fears. Together."

Silence fell in the room. She knew Jordan and Dyson's crewmates were watching from behind her, but all her attention was focused on the man in front of her, the one who held her heart in his hands and had the power to cradle it or crush it.

Slowly, Dyson lifted his hand and pushed up the sleeve of his T-shirt revealing a small, orange, round bandage that was stuck to his upper arm. A huge, blindingly brilliant smile lit his face as he stared at her.

"I guess we had the same idea then, because I faced one of my own fears today."

Her lungs seized, heart stopping as the implication of what he was saying sunk in. Her jaw dropped, hope filling every cell in her body.

"You...you got the shot?"

He nodded. "And I already have my next one scheduled."

"For me?"

"For us," he corrected moving until he was standing right in front of her. "For you, for me, for us. Because I love you, too, Lexi. I didn't intend to. I never wanted to fall in love again, but life rarely gives us what we want. It throws us curveballs, rips our heart out, and if we're lucky, give us the tools to help us heal ourselves. I've had a lot of pain in my past. A lot of people leave me. Some didn't mean to and some knew it was for the best, even if I didn't at the time."

Tears filled her eyes, her heart breaking and hoping, as the words fell from his lips like a waterfall of promise. "But you know now?"

He nodded, stepping closer until they were inches apart. "I know now. And I know why you ran, why you were afraid. I'm sorry I wasn't even willing to talk about it then. But now, I know that sometimes, the thing that scares you the most is the exact thing you need to go for. Because if you let it slip away, if I let you slip away, it would be the biggest mistake of my life."

She choked as a sob tore from her throat. Dyson's eyes misted over as he pulled her into his arms, pressing his forehead against hers.

"I love you, Lexi. I am so sorry I let my fear get in the way."

"Me too," she said as tears poured down her cheeks. Her nose dripped, dang it, why couldn't she cry all pretty like the stars in the movies? She was going to be a slobbering mess by the time he finished.

He touched his fingers to her chin to tilt her head up. His lips touched hers and she thought she might actually die. Kissing Dyson again, after she feared she never would, was the sweetest thing she'd ever tasted. Her soul filled with the brightest joy imaginable, threatening to burst from her body in an explosion of pure happiness.

A cheer went up around them. A few hoots, whistles, and she could have sworn she heard Díaz say something to Ward about a car wash. She had no idea what that meant, but it didn't matter. Nothing mattered right now except the man holding her in his arms.

She pulled back slightly, staring up at him. "I can't believe you got the shot already."

"My sisters had to hold me down, but I did it, because I love you and loving you means loving Lucifer, too. So, what's a little horrifying giant needle prick every once in a while, if I get to be with the woman I love."

She would never get tired of hearing him say he loved her.

"You could have waited." She'd been willing to work on it with him, help him through the fear.

"Says the woman sporting full clown regalia," he said, bopping her red nose.

She laughed softly. "Yeah, well I'm counting the seconds to when I can take this freaky thing off."

He grinned, leaning in close to whisper in her ear. "My shift ends in six hours. I'd be happy to help you with that."

"Dude, you know we're all still here, right?" Ward

snicked, yelping as a soft smack sounded in the air. "The hell, Díaz? What was that for?"

"For being an ass; mind your business and help me dish out the food."

Ward grumbled, following Díaz and the others into the kitchen area. Lexi nodded as Jordan gave her a thumbs-up and followed the rest.

"So this is for real then?" she asked, turning back to Dyson. "You and me?"

"Yeah." Dyson pressed his lips to hers again. "Let's do this. No more faking, no more fear. You and me."

"And Lucifer."

"And Lucifer," he laughed softly. "Let's Face-It together, Lexi."

She nodded, smiling as more tears leaked from her eyes. "Yes, together."

Epilogue

Four months later

"This is the last box," Dyson said, kicking the apartment door closed with his heel.

"Great, because the kitties are starting to get restless. If Lucifer showed Queenie how to climb the bedroom curtains, I'm going to cut off his catnip for a month."

Dyson passed by her, kissing her cheek before he placed the large box in his hands on the living room floor with the others.

"No you won't, because you're a pushover for the fur babies."

He was right. She totally was. They had her wrapped around their furry tails. Yes, tails plural because two months after they started dating—for real—Dyson was on a call where a litter of kittens had gotten swept into a storm drain during a heavy rain. The firefighters of Station 42 made a successful rescue of five adorable kittens. Since no one claimed the sweet angels after a quick checkup by a vet, the crew decided to adopt them. Dyson picked the runt of the litter, a sweet little gray kitten with pale blue eyes and a tiny white mark on her head between her ears that looked like a crown.

"She looks like a little queen," Lexi had squealed when Dyson brought her home.

The name stuck and lucky for everyone, Lucifer didn't mind sharing his home or humans with another cat. Her devil boy had taken it upon himself to teach Queenie everything he knew. Unfortunately, that meant the bad things, too, like chewing on her favorite pair of heels and clawing the curtains. But she loved her cats and she loved Dyson so you wouldn't catch Lexi complaining.

"Huh." She glanced around at the pile of boxes, counting around fifteen of them. "I thought you'd have more stuff."

Jordan and Angel had been apartment hunting for a place of their own and finally found one. When their lease was up last month, he packed and left while she renewed it with Dyson. There were tears, hugs, wine, and the delicious, but ill-conceived choice of a chocolate going-away cake. It was fine, she'd endure a migraine to celebrate the end of an era with her bestie. It was weird not seeing him every day anymore—they'd lived together since college—but he and Angel moved to the fifth floor, so he wasn't that far away.

Lucky for her, Dyson's lease just also happened to be up...in three more months, but he found someone to sublet when she asked if he wanted to move in. The past four months had been amazing. They had their disagreements like any couple, but they'd both agreed to have open and honest communication at all times. She wasn't afraid to ask for the things she wanted, because she knew Dyson wanted to please her as much as she wanted to please him and that they could work through anything together. She missed him when he had his shifts, but she knew his job was important, just like he knew how vital hers was. In fact, he even managed to get the Kincaid Foundation to donate a very generous annual sum to the center.

She had no idea his crewmate Kincaid was the son of *the* Victoria Kincaid-Hayes.

"Not much room for stuff in my studio," Dyson said, referring to his old place. "Once I got rid of my furniture, I realized most of what I own is just clothes and books."

And, since she loved him, she cleared off two whole shelves of her bookshelf for him. If that wasn't true love, she didn't know what was.

They also went out last weekend and bought a new dresser for him. One that fit better in her apartment—their apartment. Lexi also sold her bed so they could buy a king-sized bed.

Her nipples tightened just thinking about breaking the bed in tonight. She couldn't wait. Maybe she could convince Dyson to try it out before they started unpacking. *Ha!* Like she'd even have to try to convince him. Four months later and still all she had to do was wink at him and he was whisking her to the bedroom, tearing their clothing off on the way. Not that she was complaining. Sex with Dyson made her feel things she didn't even know were possible. Pleasure, of course, but also comfort, safety.

Being in his arms was the most secure and whole place she'd ever felt.

A small crash came from the bedroom. Lexi winced as she imagined what the cats could have possibly destroyed now. Probably knocked over the pictures on her dresser again. They replaced all the glass with plastic after Queenie broke the fifth one. Sometimes you had to cat-proof your pictures.

"Should I let them out now?" She moved toward the bedroom door where she heard the unmistakable sound of cat claws against fabric. *Oh shoot!* Too bad they didn't make catproof curtains.

"Actually." Dyson hurried over to the bedroom door, one hand behind his back. "Why don't you go ahead and order us dinner. Whatever you want. I have…something I need to give the cats."

Okay, that was weird. Dyson was not one to hand over the dinner reins. He was actually pretty picky about where and what he ate, she'd learned over the months. She leaned around him, trying to see what was behind his back, but all she saw was a small brown box.

"Did you buy them more toys?" She sighed. "And you call me a pushover. You have to stop spoiling them."

The man could not stop buying toys. She was fairly certain the cats had more stuff than they did at this point. Dyson had been taking his allergy shots for a while now and thankfully they were working out wonderfully. No side effects, and the doctor even said he could eventually increase the time between shots as his body adjusted. She went to every appointment with him, held his hand, whispered naughty things in his ear to distract him. A little silly, but he said it worked and she'd do anything for the man she loved. The same as he did for her.

"No, I mean yes, well…both."

"Both?" She laughed. "Okay fine, but I'm ordering sushi and getting red snapper."

"Whatever you want, sweetheart."

Okay, now she definitely knew something was up. Dyson hated sushi. But she couldn't call him on it because he opened the bedroom door and disappeared, shutting it firmly. She could hear the protests of the cats, but he must have bought them toys or catnip because they soon quieted down. Curious, but not worried, Lexi grabbed her cell phone and ordered from her favorite sushi place. Lucky for her they delivered and had dishes other than sushi. She got a few rolls for herself and an order of beef teriyaki for Dyson.

When she finished placing the order, the bedroom door creaked open. Queenie came bounding out of the bedroom with a brand-new pink collar with shiny sparkles all over it.

"Did your daddy buy you a present?" she asked as she bent and scooped up the cat.

"Meow!"

Queenie swiped playfully at her face and Lexi smelled the distinct scent of the kitten's favorite treats on her paw. The bedroom door opened fully and Dyson came out with Lucifer in his arms, the cat enjoying the head rubs, preening like a god being adored by his worshipers.

"I see Queenie has a new shiny. Did Lucifer get snazzy new duds too?"

Dyson dipped his chin. "He did, and it comes with a shiny for you, too."

Oooh, she liked shinies. Reaching out her arms, she took Lucifer when Dyson passed the cat over. Lucifer made a sharp mewl of protest but settled into her arms. As long as he was being shown affection, he was happy. She inspected his new collar. A beautiful silver one with blue stars etched into the band. As she moved down to the front, she noticed his tag was missing and in its place was a very shiny pearl engagement ring.

She gasped, loosening her hold on Lucifer when he hissed in protest after she hugged him a little too tight in her excitement. She glanced over to see Dyson had gotten down on one knee in front of her.

"Lexi Martin. I used to think love was for other people. Not me. I thought I was broken or had done something wrong to have the people I love leave me, but then I met you and I realized sometimes we lose people because life can be cruel and sometimes we lose people because they're not the ones for us. Not the ones who make us better. You make me better, Lexi."

She sniffed, warm wetness rolling down her cheeks only to be cleaned off by a rough cat tongue as Lucifer licked her tears. Her sweet kitty, thinking she was sad. He didn't realize she'd never been so filled with joy in her life.

"You make me stronger, braver, and happier than I ever thought possible," Dyson continued. "And even though I could never be good enough to deserve you, I hope I make you better, too, and you'll consider letting me be your husband and doing my best to make you happier every day."

He was wrong. He did deserve her. They deserved each other because they loved each other. Nothing would make her happier than marrying Dyson.

"I hope you meant to say that out loud," he grinned hopefully. "About being happy to marry me?"

She nodded, yelping when Lucifer clearly got tired of her not paying attention to him and jumped from her arms.

"Shoot," Dyson stood, glanced after Lucifer who ran to the bathroom where the litter box was. "I shouldn't have put the ring on the collar. I can't put it on your finger now. It was supposed to be sweet, like a cute gesture."

"It was," she assured him, wrapping her arms around his neck. "It's not like Lucifer is going anywhere; we can get the ring later. Right now, I want to kiss my future husband."

With a wide smile, Dyson wrapped his arms around her waist and dipped his head. "Always happy to give you whatever you want, sweetheart. All you have to do is ask."

His lips pressed against hers and she opened, welcoming him in. Pouring all her love into the kiss. When she pulled away, they were both breathing heavily.

"I love you," she whispered.

"I love you too, so damn much."

She gave him a sassy wink. "Guess we have even more reasons to break in the bed tonight."

He growled, pulling her closer until he could press his hardness against her. "The only reason I need is you."

And all she needed was him.

Forever.

Acknowledgments

A big thank you to my readers, without you I wouldn't be able to do what I love. Thank you for letting my characters live in your hearts and minds. Shout out to my amazing agent Eva who always has my back and gives hard truths like telling me when a character needs to be cut (RIP Tara, you were one sister too many). All my appreciation to my editor Stacy Abrams, you are a freaking rock star and I cherish you. Bree, I don't know how you do it but every cover you make knocks the last one out of the water. I love them, thank you! A big thank you to all the staff at Entangled Publishing for all their support, hard work, and dedication on this book. Hugs and loves to my kiddos, thanks for the snuggles when mommy has a bad writing day. As always thank you to my rock, my sounding board, my own happily ever after, my spouse. There isn't anyone I'd rather ride this journey called life with, love you babe!

About the Author

Bestselling author Mariah Ankenman lives in the beautiful Rocky Mountains with her two rambunctious daughters and loving husband who provides ample inspiration for her heart-stopping heroes.

Mariah loves to lose herself in a world of words. Her favorite thing about writing is when she can make someone's day a little brighter with one of her books. To learn more about Mariah and her books, visit her website, www. mariahankenman.com, follow her on social media, or sign up for her newsletter https://bit.ly/31yMv07

Discover more Amara titles...

MANSPLAINER
a Last Man Standing novel by Avery Flynn

As the only Beckett cousin who is still unattached, I'm a shoo-in to win the bet with my cousins to be the last man blissfully not in love by Christmas. Of course, I know they're still going to make me follow the rules of our bet and go on six dates with the same woman—but I've figured out a way out of that too. I'm getting married. Is it love? Not even close. Chelle Finch needs a temporary husband and I need to win this bet. We agree to put a ring on it knowing that in six months this marriage of convenience will end in divorce. Except, somehow dating my wife has me realizing that I don't ever want to take this ring off if it means losing her. What does the guy who can talk his way out of anything have to do to sweet talk his temporary wife into forever?

PLAYING DIRTY IN ALASKA
a Captivity, Alaska novel by Samanthe Beck

With her family's airfield in her hands, bush pilot Bridget Shanahan knows it's time to step up and be a Responsible Adult™. She wasn't counting on Archer Ellison III blowing into her tiny town of Captivity, Alaska, every inch the hot-as-hell mistake from her past. She's the prize he's after and the CEO *never* loses...which is really inconvenient, since falling for Archer again is the least responsible thing she could do.

April May Fall
a Mommy Wars novel by Christina Hovland

April Davis is a social influencer with a reputation for showing moms how to stay calm and collected through yoga—but behind the scenes, she's barely holding it all together. Then a live video of the "always calm" April, while she's most definitely not, goes viral...and her calm jumps ship quicker than her kids running from their vegetables. She's going to need a boatload of margaritas just to find her way back to herself again.

Aggie the Horrible vs. Max the Pompous Ass
a novel by Lisa Wells

Wild-child Aggie Johansson shows up for an interview with golden-boy Max Treadwell with one goal—to not be offered the position. While she hates to disappoint the matchmaking grandmothers who'd pressed Max to hire her, she wants nothing to do with a pity job.

The last thing entrepreneur Max Treadwell wants is to hire bizarre and annoying Aggie, who's gone through half-dozen employers already. He might've promised Grandmother, but if Aggie doesn't take the job because he's more than a little un-charming, that won't be his fault.